W9-CYC-260

Dateland

Dateland

Jennifer Parello

McKenna Publishing Group

Indian Wells, California

14.00

Dateland

ISBN: 978-1-932172-28-7
LCCN: 2007931746

Cover design by Melanie Bender

First Edition
10 9 8 7 6 5 4 3 2 1
Printed in the United States of America

Visit us on the Web at: www.mckennapubgrp.com

For Holly Tarr, Laurie Attea, and Lauren Love.

Special thanks to Dr. Lene Larsen.

CHAPTER 1

My date with Claire—the first date I went on since my breakup with Jean—did not go well. It was, in fact, a disaster. And, as with all true disasters, there were witnesses to document the horrible events for future generations.

"It could have been worse," said Tricia, my best friend and law partner. We were standing on a street corner after the date had come to a miserable end, watching a cab carry Claire into the false twilight of the city night. "You could have fallen in love, stopped having sex, and grown to resent each other." She sighed dramatically at her own sorry plight and rested her head on my shoulder.

It had started out as a good day. When I woke that morning, a fat band of sunshine was streaming through the bedroom window. It was the first time in weeks that the sun had blasted through the steel-gray curtain that hung over Lake Michigan. The sun had been missing for so long that a newspaper published a running tally of the number of days it had been since the sun had last shown its hot face over Chicagoland.

I stretched in the sunlight, happily noting that I had been awake for a full five minutes and, in that time, I had had only two pass-ing thoughts about Jean. And in neither instance had I pictured her having sex with Michelle, the woman she left me for. This so delighted me that I grabbed my cat, Norm, and buried my face in his soft belly. Norm, obviously caught off-guard by my sudden affec-tion, stiffened and tried to jump out of my arms. In the six months since my breakup with Jean, I had touched Norm about a dozen times, and then only by accident. I was lucky if I remembered to brush my own hair, let alone pet the cat. During the darkest days following the breakup, I considered packing him off to live with my parents. Ultimately, though, I figured he'd suffer less from my uneven attentions than he would from my mother's attempts to reason with him.

With my arms wrapped around Norm's squirming body, I laid in bed, listening to the sounds from the apartment above. The walls in the old two-flat did little to muffle the noise generated by Tricia as she stomped and hollered her way through her morning routine. In the midst of Tricia's racket, I could hear Anne dumping food into the many pet dishes scattered around the apartment. This was quickly followed by a parade of paws, hooves, and talons click-clacking across the hardwood floors. At last count, Tricia and Anne had nine animals, all of which were named after chemical elements, and many of which were of undetermined species. Tungsten, the most recent addition to the household, looked like a cross between a very fat ferret and a half-eaten apple.

"Let's call him a cat and be done with it," Tricia said impatiently the week before, as Anne and I turned Tungsten this way and that, trying to figure out his place on the food chain. Tricia hated ambivalence of any kind, except when it came to her relationship with Anne. She had spent the past ten years wringing her hands, agonizing over whether she and Anne belonged together. Occasionally, Tricia would leave, only to return a few weeks later, moaning and howling until Anne agreed to take her back.

It had been three years since their last breakup and, as Anne told me on the day we found Tungsten shivering and gnawing on his own ropy tail under the porch, "We're due for another one. Tricia keeps telling me how unhappy I am." She chuckled grimly as she crouched down to the pavement to coax Tungsten out from behind a garbage can.

I gave Norm a kiss on his head and jumped out of bed. Norm followed me into the kitchen where he rubbed against a teetering stack of unpacked boxes while I poured food into his bowl and sang him a song about the character flaws of mice. Several times over the past few months I had forgotten to feed Norm. I'd often find him sitting at his bowl, staring at it, willing for something to happen. As a result, he had gotten into the habit of gobbling down his food as it fell from the bag, probably because he didn't know where his next meal was coming from. He would eat so much, so quickly, that he'd end the feeding frenzy by staggering into a corner and throwing up.

"Congratulations," Tricia said after witnessing a mealtime, "your cat has an eating disorder."

But on this morning, Norm must have sensed a tentative step back toward stability. Instead of indulging his bulimia, he sniffed at his food with indifference and took only a few dainty bites before joining me in the living room, where I was drinking a cup of coffee at a card table, the only piece of furniture in the room. Nearly everything else I owned was stored in my parents' attic or buried in one of the dozens of unmarked boxes leaning against the apartment walls. Many of the boxes were torn and their walls were caving in—victims of my aborted attempts at unpacking. The towers of damaged cardboard gave my apartment the feel of a sad downtown in an industrial city, which should have depressed me, but instead made me feel cozy.

Just as I stood to get another cup of coffee, I heard Tricia slam her front door and clomp down the stairs to my apartment landing. I froze as she pounded on my door and rattled the knob. She called my name a few times before finally giving up and heading outside to catch a bus downtown. In the past six months, I had rode to work with Tricia only twice. I liked to use the quiet of the bus ride to collect my thoughts, something that was impossible to do while sitting next to Tricia. Most people would have figured out by now that I was trying to avoid them. But Tricia simply couldn't believe that anyone would deny themselves the pleasure of her company. So every morning I was forced to either sneak out of the house before her or hide until she left for work without me.

I tiptoed to the front window and peeked at Tricia through a rip in the dingy shade. She was wearing the ratty beaver coat she bought from a thrift store the day we opened our law practice, dragging the coat's hem in the snow that covered the front path. Our neighbor, Mrs. Sternansky, a woman who had filed police complaints against us for everything from unlicensed pets to unorthodox Christmas decorations, was shoveling her sidewalk, being very careful not to clear any snow past her property line. Tricia called out a cheery good morning, forcing Mrs. Sternansky to raise her meatloaf-shaped head and growl something in return. Tricia crossed the street to the bus stop, where she chatted with one of the many crazy people who lived on our block—a guy who wore aluminum foil mittens year 'round and sang patter songs about the stuff he found in dumpsters.

* * * * * * *

By the time I arrived downtown, the sun had disappeared again behind a bank of storm clouds. The dark sky made our office building look even more menacing than usual. The building was one of the world's first skyscrapers. It was built in the 1800's by an architect who designed the granite walls to be several feet thick to hold the then-towering sixteen stories. As a result, he created a hulking fortress that looked like it wanted to beat up every other building on the block.

When I walked into the office, Tricia was standing over our secretary's shoulder, munching a piece of toast and shouting out wrong answers to the *Tribune's* crossword puzzle. Tricia had a brilliant legal mind, but she was a moron when it came to games-manship. She did not understand that games had rules you had to obey. Therefore, you can't stuff a nine-letter word into a six-letter space and you can't take two consecutive turns at tic-tac-toe just because you want to win.

"8 across is Lindbergh," Tricia yelled, spewing crumbs all over the room.

"L-i-n-d-b-e-r-g-h," she spelled, jabbing her finger at the puzzle, leaving a greasy fingerprint in each empty space.

"It is not, you fool," Lonnie said. Lonnie wiped the toast crumbs from the desk surface, being careful not to chip her long, colorful fingernails on the wood. Then she fluffed out the paper, and laid it down on the other side of the desk, out of Tricia's view.

"Well, look who decided to show up this morning," said Tricia, as I dropped my briefcase on the floor. She stuffed the last bit of toast into her mouth and clapped her hands together as if she were cleaning erasers, giving Lonnie's desk a final spray of crumbs. "You've missed a lot of excitement around here."

Lonnie rolled her eyes. "I had nothing to do with it, baby. It was all this one's deal," she said, jerking her head in Tricia's direction. Tricia waved her hand dismissively, causing about ten ceramic bracelets to rattle around her wrist. She walked out from behind Lonnie's desk and grabbed me by the shoulders.

"Guess what you're doing tonight," she asked, grinning like a maniac. Ever since my breakup with Jean, Tricia had a lot of sug-gestions on how I should spend my evenings—most of which involved drinking and leering at women with her.

"Playing bridge," I answered, squirming out from under her grasp. I played bridge twice a week in the suburbs with my parents. Tricia did not approve of card games, the suburbs, or my parents.

"Bridge!" Tricia said with a snort. She held out her wrist and loudly tapped the face of her watch. "You're thirty-three years old, Julia. Isn't it a little early for you to be entering your Golden Years?" I brushed past her and picked up a stack of mail from Lonnie's desk. I ignored Tricia, hoping she would turn her attention back to Lonnie.

"You are not playing bridge tonight," she said. "You, my friend, are going on a date! With Clarice Lingraman!" She wedged herself be-tween the desk and me and waggled her eyebrows suggestively.

Tricia never got anyone's name right, so first I had to figure out who she was referring to before I could focus on this date nonsense. I dropped the mail back on the desk and looked at Lonnie for help.

"Claire Larsson?" I asked.

Lonnie nodded. "Mmmmmm hmmmmm. That's the one."

Claire Larsson was one of our real estate clients. I represented her several months before when she bought a house. I had met Claire only twice. The first time was the day she came to our office and hired me to handle her purchase.

Most law firms assign clients to attorneys based on the lawyer's specialty. An attorney skilled in real estate law usually advises clients looking to buy property, while a family law attorney takes divorce cases. Our firm handled things a bit differently. Tricia had spent a considerable amount of time training Lonnie on our very different tastes in women. It was Lonnie's job to assign us female clients based on their looks, and not their legal needs. Tricia got any client who had a chip on her shoulder and wore ugly eyeglasses. Women who used lipstick and bathed regularly were sent to me.

Claire certainly fit within those vague parameters. She had the slightly over-fed prettiness of a busy PTA president. She was blonde, but a Midwestern blonde, which is very different from the sleek and dangerous blondes of the East Coast or the oversexed and fun-loving types bred in California.

"She looks like she was milked out of a cow," Tricia said, not unkindly, after meeting Claire. We were both shocked to learn that Claire had found us through our ad in a gay newspaper

"But she can't be gay," said Tricia, shaking Claire's client form, which asked where she had learned about the firm. "She was wearing Espadrilles, for Christsakes."

I didn't see Claire again until the day we closed on her property. Unfortunately, the closing took place the week after my breakup with Jean. I sat next to Claire, pushing papers at her that I had never even glanced at, telling her in my zombie voice, "Sign here. Sign here." At one point, she reached over and tucked in a tag that was hanging out of my blouse, and then she gingerly patted my back. I almost burst into tears at the gesture, which in my state of despair seemed like a saintly act of kindness.

A few weeks later, Claire called me at the office. I shook my head in a panic when Lonnie tried to hand me the phone. I was certain she was calling to tell me that I had screwed something up at the closing.

"Does she sound mad?" I asked Lonnie after she hung up the phone. "Does she sound like she wants to sue me?"

"She sounds like she sounds," Lonnie said. "Call her back if you're so interested in her mood."

I returned her call late at night when she wouldn't be in her office. I left a message that I'd be out of the country for a while. I didn't hear from her again until that morning.

"I answered the phone because this one," Tricia said, pointing at Lonnie, "was much too busy to do her job."

"Too busy fetching your damned breakfast," Lonnie sniffed, not bothering to lift her head from the crossword puzzle.

"Anyway," Tricia said, slapping her hands together, "we had a nice chat. She wants to take you to dinner for doing a good job on her closing, which we all know is ridiculous. I told her that you weren't busy tonight—which you are not. She'll be here at six." Tricia crossed her arms against her chest and smiled smugly.

I stared at her for a moment in disbelief. Tricia had always taken an unusual interest in my love life, but her actions were generally restricted to peppering me with questions about my lovers' sexual peccadilloes. This was the first time that she had actively recruited for me.

"You idiot," I said, finally.

"Mmmmm," said Lonnie, chuckling over the newspaper. "What have I been telling you all these years?"

"Oh, come on, Julia, it will be fun. She's very cute and you need to start hanging out with people who are under age 65."

I pushed past Tricia and reached for Lonnie's Rolodex.

"What are you looking for, hon?" Lonnie said, looking up from the puzzle and tapping a pen against her teeth.

"Claire's number," I said. "I'm calling her to cancel."

"Sorry, baby, she got there first." I looked up at Tricia who was holding the card just beyond my reach and dancing it teasingly in the air.

I lunged for the card, but Tricia jumped back and I tripped over the coat rack.

Tricia stuffed the card into her bra. "You've been moping around in a funk and feeling sorry for yourself for months. Not having any fun. Barely talking to me or Lonnie. Isn't that right, Lonnie?"

"I'm staying out of this one," Lonnie said, burying her face in her coffee mug.

I looked Tricia up and down in a way that I hoped made her feel bad about herself, and I walked into my office. As I shut the door, I heard Tricia tell Lonnie in a stage whisper that they should leave me alone for a while. Two seconds later, Tricia crept into my office on exaggerated tiptoe and knelt on the floor beside my desk.

"Are you really mad or just pretend mad?" she asked. I didn't know the answer, so I glared at her, just in case.

She looked up at me pleadingly for a moment. "Fine," she said, suddenly officious. She jumped to her feet and fumbled in her breast pocket for Claire's number. "Wallow in it." She threw the card at me and stormed out of the office, slamming the door behind her.

* * * * * * * *

Over the past several months, Tricia had been almost frenzied in her attempts to cheer me up. She tried to drag me to lesbian bars every weekend. She composed personal ads that described me with such outrageous adjectives as luscious, feline, and ripe. And she took every opportunity to badmouth Jean, reminding me, for example, that Jean had affected a British accent after a weekend trip to London. I should have appreciated Tricia's efforts, but instead I treated her every gesture as an irritant and regarded every invitation as an obligation. Worst of all, I suspected that Tricia's campaign to get me interested in other women had contributed to her own feelings of restlessness with Anne.

I put my feet up on my desk and watched an El train rattle past the window. I realized that my dark, little cloud routine was wearing thin not only on Tricia, but on myself, as well. Maintaining a bad mood for six months was exhausting and not very good for my complexion. Maybe Tricia was right. Maybe it was time to have some fun.

I picked up Claire's card and stared at her name until the type blurred and gave me double vision. I didn't think I was capable of falling in love again, so why not chose this smart, nice, slightly awkward woman who was obviously interested in me? I could be as happy with her as I could with anyone else. And, I thought, smiling to myself, Claire was pretty. Certainly pretty enough to make Jean jealous.

The more I thought about it, the more excited I got at the prospect of going out that night. I hugged myself and twirled around in my chair. Just then, Tricia walked into my office with a stack of files in her arms. She had pinned her hair up in a bun, which meant she wanted to be taken seriously.

"Here," she said, slapping the files on my desk, "you need to go through these. I don't have the time to do it myself." This was the same stack of files that had been sitting on her desk for a year. They contained closed cases that needed to be filed. Whenever Tricia wanted to appear overworked, she'd haul out these files and make a big production about how much time it was taking her to clear them.

"I'll get right on it," I said with a laugh. Tricia grabbed her chest and collapsed into a chair. She shook her head in mock disbelief and called out to Lonnie: "Get in here. There's something wrong with Julia." Lonnie grunted a reply and ignored the order.

Tricia leaned back in the chair and kicked her big, clumsy feet up on the desk. She was wearing leather pumps, which, like most of her shoes, were so weatherworn that the heels were ground into nubs and the toes curled up, making them look like elf shoes. "It's just a date," she said. "You don't have to marry her." I smiled and shrugged my shoulders with what I hoped appeared to be indifference.

For the first time that day, I noticed that Tricia was wearing a skirt. We had what you might call a "casual" workplace. We considered anything short of full-frontal nudity appropriate business attire. Today, though, Tricia, who bought clothing that was at least one size too small as an incentive to lose weight, was spilling out of a short wool skirt and filmy blouse. I reached over and ran my hand up and down her calf. "Stockings?" I asked. "What gives?"

She smirked and pulled the pencil out of her bun, causing her hair to cascade in a honey wave over her shoulders. Tricia wasn't particularly vain, but she was extremely proud of her hair, which was long, curly and the color of cognac. She couldn't walk past a mirror without stopping to smooth a cowlick or tuck a strand behind her ear. Once a week she treated her hair with expensive conditioners and wrapped it in a turban, which gave her the slightly exotic look of a fading European film star. The rest of her appearance suffered for all the attention she paid to her hair. Her clothes, purchased exclusively at thrift shops, were usually wrinkled and covered in cat hair.

"Guess who else has a date tonight?" she said.

"With who?" I asked incredulously.

She covered her face with her hands and convulsed with laughter.

"Oh, God. Not Bunny," I said.

Tricia's face was fever red from laughter and, I hoped, shame. "I know what you're thinking, but you're wrong," she said, waving her hands furiously. "I'm just going to have sex with her. That's it. No relationship. We have already agreed to these terms." She pounded her fist on the desk to make it sound official.

"You've got to be kidding," I said. Tricia and Bunny fell into bed every couple of years. Their affairs always played out in three stages: loud lovemaking in public places, followed by exchanges of bad poetry about the absurdity of their love, and culminating in competitive threats of suicide. By stage three, after being subjected to the poetry of stage two, I was handing Tricia straight-edged razors and begging her to jump off ledges.

"Does Anne know about this?" I asked sharply. I tended to take Anne's side in any dispute, partly to irritate Tricia, but mainly because I couldn't understand why Tricia was bent on destroying their relationship. The fact was that Tricia and Anne had a nearly perfect relationship. They both loved wine and drank it to excess. They snickered at people who exercised regularly. They enjoyed vacationing in places with shaky political climates. And they fought just often enough to keep things interesting. Their biggest problem was that Tricia couldn't accept that she was in a happy relationship.

"Of course she does," Tricia snapped. We glared at each other for a moment until she rolled her eyes and tossed up her hands in resignation. "Well, she doesn't know about Bun, but she knows that I'm dating other people."

"Don't worry," she said, smirking at me, "we've decided to stay together for the children." I smiled with genuine relief. Tricia and Anne's breakups were as hard on me as they were on them. "We're going to have an open relationship."

"I thought only gay men are allowed to do that."

Tricia shook her head slowly and lifted a glass off my desk. She rolled it back-and-forth across her forehead. "You know what's weird? Anne thinks it's a good idea. I was expecting her to freak out. Maybe even ask me to leave." She knocked the glass gently across her forehead. "What do you think she's up to?"

"Maybe she's met someone on the Internet," I said. Anne was terrified of computers. Tricia, however, considered herself to be something of a technophile because she kept a computer on her desk, though she used it for little more than a place to hang *New Yorker* cartoons and to surf the Web for free pornography.

"Oh, come on, she doesn't even know how to turn one on," Tricia said with a snort. "She thinks that if she pushes the power button the computer will spring to life and run around giving us orders." She began gnawing on her thumbnail, something she did when she was trying to work through a problem. "No, I think it might be reverse psychology. Like if you give a little kid a lot of freedom, they won't want it." She pondered the idea for a moment, nodding her head in agreement with herself.

"How do you think she's going to react when she finds out about Bunny?" Anne hated Bunny, and with good reason. Anne and Bunny had been friends before Bunny and Tricia started their first affair.

"She'll probably throw me out," Tricia said with a shrug.

"Is that what you want?"

"No," she said, flinging her arms wildly in the air. "I want to date. Not just Bunny. I want to date lots of women. I want to have some fun. I want to have sex. I'm thirty-six years old and I haven't had a non-self-induced orgasm in months."

"So, you and Anne are going to live together and date other

people?"

"It should make for some interesting dinner parties," she said lightly. Tricia grabbed my knee and shook it. "Do you realize that this will be the first time in the history of our friendship that you and I will be single at the same time? We'll be just like Mary Tyler Moore and Rhoda."

"As long as it's understood that you're Rhoda," I said.

* * * * * * * *

At five o'clock, Bunny slunk through the old, heavy door of our office. She was wearing her usual uniform: baggy, black pants; a white, man's business shirt; and a shapeless, black jacket. And, of course, thick glasses with heavy frames to advertise the fact that she was a serious artist. Although her name was Bunny, she more closely resembled a creature with an exoskeleton. I had to fight the urge to call her Cricket or Aphid. She was small, wiry, and her limbs did not seem to fit into their sockets. Her face and fingers were stained yellow, the telltale signs of a dedicated smoker, and her shoulders were set in a perpetual slump.

Bunny approached Lonnie's desk warily, like a sick dog would, doing her best to avoid eye contact. "Where's Tricia?"

Lonnie and I stood shoulder to shoulder, both rendered speechless by Bunny's charm. After a moment, Lonnie chuckled softly, grabbed her coat, and said, "That's enough for me today."

I took a deep breath and stuck out my hand. Bunny stared at it as if it was electrified. She sighed deeply before reluctantly dropping her hand into mine. I grabbed her clammy paw as tightly as I could and shook it senseless.

Just when I thought Bunny and I would have no choice but to engage in painful small talk, Tricia popped her head out of her office. "Get in here, you," she said huskily. I retreated to my office, but even after I closed my door I could hear giggling, the clinking of ice cubes, and other sounds that I did not want to identify. I made as much noise as possible, hoping to remind them of my presence and shame them into silence, but nothing could quiet their ardor.

Finally, I settled in at Lonnie's desk and began sorting out Tricia's closed-file mess. I have found that tedious, clerical work can be much more fulfilling than many more mindful pursuits. And once you've finished stuffing envelopes or organizing a stack of forms, you always have something tangible to show for your efforts, unlike many intellectual tasks, where all you end up with is a headache. I became so absorbed in my filing project that I didn't hear Claire walk into the office.

"Julia?" she said softly. Her voice startled me. I tossed a file into the air. A dozen papers flew out of the folder and scattered on the floor around the desk. As I stumbled out of the chair to pick them up, Tricia burst through her office door. Bunny followed, sulkily buttoning her shirt.

"Clairy!" Tricia exclaimed. She wrapped her arms around Claire and hugged her hard. Tricia pulled away from her and held Claire at arm's length. "I love that blouse," Tricia said, reaching up to straighten its collar.

Claire had clearly made an effort to shed some of her suburban shine for our date. She was wearing black jeans and loafers. Her mustard-colored silk blouse was opened daringly low to reveal an ample bosom. She was maybe ten pounds overweight, but the extra pounds gave her a dreamy, voluptuous quality, like someone floating just below the surface of water. Suddenly, I felt dizzy and nauseous. I grabbed hold of the edge of the desk to steady myself.

"So," Tricia said, cocking her head at Claire flirtatiously. "Where are you off to?"

"I'm not familiar with the area," Claire said, hesitantly. She tugged on a thick strand of hair and smiled at me shyly. "I was hoping you could suggest a place."

Before I could answer, Tricia exclaimed, "Good, then it's settled. You're coming with us to Shangri-la." I shot Tricia a dirty look, but, secretly, I was relieved. I wasn't so sure that I could do this alone.

* * * * * * * *

Shangri-la was my favorite bar in the city. It was a throwback to 1950's swank, with Easter Island heads guarding the front entrance, red banquettes shaped like clamshells, and canned tiki music playing in the background. The cocktails had dangerous names and were served in glasses that looked like man-eating plants.

When we arrived at the bar, I slid into our regular booth, only to be ordered out by Tricia. She directed Bunny to sit at the far end of the booth. Tricia sat next to Bunny, and she told Claire to sit next to her. Finally, I squeezed in next to Claire, who tried to adjust her body so it was touching neither mine nor Tricia's. "Now this is cozy," Tricia said, snuggling against Bunny's shoulder. Bunny sneered off into mid-distance.

Tricia signaled the waiter and we ordered Mai Tais. Claire asked for a glass of Chardonnay. "You don't come to Shangri-la for the wine," Tricia said. "Have a Mai Tai."

"She can have whatever she wants," I said.

"It's okay," Claire said with an uncomfortable laugh. "I'll try a

Mai Tai."

"Three Mai Tais," Tricia told the waiter triumphantly. "And, sweetie," she said, rubbing Bunny's thigh, "what will you have?"

"Scotch," Bunny barked.

Tricia turned toward me and mouthed, "She's so butch."

As soon as the drinks arrived, Tricia raised her glass and said, "To new love." I set my glass down and glared at her.

"So, Claire," Tricia said, shifting around in her seat so that she was practically sitting on Claire. I could feel Claire's body tense as if she were bracing herself for a blow. "You don't look like a scientist."

Claire exhaled in relief. She must have been expecting a question about her bathroom habits. "I'm a biologist. It's the physical scientists who tend to look a bit abstract."

"What's your degree holding," Bunny asked suspiciously. When Claire answered that she had a doctorate in entomology, Bunny groaned and rolled her eyes. Bunny was a failed doctoral candidate. Her doctoral review committee had rejected her dissertation on grounds that everything about it—including the title—was incomprehensible. Bunny claimed to be delighted by the rejection, heralding it as an endorsement of her brilliance. "They should replace the letters Ph.D. with the word sellout," Bunny said to Claire.

Claire stuttered and looked around the room in a panic. I briefly considered punching Bunny in the face. Instead, I drained my Mai Tai and signaled the waiter for another round.

"Oh, don't pay any attention to Bunny. She's a very angry person," Tricia said, leaning into Claire conspiratorially. "Have you ever had sex after a fight? Isn't it terrific? Well, that's what it's like with Bunny all the time." She grabbed Bunny's face, and kissed her hard on the mouth. Bunny's eyes softened and she mewed with pleasure.

"Entomologist. You study insects, right? Or is it fish?" Tricia asked, turning her attention back to Claire. Like most outgoing people, Tricia had a talent for making shy people feel comfortable. She did this mainly by asking lots of questions and then answering them herself, giving the shy person the impression that they were actually participating in the conversation.

"Maybe you can settle an argument between my good friend Julia and me," Tricia said. "Isn't it true that fleas can be trained to pull little wagons and walk on tight ropes?"

"Well," said Claire, glancing nervously at me, "I wouldn't use the word 'train.' But they can be manipulated to perform stunts that rely on their instinctual behaviors."

"Aha!" Tricia said, pointing her finger accusingly at me.

"Do you even understand what she just said?" I asked.

"She said that I am right and you are wrong." Tricia grabbed a drink off the waiter's tray and launched into a tale about an uncle who ran a flea circus. The cast of characters included Asian gangsters, identical twins who were both named Santa, and a very fat woman with no thumbs. Like most of her stories, it was highly improbable, but it contained just enough basis in fact to be wildly amusing.

* * * * * * *

In no time, Tricia and I were drunk and dribbling on ourselves. Tricia told silly stories and I laughed too loudly, hoping that if I pretended to have a good time it might rub off on Claire, who was clinging to her drink as if it was a life preserver.

Bunny sat at the end of the banquette, sullenly waiting for Tricia to pay attention to her. She shifted in her seat every few seconds and savagely ripped at cocktail napkins. After about an hour, Bunny shot up from the table, manfully adjusted her trousers, and marched into the men's room.

"What's she up to?" I asked, grabbing a Mai Tai off the waiter's tray.

"God only knows," said Tricia, craning her neck toward the bathroom, her eyes crazy with excitement.

A few seconds later, a man came flying out of the restroom, closely followed by Bunny, who planted herself in the middle of the room and loudly accused him of not washing his hands.

"Isn't she something?" Tricia said, raising her glass in Bunny's direction. Bunny stomped to the table, grabbed Tricia's arm, and yanked her to her feet. Tricia held up a hand in a halting gesture as she quickly drained her glass. Then she let Bunny lead her off to the ladies' room.

It was the first time all evening that Claire and I had been alone. I cleared my throat and fiddled with the fruit-laden spear in my drink.

"I'm sorry about all of this," I said, waving my hand over Tricia and Bunny's empty seats.

"No, no, I'm having a nice time," Claire said, unconvincingly. She bit her lip and looked down at her hands, which were folded neatly in her lap.

"So am I," I said, staring at my sweating glass, resisting the urge to gulp down the rest of the Mai Tai. It suddenly occurred to me that I had been drinking much more than usual lately.

"Really?" she said with genuine surprise. She swiveled in the banquette so that she was facing me. Her lips were full and stained red from the few sips she had taken from the cocktail. "I'm not very brave. But a friend of mine convinced me to call you. And this friend, her name is Nadia, she has been nominated for a Nobel Prize. That's how she got me to do it. She said, 'Listen to me. I've been nominated for a Nobel Prize. I know what I'm talking about. Ask her out to dinner.'" Claire laughed. She picked up her drink and took a careful sip.

"Did she win?" I asked.

"Nadia? No. She was nominated with a team of American chemists. But they lost to two Russian researchers. And the funny thing is that Nadia is Russian. Of course, I mean it's funny in the ironic sense."

"Have you won a Nobel Prize?"

"Me? Oh, God, no. Oh, you're just teasing me." She slapped me playfully on the arm. Her light touch burned pleasantly into my flesh. "My research is not taken very seriously. People are only interested if you find new ways to kill insects. I became an entomologist because I like insects. They are fascinating! They are our friends!" She pounded the table lightly with her fist. The movement caused her breasts to bounce pleasantly under her blouse.

"Did you know that only one percent of all insects are pests?" she asked. I shook my head. "Of course not. No one knows that. People just want to kill them all." She frowned into the distance and distractedly stabbed a shrimp fork into the table.

Her passion caught me by surprise. It filled me with a warm, almost sleepy feeling. If there had been a bed in the restaurant with flannel sheets and a thick wool blanket, I would have taken her by the hand and climbed in. I would have asked her to talk of nothing but insects until I fell asleep.

"I've always been rather fond of spiders," I said.

She looked up at me from over the top of her drink and smiled slyly. "Spiders are arachnids, not insects."

Then our eyes met in that way that eyes sometimes do. A powerful moment of connection that makes you feel as if you are destined for each other. I had built a relationship with Jean on little more than a thrilling exchange of glances. Somewhere, deep within my rum-soaked brain, a voice told me that I should know better. But, of course, I told that voice to shut up.

I inched toward Claire and allowed my body to melt slightly into hers. She didn't pull away, so I moved closer. We both reached for our drinks. She jiggled the soggy fruit in her glass and glanced at me self-consciously. I took a deep breath, and set down my glass solidly. And then I kissed her. As I did, I realized I was making a huge mistake. But I couldn't stop myself. It was like knowing you are about to hit freezing cold water after you've already jumped off a diving board.

The kiss caused Claire to reel back into the banquette. She tried to leap to her feet, but she slammed into the table. She scooted out of the banquette. Her eyes were huge and filled with terror as she excused herself to go to the washroom.

"Sorry," I said weakly as I watched her scurry away. As soon as she got to the bathroom door, Tricia and Bunny emerged in a cloud of cigarette smoke. "Claire!" Tricia exclaimed, as if she hadn't seen her in years.

When Tricia and Bunny returned to the table, I had my head buried in my hands.

"What's wrong?" Tricia asked with concern. One of the things I loved about Tricia was that she knew when to take me seriously.

"I'm an idiot."

"Join the club," she said gently. Tricia slid next to me and wrapped her arm around my shoulder. I whispered what had happened, stealing glances at the bathroom door, nervously anticipating Claire's return.

After a few minutes, Claire emerged from the bathroom. Her face was washed clean of the light makeup she had been wearing and her eyes were puffy and red. Tricia grimaced at the site of her and whispered, "Jesus." Claire didn't look at me when she announced that she was leaving. "It's started to snow again, and I have a long ride home," she said in a strained tone.

* * * * * * * *

Tricia tried to lighten the mood as we left the bar by giving one of the big Easter Island heads a sloppy kiss. She grabbed Bunny's hand and skipped up the stairs with Bunny dragging behind her like an anchor.

Claire and I stood silently under the restaurant's awning, watching Tricia and Bunny as they tried to hail a cab. Bunny slouched in the street with her hands jammed in her pockets, while Tricia jumped up and down and yelled at each passing taxi.

"I'm sorry," I said, finally. "I was drunk and there was all that tropical music..."

"It's okay," Claire said, furrowing her brow and shaking her head. She gazed out at traffic for a few seconds and then she chuckled awkwardly. "You probably won't believe it, but I'd like to try this again. Maybe, next time, we can make it all the way through dinner before I run out of the room."

I smiled and nodded, knowing that I would never call her. Bunny whistled to us, signaling that Tricia had flagged down a cab. Claire touched my hand and mouthed "thank you" before ducking into the backseat. Tricia bent down and waved madly at Claire, who was tugging on her eyebrow and staring straight ahead. "Bye Claire," she shouted. "Let's get together again soon."

Tricia and I stood next to each other, weaving unsteadily on our feet, our shoulders bumping together gently, watching the taxi pull away from the curb. "So, that was pretty horrible, huh?" Tricia said. As I watched Claire disappear into the city night, I felt an urge to tell Tricia just how terrible it had been—not only that night, but also every night for the past six months. But then, just as suddenly, the feeling left me.

"Well, it's a start, anyway," I said, feeling almost merry.

CHAPTER 2

I was thirty-three years old and I had never dated. By dating, I mean spending an evening with someone you're mildly attracted to that ends in nothing more than a friendly handshake, a vague agreement to go out again, and perhaps a bout of casual sex. Instead, each first date ended abruptly in a trial marriage complete with instant intimacy, a sense of spousal entitlement, and empty vows of fidelity. I would find myself making major life decisions with a virtual stranger who felt entitled to destroy my friendships and estrange me from my pets simply because she was sticking her tongue down my throat.

Karen Becker, the woman I was involved with just prior to my relationship with Jean, was a fair representative of the kind of emotionally stunted women I was attracted to. Karen was a stockbroker with a penchant for bullying underlings and making scenes in restaurants. She possessed a combination of dazzling good looks, pathological self-absorption, and testiness. In other words, she was just my type.

I met Karen in a book group at a women-owned bookshop in Andersonville, the Chicago neighborhood I lived in at the time. I joined the group out of guilt, the motivating force behind so many of my actions. The shop was on the verge of collapse and the owners established the book group in a last-ditch effort to attract customers.

Women's Words had long been a mainstay of Andersonville, which was first settled by Swedish immigrants in the late 1800's, and resettled in the 1970's by pioneering lesbians who were attracted by the low rents, lake views, and challenges inherent in living in old homes crippled by infrastructure problems. By the 1990's, after the lesbians had fixed the plumbing, the area was ripe for gentrification. Housing prices skyrocketed and corporate franchises drove out boutique businesses owned by the ethnic and social fringe. At the time I joined the book group, a monster bookstore had gobbled up an entire city block and was casting a menacing shadow over Women's Words. A tireless gang of feminist literati tried to stop development, flooding the alderman's office with petitions and taking turns reading angry poetry outside City Hall. However, the demands of a gaggle of novelists from obscure publishing houses did not hold the sway of a corporate giant that promised to bring lattes and cheap potboilers to the neighborhood.

The book group was populated by the type of people you'd expect to find prowling the aisles of a feminist bookshop—largely lesbian, with a few old '60's activists, and a couple of Yuppies suffering pangs of conscious for their contribution to the destruction of the neighborhood. The reading list was dominated by grim memoirs and nutty lesbian fiction that always featured at least one character mythologizing the joys of menstruation.

On the night Karen joined the group, we were discussing a lesbian vampire story. Midway into a debate over whether the main vampire was truly evil or simply insecure, Karen burst into the store. She was shouting into a cell phone, berating someone over what she referred to as "the lasagna incident." The group sputtered into stunned silence as Karen dragged a chair into the reading circle and snapped the phone shut with exaggerated efficiency. She reached into her briefcase, yanked out a copy of the vampire book, and tossed it dismissively across the table, proclaiming it "an utter waste of my time." Then she smoothed an errant strand of hair into her smart bob and poured herself a glass of wine from the jug provided by the store's owner. She tapped the side of the wine glass impatiently as one of the hippies meekly attempted to defend the book. I studied Karen from across the room, wondering what it would be like to kiss her.

I found out the following week. After book group, Karen briskly ordered me to have a drink with her at a neighborhood bar. On the short walk to the bar, Karen baited me into an argument over the relevance of the gall bladder. I didn't have an opinion about the organ, but I felt compelled to take a stand. The debate quickly escalated and we were soon standing in the middle of a busy sidewalk screaming at each other about the ethics of elective surgery. Suddenly, she pushed me against a wall and we engaged in a hungry make-out session that ended only after one of the lesbians from the book group discovered us and scolded me for kissing a Republican.

That evening set the tone for our relationship, which stormed on for more than two years. We argued so loudly and so often that I introduced us as Murder/Suicide, because I was certain that that was how we'd end up. Each argument ended in a marathon session of passionate sex that was fueled by rage and frustration, emotions that you try to avoid until you understand their value in the bedroom.

Our most explosive arguments centered on my refusal to move in with her. From the beginning of our relationship, Karen pressured me to live with her in her loft in the financial district, which was decorated in red, purple, and black—the colors of pain. I refused, citing our spectacularly unhealthy relationship and proudly pointing to my history of never having lived with a lover. However, given my habit of slipping into mindless commitment with any woman who kissed me, it was like a heroin addict bragging that she never drank beer.

Eventually, my resolve weakened and I agreed to her demands. I reasoned that it was the only way to end the relationship. The stress of moving day is enough to destroy the most stable relationships, and I was betting that we'd have it out in an apocalyptic battle of good verses evil before we managed to unload the U-Haul. But I was spared the final drama when a few weeks before the move, Tricia and Anne invited me to live with them in their apartment in Rogers Park, the beaten-down neighborhood north of Andersonville. I called Karen and broke up with her over the phone. I hung up before she could argue me back into bed.

In the weeks after I left Karen, I made a swaggering attempt to break my habit of serial monogamy. I was determined to date lots of women and not take any of them home to meet my parents. Tricia helped me steel my emotions by letting me practice staring longingly into her eyes for several-minute stretches. The goal of the exercise was to resist the urge to blurt out "I love you" just to fill the awkward silences.

But then Jean waltzed into my life, and I reverted to type.

* * * * * * * *

I met Jean at a Halloween party hosted by the gay and lesbian alumni association of Darrow Law School, the school that Tricia and I had attended. The party was held at a gay nightclub renowned for its forgiving lighting and overdressed cocktails. The venue was selected after months of bitter debate. The gay men in the group wanted to raid the scholarship fund to pay for a swanky affair, and the lesbians fought to hold the party in a warehouse owned by one of the female attorneys. Tricia and I sided with the lesbians until they overplayed their hand by insisting on a cash bar and off-brand snacks. After we switched allegiances, we wrested control of the food committee and hired Anne, who had recently opened a restaurant, to cater the event with her trademark comfort foods.

Tricia was already at the party when I arrived. She was sitting at the bar, chatting with Robert, a gay dandy with a sentimental weakness for dead musical-comedy stars. Robert was raised in a farm town in Iowa, but he passed himself off as a worldly dilettante who practiced law as a hobby. He was barely employed in private practice and his scant client base consisted of wealthy older women who demanded little more than a dashing middle-aged escort to take them to lunch and help them shop for picture hats.

Robert's only interest in the alumni association was the Halloween party, which gave him the opportunity to flex his decorating skills in public. Every year, he would resign from the decorating committee in a fit of pique until they agreed to his Byzantine demands, which typically involved huge outlays of cash and complete creative control. This year, he spent his entire budget on dry ice. Great chunks of dry ice were positioned on every available surface, hissing out so much mist that visibility was limited to about two feet. The effect was appropriately eerie and oddly seductive.

"You've done it again!" a small-boned patent attorney exclaimed, as he clutched Robert's arm. "It's like a fantasy bathhouse."

"Ha! And the lesbians said we would have to make do with black steamers and balloons from a party story," Robert said, spitting the words out of his mouth as if they were dead gnats.

Robert had little regard for lesbians, whom he referred to collectively as "the Sisters Grim." But he liked Tricia and me, mainly because we appreciated his fussy aesthetic. He often introduced Tricia admiringly as "the least sensible woman on the planet." And he had big plans to transform me into his ideal of the perfect lesbian— an amalgamation of Lauren Bacall and Carol Lombard with a pinch of Tallulah Bankhead for texture. The week before the party, he stopped by our office with a picture of a woman wearing a veiled pillbox hat. Across the photo he had scrawled: "It's you!"

"Oh, who wears veils anymore?" I scoffed.

"Women of mystery," he responded, cocking his eyebrow in such a way that almost convinced me to buy the hat.

I often found myself dressing for Robert's approval, and tonight was no exception. I chose my Halloween costume with his sense of drama in mind.

"Darling!" Robert exclaimed, twirling me around and taking in my costume. I was wearing a yellow rain slicker over a black leotard, yellow rain boots, and a floppy rain hat. He placed his chin in his hand and studied me for a moment. "Barbara Stanwyck in 'Stella Dallas?'"

"No," I responded with great disappointment. I was Barbara Stanwyck the year before. "I'm the Morton Salt girl. You know, from the label of the salt container."

"You're not going to be anyone's girl in that get-up," Tricia said. "You look like something dreamed up by a rubber fetishist."

"And you look like a sex toy," I said. Tricia was dressed in what could loosely be described as a costume. It was a collection of flesh-colored fabric that barely covered her torso.

"You're both fabulous, as always," Robert said with distraction. He was peering through the mist at a figure muscling its way through the crowd. He leaned into me and whispered conspiratorially, "Something wicked this way comes."

Georgia, a family law attorney who weighed at least 300 pounds, was puffing across the room like a steam engine. She was wearing her standard party outfit—big-girl jeans and a Hawaiian shirt. As usual, an extra-thin cigarette was cocked jauntily from the side of her mouth.

"That woman frightens me," Robert said with a shudder. "I once saw her lick clean a cake plate in the law library."

I was scared of Georgia, too. She had a bad habit of falling in love with women who wanted nothing to do with her. And then she compounded her misery by refusing to take no for an answer. I had been one of her victims shortly after Tricia and I started our practice, and I was still rattled from the experience. Georgia hired a private investigator to gather information about my life and then dropped unsettling bits of trivia about me into conversation. Tricia, who was initially amused by my discomfort, finally grew irritated at not being the center of attention and ordered Georgia to stalk someone else.

Georgia sucked on her cigarette as if drawing strength from it and surveyed the room. Her raptor gaze landed on a doe-like creature who was hugging a corner of the dance floor. The woman's skin had a bluish hue that suggested she wasn't getting enough oxygen. "Mmmmm," Georgia said hungrily, "she's cute!"

Tricia glanced at the woman and rolled her eyes. "Why don't you go out with that woman who has made shy inquiries about you? You know, the one who filed that suit against the doctor who fouled up her mole removal."

"Donna?" Georgia said, scrunching up her eyes and nose so they gathered tightly in the middle of her enormous face. "She looks like J. Edgar Hoover."

"You say that like it's a bad thing," said Tricia. "Hoover was a very powerful man."

As Georgia and Tricia discussed the questionable merits of the former FBI director, Robert nodded his head toward a group of unusually tall and blonde women who had just entered the club. "Why is it that you lesbians insist on wearing soft-sole shoes?" he asked, referring to the running shoes worn by most of the women in the group. "This isn't Vietnam. You don't have to sneak up on the enemy. When will you learn that nothing truly interesting is going to happen to you until you start wearing heels?" He shook his head sadly at the women, grabbed his cocktail from the bar, and vanished into the mist.

The women looked like a straight man's fantasy of a lesbian volleyball team. They had a certain strapping glamour that suggested they'd be perfectly comfortable wearing nothing but sports bras and jogging shorts to a dinner party. Their overall effect was stunning, but on closer inspection it was clear that they were aging rapidly thanks to too much time in the sun and too many late nights in bars.

"Who are those women?" I asked.

"You don't want anything to do with them," Georgia sniffed. "They eat their own."

I had seen the women several times before. They would arrive at parties en masse, rarely interacting with anyone outside their tight unit. They reminded me of tourists who went to foreign countries not to experience different cultures, but rather to let different cultures experience them.

Only one of the women stood out as being different from the rest of the group. While her friends turned inward and spoke only to each other, she waved and called out greetings to people outside the group's rigid boundaries. She flashed an enormous smile around the room, serving her group as a beacon to the outside world. When she swung her head in my direction, she caught my gaze. Her smile dimmed a few watts and she cocked her head at me curiously. After I dropped my eyes, she broke from the pack and strode across the room with a purposeful gait.

She stopped short in front of the bar and gave my costume the once over. "So, is this what you wear to court?" she asked in a tone usually reserved for speaking to preschoolers and mental patients.

"Only when it rains," I muttered, totally undone by her confidence and periwinkle eyes, which twinkled at me with bemusement. She was not as physically striking as some of her friends, but her imperfections made her seem more human and accessible. There was something soft, almost mushy about her features. But she didn't make the mistake of trying to bury her flaws under too much makeup. She wore the uniform of her friends—jeans, sneak-

ers, and a cotton tee-shirt—yet the outfit looked oddly formal on
her, as if she was some type of minor royalty who was dressing
down to mix with the rabble.

"Jean!" Georgia boomed, heaving herself off the barstool and
wrapping Jean in a hug.

Jean's face was frozen into a grimace. She clearly had no idea
who Georgia was or why she was locked in what was obviously
a predator/prey relationship with her.

"Geneva?" Jean said, finally.

"Georgia!" Georgia bellowed, dropping Jean from her embrace
with great insult.

"Oh, right," said Jean, placing her hand on Georgia's shoulder
and massaging it tenderly. "I'm sorry! I didn't recognize you in
your costume"

Before Georgia could say that she wasn't wearing a costume,
Tricia raced to her rescue. "You don't remember me, do you?" asked
Tricia, flashing the phony smile she saved for opposing counsel
and my mother.

"Of course I do," said Jean. An obvious lie.

Tricia continued to smile hard at her, but then grew bored of
the game and let her off the hook. "Well, I don't remember you,
either. So, we're even. I'm Tricia. And this is my law partner, Julia,
a woman with a lot of personal demons."

I responded in the way I usually do when forced to interact
with someone I'm attracted to. I stared at the floor and mumbled
incoherently. Jean stepped close to me and bent her head next to
mine in a bold attempt to hear what I was saying. The combination of heat from her body and her musky perfume caused me to
fall back against the bar.

"Having another one of your spells, dear?" Tricia asked with mock
concern. She gave me a chance to recover by turning her attention
back to Jean. "So, Jean, you're not an attorney, are you?"

"No, she's a sales rep for Pigglet Wines," Georgia said. "She was
their top salesperson for six consecutive months this year." Pigglet
was owned by a celebrity debutante, who purchased the vineyard
with earnings from a reality television show she starred in. The
wines were fermented just this side of grape juice, but they were
remarkably popular thanks to cute labels that featured the winery's
mascots—baby pigs suckling at their mother's teet.

"How do you know that?" Jean asked Georgia, looking more
frightened than curious.

"Oh, I have my ways," Georgia said, rocking on her heels, delighted to have finally caught Jean's attention.

Tricia reached over and slapped Georgia across the back of her
square head. "This is why women think you're odd," Tricia said, grab-

bing Georgia by the arm and yanking her off the stool. "Excuse us, but Georgia needs a spanking."

Jean tossed her head back and laughed mirthlessly in relief. "Don't leave," she said, reaching out to stroke Tricia on the arm. "I didn't mean to intrude on your little party. I just wanted to tell Julia that I like her costume." She took a step back and looked me up and down. "I still have no idea what you are." She chuckled and walked away.

It took her several minutes to walk back to her clutch of friends. Several admirers stopped her along the way and Jean's eyes widened in surprise and delight each time someone in the crowd called her name. As she made her way across the room, she touched dozens of people, each of who melted slightly after she made contact. She knew the power of a light caress, and she used it expertly to make an instant connection. She had used the technique on Tricia and Georgia, but she had refrained from touching me. I interpreted that as a sign that she wanted something deeper than a casual touch.

When she finally returned to her friends, they opened ranks and folded around her. It was like an exploratory vehicle being welcomed back to the mothership. The group moved toward the exit, and I was delighted when Jean glanced back at me before she walked out the door.

* * * * * * * *

I didn't speak to Jean again until the following summer. It was the summer that Tricia, Anne, and I played on a softball team organized by our friend Carmen, an impish native of Malaysia with boyish good looks and zany sensibilities. Carmen was a compulsive joiner who collected friends the way other people collect saltshakers—the only requirement being that they were cute, colorful, and odd. As a result, our softball roster was a weird mishmash of the wildly different factions of Chicago's lesbian community. Our pitcher was a member of a Black Pride poetry club. First and third bases were covered by Orthodox Jews from the Or Cadash group. And a few anemic creatures from the Vegan Society stumbled their way around the outfield.

Carmen had never managed to befriend one decent athlete and our team suffered as a result. We were by far the worst team in the league. The closest we came to winning a game was when we played a team of overweight asthmatics who spent the game alternately sucking on steroid inhalers and filterless cigarettes. We played them on an ozone-alter day, which worked in our favor, but we still lost by five runs.

Early in the season, a woman wearing crisp athletic shorts and a whistle showed up at our dugout. She stood with her hands on her hips surveying the team, which was sprawled out on the bench, staring meaningfully at the ground and talking about anything but softball. As I quietly prayed that we wouldn't have enough players to start the game, the woman gave the whistle a loud, extended blast.

"I have one question for you. What are you made of, ladies?" she demanded. We looked at each other in confusion. We had no idea who this person was or why she was asking us existential questions this early on a Sunday morning. "Did you hear me?" she barked. "I asked what are you ladies made of?"

"About ninety-six percent water and the rest is pure cowardice," said Pam, our catcher, as she struggled into her gear. Pam had the soft prettiness of a pre-Raphaelite Madonna and a deceptive timidity. Her habit of making wisecracks in sotto voice captured the admiration and affection of Anne, Tricia, and me, and by mid-season she had easily won a place among our tribe of friends.

The woman with the whistle squinted her tough eyes at Pam and squared her shoulders as if preparing for battle. Pam squeaked and sank behind me for protection. Just then, Carmen trotted to the sidelines, giggling into her hand mischievously. "This is Delores, our new coach."

Delores accepted the introduction with a curt bow. "You can call me Coach, ladies," she said, getting a faraway look in her eyes. "And I'm here to make you into a winning team!" As Coach rattled off her credentials to a stupefied audience, Carmen pulled me aside and told me in an excited whisper, "She's been kicked off every team in the league for excessive enthusiasm."

Coach would show up at the field hours before the game started, checking out the competition in the dumb hope that she might be able to teach us something that would help us win a game. She'd formulate complicated playing strategies and present them to us in the form of charts and graphs, while we sat listlessly on the sidelines. At the end of her lectures, Coach would open the floor to questions. The only question we ever asked was why we weren't allowed to use Coach's lucky bat, the precious piece of wood she carried to every game in a leather satchel. Coach would never answer the question. Instead, she'd nod her head earnestly and harkened back to her own glory days on the field, slipping into some strange fantasy world populated by women that she mistily referred to as "the girls."

The fact that none of us paid any attention to her didn't bother Coach in the least. And her demented fantasy that we were improving under her care could not be dimmed by the fact that we continued our aggressive losing streak. Coach would prowl the sidelines, clapping her hands and cheering us on manically as we fumbled balls, swung at the dirt, and yawned our way through the game.

Our team stood in sad contrast to Jean's team, which had won the league championship for several years running. Her teammates would scamper onto the field looking more like gazelles than softball dykes. They wore professional looking uniforms bearing the logo of their sponsor, Big Martha's Bar. Our jerseys, on the other hand, were cheap polyblend tee-shirts that Carmen picked up at a shop that specialized in damaged and irregular clothing. They featured the name of our firm—DeTorelli and Polanski—along with a pair of crutches and a Band-aid. Tricia thought the emblem might help us solicit personal injury cases from wounded players. Most of our members refused to wear uniforms, though, citing complicated political or dietary concerns.

We didn't play Jean's team until mid-season. My regular position was shortstop, but I switched positions with Pam for the game so I could play catcher. The catcher is the most social of all positions and I saw it as an opportunity to flirt with Jean each time she stepped to the plate.

As Tricia helped me put on the catcher's gear, we overheard Jean's teammates moaning about having to waste their vastly superior skills on a team as unworthy as ours. They consoled themselves with the fact that they'd beat us by the slaughter rule, which would allow them to spend a long afternoon at Big Martha's Bar.

"Those bitches," Tricia said, sneering at the infield. She called the team together, which was about as easy as corralling hamsters. When we finally gathered in the dugout, Tricia gave a pep talk that managed to inspire killer instinct in women who believed that compromise and acquiescence were the only ways to win at any contest.

"Are they going to beat us?" Tricia said as she paced across the bench. "Of course they are. But are we going to let them beat us by the slaughter rule? No way!" Coach, who had tears in her eyes by this point, pulled her lucky bat out of its satchel. "I want you to use this today, ladies."

We took the field, and for the first time all season my teammates jogged to their positions with gusto and purpose. Usually, we skulked reluctantly from the sidelines only after the umpire threatened to penalize us with delay of game. The first two batters made hits, but my team fielded the balls with amazing efficiency and held the runners at second. Jean was the third batter. She stepped up to the plate and blasted me with a smile. "My team thought you'd be an easy win, but I told them 'Don't be too sure. The catcher is the brains of that outfit.'"

She dug in her spikes and wiggled her butt longer than I thought was necessary. When the first pitch came in as a strike, she turned and smiled at me again.

"You'd better stop smiling at me and watch the ball," I said. She laughed and swung at the next pitch, hitting a pop-up that I caught easily. I reached over and tagged her with my glove.

"That's not necessary," she said, helpfully, as if I'd never played the game before. "You don't have to touch me after you catch a fly."

"But what if I want to touch you?" I said. The umpire pushed her hat back on her forehead and exclaimed "oooh!" at my cheekiness. Jean reached over and playfully tugged my cap over my eyes.

My team continued to play well, hitting and fielding if not like good players, then at least like mediocre ones. Jean's team seethed, getting so angry that they made stupid mistakes. Only Jean treated our miraculous turnaround with good humor. She congratulated us when we made good plays and sided with us whenever an umpire made a questionable call.

By the sixth inning, though, my team had lost interest in the game. One of the outfielders missed an easy catch because she was kneeling on the ground, reciting a haiku to a squirrel. Anne, who was playing second base, was chatting with Pam when a ball flew past her. She shrugged as it sped by and continued her conversation. My attention was completely focused on Jean, so if she wasn't on the field, I was searching for her on the sidelines. As a result, I missed a few tags at home plate. But the errors were a small price to pay for the rewards of my surveillance. I was thrilled to catch Jean peeking at me self-consciously after she dodged the embrace of her girlfriend and, later, when she removed her girlfriend's hand from her knee, I could barely contain my joy.

Despite our disintegration in the final innings, we managed to hang on through a regulation game. So, even though we were beat by seven runs, we considered it a moral victory. And Jean's team regarded it as a defeat.

* * * * * * * *

Unlike most teams, my teammates had no interest in spending time together after the games. But following the game against Jean's team, we were energized with a sense of esprit de corps. So when Carmen asked if any of us wanted to go to Big Martha's Bar, we all cried, "Yes!" in a rare moment of unity.

Big Martha's was a fortress of intimidation. It was dominated by loud, sporty girls who lived in their spikes and knew all the bartenders by name. The regulars would drink free shots by the trayful and stare menacingly at any strangers who made the mistake of wandering into the place. The bar itself was nothing special. It was a squat, ugly brick building in a marginal neighborhood that was filled with half-broken furniture and decorated with Christmas lights and posters of sex symbols from the 1980's. Behind the bar was a wall filled with photos of sports teams sponsored by Big Martha's—champions all! That wall of toothy aggression put you on notice that if you couldn't swing a bat or catch a football you weren't welcome here.

Tricia, who refused to feel out-of-place anywhere, burst through the doors of Big Martha's like a cowboy sheriff looking to clean up the joint, and the rest of the team followed meekly in her wake. A few minutes after Tricia commandeered a table by the grimy windows, I spotted several of Jean's teammates walk into the bar and head toward the patio.

Most of Jean's team was huddled at a table, sulking over their lite beers. The beer had not yet had its healing effects and they were quietly grumbling about each other's poor play. Jean was not on the patio and I assumed she was making amends with her girlfriend, who fled the field in tears in the last inning after Jean rebuffed a kiss. When I turned to go back into the bar, I ran smack into Jean.

"You!" she said. "I blame you for this!" She swept her arm in the direction of her teammates. "You are the mastermind behind our humiliating victory."

Her team looked up from its collective gloom, and it was as if the sun had appeared after a long, gray winter. They each called out her name loudly and in different derivations—Jean, GeGe, Jeano, Geelee—so it sounded as if they were arguing with each other.

"Join us for a drink," she said, ignoring them and focusing on me. She was carrying two glasses of red wine and she handed one glass to me. "My private stock," she said with a wink. "I keep a few bottles at the bar." I took a sip of the wine and had to restrain myself from spitting it out. It tasted like a combination of melted popsicle and bubblegum. It was the Pigglet brand.

We sat down at the table and Jean made a comic confession about how she was solely responsible for every error made during the game. She was a genius at self-deprecation and her friends responded by teasing her in a way that made it clear they adored her. Jean merrily launched into a story about the time she almost single-handily lost a championship game for her team, but she stopped in mid-sentence when a stunning woman with cropped blonde hair walked onto the patio.

"Hey, Michelle," Jean said quietly.

Michelle nodded humorlessly. She sat at the other end of the table and lit a cigarette. Michelle was the most physically attractive member of the group. The only thing that kept her from being movie-star beautiful was the fact that she never smiled. I had watched her over the past few months and noticed how her friends deferred to her, and also how she and Jean rarely interacted.

Michelle stubbed out the match and looked up at me from across the table. Her gaze was unsettling. It was the type of look that a dog gives you while it's deciding whether to bite you. "Where's Laura?" Michelle asked Jean.

Jean shook her head and rolled her eyes dramatically. "She's having the vapors. I had to take her home."

"Is that your girlfriend?" I asked, with more interest than I intended.

"Mmmm," Jean said, noncommittally. "We're dating."

Michelle scoffed loudly. "Is that what it's called?"

The group laughed heartily and I felt Jean tense next to me. She finally joined in with a forced chuckle. Then she clutched my arm and pulled me close to her. "I was hoping you'd be here," she said, confidentially. "I have a legal problem I'd like to discuss."

"Sure, what is it?"

"Oh, not here," she said, stealing a glance at her friends. "I have to leave in a few minutes, and there's no privacy...." I would later learn that this was one of Jean's patented moves. She was famous for popping into places for a few minutes, spreading joy and then leaving before anyone could tire of her. Our entire relationship was based on brief encounters and quick escapes.

"Can we meet next week? How about over dinner? I was injured recently and I'd like your advice on what to do about it."

I got up from the table and wandered back into the bar. Anne and Pam were still at the table, drinking martinis. Anne was wearing cut-off chef whites. She wore chef whites for everything from pajamas to formal wear. She hated wearing shoes and insisted on playing softball barefoot. Her filthy feet were just barely covered by a pair of ancient flip-flops, a reluctant concession to the bar's relaxed health code requirements.

"Where's Tricia," I asked.

"She's raging around here somewhere," Anne said. "She is certain that the bartender is watering down our drinks. She's already started to refer to the bartender as 'the defendant.' You'd better calm her down or there's going to be a brawl."

I glanced around the room and spotted Tricia shoving her cocktail at the vegans, trying to force them to check its alcohol content. "Julia," Tricia yelled across the bar, "taste this. Does it have any gin in it?" She shot a dirty look at the bartender, a woman who was constructed of muscle, tattoos, and scar tissue.

I yanked the drink out of her hand and took a sip. Then I spit it out. "Are you kidding?" I said, handing her the drink. "It's pure alcohol."

"Really," she said, sniffing the drink suspiciously. The bartender smirked at Tricia.

I shoved Tricia into a window seat and slipped in next to her. "We may have a new personal injury client," I said.

"Excellent," said Tricia, licking her lips. "Any broken bones involved?"

"Don't know. I'm meeting her next week to discuss it."

Just then, Jean walked up and leaned her face so close to mine I thought she was going to kiss me. "See you on Wednesday," she said.

"That's not a client. That's a date," said Tricia. We craned our necks to watch Jean make her way out of the bar. A gay man walking into the bar grabbed her in an embrace and they chatted animatedly together.

"So, what do you think?" I asked, trying not to sound too excited.

"She seems like the type of woman who is more interested in finding a consort than a girlfriend," Tricia said with a shrug, turning her attention back to her drink. "But she might be good in bed. Better bill her hourly, though. I can't afford to be working for free just so you can have a decent sex life."

* * * * * * * *

Jean was forty-five minutes late for our meeting. By the time she arrived, I was closing my briefcase and turning off the lights. She flew into the office full of apologies and good cheer. She sighed in happy exhaustion and collapsed against the wall. "You look nice," she said, eyeing me appreciatively.

I had dressed carefully for the evening. The night before, I tried on almost every outfit in my closet. I settled on linen slacks and a silk sweater that could be businesslike or sexy depending on what bra I wore under it.

Jean was wearing a suit heavy on brocade and light on subtly. I was expecting that she'd favor something sleek and stylish and in the color of expensive nuts. But the suit was pink, bulky, and overly feminine. It looked like something the wife of a senator might wear.

Jean declared that she was starving for a drink, so we left the office and headed for a restaurant several blocks away. We landed at a trendy restaurant known for its bad food and inflated prices. When we walked in the door, the maitre d' slapped shut the reservation book, tossed his arms around Jean and gave her a kiss on each cheek. They chatted gaily, gossiping about what celebrities had recently eaten at the restaurant. I quietly stood beside her, searching the room for movie stars.

Once we were seated, Jean ordered a bottle of wine without looking at the wine list. I recognized it as one of the Pigglet brands of wine, the same sickeningly sweet wine I tasted at Big Martha's. When the wine arrived, she placed her elbows on the table, rested her chin on her hands, leaned forward, and said, "So, I guess we should talk about my toe."

Several months earlier, a truck from Trident Towing—the most hated and feared towing company in Chicago—rolled over her big toe as she was crossing the street. The tip of the toe was crushed and part of the toe was amputated. She had spoken with a few attorneys, but hadn't chosen anyone to represent her.

"Now, instead of a toe, I have a nubbin," she said. "It's actually quite cute."

"Well, we don't want the jury to know that," I said. "From now on let's refer to it as your devastating loss."

I explained that Tricia and I had a general practice, but Tricia was interested in picking up more personal injury work. It was the only way we'd ever become millionaires, she said. The few injury cases that we handled had settled out-of-court for small sums. I wasn't interested in personal injury work, but agreed to take on some cases to please Tricia, who longed to be a trial attorney. Personal injury cases required a huge investment of time and cash and it could take years before we saw any payoff.

"So that would mean a lot more dinner meetings?" Jean asked.

"Well, yeah," I said.

"You're hired," she said.

After dinner, which was typical for those types of restaurants—the food looked more like something you should wear than eat—Jean walked me back to my office. As I stood in the entryway, wondering whether I should shake her hand or hug her, Jean kissed me.

"There," she said, as if she had just accomplished some type of manual labor, like laying a tile floor.

I grabbed her by the waist, pulled her into me and kissed her. She placed her hands on the front of my sweater and rubbed her palms against it gently. "Let's go," she said. She took my hand and waved down a cab, which she directed to a swanky hotel.

Later that evening, while we were lying in an impossibly large canopied bed, she showed me her toe. It was cut off at the knuckle and appeared to be red and swollen. I moved to the opposite end of the bed and I kissed it on its flat, angry face.

* * * * * * * *

When I woke the next morning, Jean was gone. She left a note that read: "Thanks for teaching me the true meaning of litigation." I folded the note carefully and slipped it into my briefcase.

I arrived at the office late, wearing the same outfit I had on the day before.

"You slut!" Tricia proclaimed gleefully. Lonnie looked up from her newspaper and tsked-tsked loudly.

"Lonnie, I had to sacrifice my body for the firm," I said. "We've got ourselves a nice, little P.I. case."

Tricia grabbed my wrist and looked at me expectantly.

"It's a good one," I said. And I told her about the toe.

"A missing limb!" Tricia exclaimed.

"It's not a limb. It's a toe," I said.

"When I get done with it, it will be a limb!" she said with supreme confidence. "And we'll be going after Trident Towing. That's like representing a client against Methostopholese. So, tell me about it."

"The toe? Well, it looks pretty bad, but it's not like she's crippled because of it."

"Not the toe. The date."

I told her about dinner and the kiss and the hotel.

"You slut!" she said again. "Do you think she has a girlfriend?" Tricia said, squinting hard at me. Lonnie looked up with concern.

"I think so," I said. "She's dodgy about it."

"Well, don't worry," Tricia said. "It's not your problem. It's hers. Now, when am I going to meet that million-dollar toe?"

CHAPTER 3

Jean and I were together for fifteen months. And until I discovered that she was sleeping with Michelle, I thought we were happy. Sure, we had our problems, but we dealt with them as any two adults would—with equal measures of patience, understanding, and deep denial. In hindsight, I realized that the warning signs were there from the beginning.

The first few months of our courtship were idyllic if you didn't count the fact that most of our intimate moments were played out in public. Jean refused to go to my apartment because she claimed she wouldn't feel comfortable sharing a bedroom wall with Tricia and Anne. However, I felt this was an odd concern coming from a woman who felt perfectly comfortable stuffing her hand down my shirt in a crowded nightclub and making out with me in front of a group of school kids near the birds of prey exhibit at the Lincoln Park Zoo.

These were the weeks before her girlfriend moved out of Jean's apartment, when Jean was still concocting elaborate lies about why we couldn't go to her place. When she finally ended the relationship with Laura, I was sorry I had pushed for the breakup. Once we began dating openly, the power dynamic shifted in Jean's favor and the spotlight of her affections began its slow swing in the direction of a new, unobtainable star.

* * * * * * * *

Jean and I were together for five months before she met Anne and Tricia. We made dozens of dinner dates, but Jean always begged

41

off at the last minute. I explained to Tricia that Jean had a habit of double booking herself, and not to take the cancellations personally. But Tricia wasn't buying it.

"If she can't commit to dinner, how can you expect that she will commit to you?" asked Tricia, always looking to stir up trouble. In retrospect, I should have let the matter rest, because when we finally did get together with Anne and Tricia it was a nightmare.

Jean was scheduled to come to our office that afternoon for our first meeting about her crippled toe. Tricia had filed a lawsuit against Trident Towing and we needed to start the discovery process. After the meeting, we planned to go to Anne's restaurant for dinner.

Before she opened her restaurant, Anne worked as a chef at a series of overpriced, overrated restaurants with stupid one-word names that didn't have any relevance to food: Tiny; Branch; Alone. She quit her job at Loud a few weeks after her last breakup with Tricia and opened a cafe that catered to the homeless. The restaurant was called The Depression for several reasons. It was borne out of Anne's despair over her breakup with Tricia and it reflected the type of food on the menu—hearty meats, stews, and casseroles, homemade breads, and cream pies—all created from recipes Anne's grandmother used at a roadside diner in Detroit in the 1930's. To fund the venture, she had a few seatings weekly for paying customers, who were served the same meal as the homeless. By the time Chicago's leading alternative newspaper rated the heavy food the best hangover cure in town, lines were forming around the block on the nights it served paying customers, and some people feigned destitution just to sneak in on the homeless-only nights. After Tricia and Anne reconciled, Tricia convinced Anne to expand into a neighboring building to accommodate paying clientele daily.

At six o'clock, when Jean still hadn't arrived at the office, Tricia tossed me my coat and ordered me to turn off my computer. I protested lamely, but I knew she was right. Jean's casual indifference to time was a major source of friction between us. I fretted constantly about being late to appointments and insisted on arriving at the airport at least two hours ahead of any flight. Jean was the person you'd see sprinting through airports, yelling for the stewardess to hold the door, and slamming into her seat moments before takeoff, chuckling to neighboring passengers about her close call.

As Tricia and I were leaving the office, the phone rang. Tricia tried to pull the door shut, but I squeezed past her and lunged for the phone. It was Jean.

"Change in plans," she said without a care in the world. I could hear a lite rock station in the background, and I could picture her bopping her head to the music and checking her reflection in the rearview mirror every few seconds. We had different tastes in music.

She liked syrupy ballads that were often featured as background music for greeting card commercials. I preferred songs written by the great lyricists of the '30's and '40's and performed by big band singers who were destined to become obese, drunk, or broke in their later years.

"I have to cancel dinner tonight," she said. "I've got to meet a client at Issue." Issue was the restaurant of the moment. Everything about it was hard and cold—the furniture, the wait staff, the food.

"You can't," I snapped with not as much fury as I would have liked. Tricia was standing beside me, silently demanding that I turn the phone over to her.

"I'm disappointed, too, but what can I do?" Jean chirped. "It's business." Jean used the "it's business" excuse for everything from a legitimate sales call to staying out until all hours with a friend who may or may not open a bar in the next ten years.

"How about this," she said, correctly interpreting my silence as a sign that I was not going to let her off the hook. "How about you meet me at Issue and we can eat there? I'm just pulling up now, so I can take care of my client by the time you get here." I hung up and told Tricia in as casual a tone as I could muster that we would pick up Anne and meet Jean at Issue.

"We're eating at The Depression," Tricia said, poisonously.

"Look, don't make waves for once, okay?" I pleaded. "Try to keep an open mind about her. Honestly, she's no more impossible than you are." It was the wrong thing to say. Tricia insisted on being the most impossible person in any group.

"I don't like this one bit," Tricia said. "The only reason—and I mean the only reason—I am putting up with this nonsense is because I am in love with her toe."

When we arrived at the restaurant, Jean was in the bar chatting with Issues' owner, a man who looked exactly like the robot who was the villain of a movie Anne and I watched the night before. The robot in the movie pretended to be compassionate and empathetic. But it was all an act. His real agenda was to steal people's tongues. I dozed off before I learned what he did with the tongues. Jean spotted us and gave a comic double take before leaping from her stool and walking to us with her arms extended.

"Look at me!" she exclaimed. "I'm early for once."

The evening went downhill from there. Jean was nervous, but she tried to cover it up by dominating the conversation. Tricia stared at her from across the table with a dead expression. Jean ordered a bottle of wine—thankfully, not the Pigglet brand—but when the waiter tried to pour some into Tricia's glass, Tricia held her hand over it protectively. "No, thanks, I'll just drink water," which was like a cat refusing catnip.

I tried to salvage the evening by announcing that Trident's attorneys had called that afternoon with a settlement offer. It was for a measly $10,000, but you rarely received an offer this early in negotiations. It was an excellent sign that they didn't want to go to trial.

"How high do you think they'll go?" Jean asked me. Up until that point, Jean took almost no interest in the case. She considered her toe little more than a curio, an odd bit of china to take out of a cabinet occasionally and tell the story of how you came by it. But the prospect of collecting a sizeable settlement finally caught her attention.

"We're not settling for anything under a half a million," Tricia said, challenging me with her eyes. The settlement amount had been a point of contention between Tricia and me. I thought we should hold out for $200,000. But Tricia wanted to set the bar at an unreasonable amount, which would force us to go to trial.

Jean let out a small whoop and threw her arms around me. "We could buy a house," Jean said, giving me a kiss.

"House?" Tricia said, cocking her eyebrow.

The next day, Tricia placed a vase of flowers on my desk.

"What's this for?" I asked.

"It's a housewarming present," she said. I dropped my head into my hands and moaned.

"At what point were you going to tell me that you were buying a house with that woman—before or after we signed a mortgage together?" she asked. Tricia, as usual, was over dramatizing the situation. Tricia, Anne, and I had spent a couple weekends looking at two-flats with our realtor, Diane. But we did it mainly because we enjoyed spending time with Diane, a middle-aged adulteress who amused us by giving us tours of the empty homes she used as rendezvous spots with her lovers.

"I am not buying a house with her," I said.

"I don't know why not," she said. "You're already living with her."

I had started a slow but steady migration of my belongings to Jean's apartment immediately after Laura moved out. I returned to my apartment for an occasional change of clothes and to check on my cat, Norm, who was not welcome at Jean's home because she was allergic to animals. "Well, that tells you something right there," Tricia said, as if the allergy was a mental disorder. Unlike my other girlfriends, Jean did not pressure me to move in. She never even mentioned it until the dinner with Tricia and Anne. Initially, I was relieved that she didn't ask me to live with her. Later, though, I began to feel insecure and I started dropping subtle hints, ones that she either failed or refused to pick up on.

I pulled my checkbook from the desk and opened it to show Tricia that I was still paying rent on our apartment. She yanked it out of my hand and tossed it across the room. "You're just using our apartment as a life raft. Yes, you, Miss 'I'm-so-superior-because-I'm-not-a-stupid-lesbian-who-moves-in-with-my-girlfriend-after-the-first-date.' You're just like the rest of us fools now."

"We're not buying a house together," I said. "Jean just got excited by your very overly optimistic projection of a settlement amount."

"All I'm saying is that you'd better be careful," she said in a gentler tone. "I can't believe I'm going to say this, because I don't like you very much right now and it pains me to give you any advice that might save you from making a terrible mistake. But even if I don't like you, I do love you. So, here it is: From day one I thought the relationship wouldn't last because you would grow bored with her. But what I realized last night is that she is never going to give you the chance to get bored with her. She'll leave you before that happens."

Tricia began to walk out of the office, but she stopped short and leaned against the doorframe. "And what the hell was that cocktail dress all about?" she said, referring to the sleeveless black dress Jean wore to the dinner. "You may want to inform her that she is not Audrey Hepburn. I mean, come on! Accept your limitations."

* * * * * * * *

A few days after the confrontation with Tricia, my mother called me at Jean's apartment. It was a Sunday, and we were spending a rare morning lounging around, reading the papers and eating bagels. Typically, our weekends were packed with commitments with Jean's friends—brunches, followed by shopping, and ending with long, drawn-out dinners with large groups of people that had me longing for bed.

After the fiasco at Issue, Jean was eager to placate me. So, she promised to turn down invitations and spend a quiet day alone with me. But when the phone rang, she leaped from the couch as if reacting to a fire alarm and she grabbed the receiver, grimacing an apology as she did so. I couldn't have been more surprised when she handed me the phone. "It's your mother," she said, practically singing.

I looked at her in horror, unable to move or speak for a moment. As soon as the shock wore off, I took the phone and placed my hand over the mouthpiece. "How does she know I'm here?" I asked Jean.

"Because Miss Tricia told me so," my mother called out through the receiver. "Believe me, I was just relieved to learn you weren't dead. I've been trying to get a hold of you for weeks." I had just spoken to her on Friday. Ever since I came out to my parents, they had been unnaturally concerned about my whereabouts. My mother mentioned Jeffrey Dahmer every chance she got and the words "rough trade" entered her vocabulary. I considered delineating the differences between gay men and lesbians, but I knew it would open a whole new can of worms.

I came out to my parents when I was in my mid-20's at a carefully orchestrated dinner at my uncle's restaurant. I figured that they'd be reluctant to kill me there. After I stumbled through my announcement, my mother shot my father a glance that said, "Behave yourself." My father, who looked like he wanted to brain me with a bottle of Chianti, silently seethed and didn't speak to me the rest of the evening. Later that night, my mother pulled me aside and said, "Don't worry about your father. He'll figure out a way to blame this on me, and you'll be off the hook."

"I was just calling to see if you received your Scandinavian Club newsletter," my mother said. My grandparents moved to the United States when my mother was a baby, but my mother acted as if she had never left Denmark. All her friends were Danes, Swedes, and Norwegians. Her social life revolved around the Scandinavian Club, which was located in Forest Pond, the suburb my parents lived in. In the most recent election, my mother's best friend Neva was elected club president, but my mother was the real power behind the throne. Neva's reign started out smoothly, but a dark cloud moved over her administration when the German Club suggested that the two clubs merge into one club. My mother thought the German's motive—apart from the innate German need to conquer—was to take over the Scandinavian clubhouse, a lovely old home that was donated to the club by a spinster member decades earlier. The recent newsletter focused on the latest threat by the Germans.

"Did you read the article Nettie wrote?" my mother asked. From her tone it was clear she was not happy with the article. "Every sentence ended in a punctuation mark. How are you supposed to know what's important and what's not? 'The Germans want to take over the club! It's Ingrid's turn to bring pastry to the needlepoint circle!' That's the last time we let a Swede cover any important news." My mother had a low opinion of Swedes. Although many of her friends were Swedish, she ridiculed them in private and spoke to them slowly, like you would to a mentally disabled person. Normally, I enjoyed encouraging my mother's tirades against the Swedes and Germans, but I didn't want Jean to think I shared my mother's crackpot prejudices.

"So, Mom," I said, changing the subject. "How's Eric?" Eric was my younger brother. He still lived at home in an old boathouse he converted into a bachelor pad. My mother sighed dramatically, her standard response to any mention of my brother. They were both high-strung and demanding and they drove each other crazy. My father worried constantly about keeping the peace, not realizing that they thrived on the conflict. Eric worked at my dad's construction company and he was always scheming of ways to transform the business from one that specialized in building cheap, ugly apartments into a Trump-like enterprise that wouldn't consider a project that was under fifty stories tall.

"You're brother is dating someone. God only knows who," she said. "Probably another cocktail waitress. I just hope he's up-to-date on his penicillin shots." When Eric was in college, he dated a girl who held a summer job as a waitress at Bennigans. From that time on, my mother predicted that he would marry a topless dancer.

My brother and I looked exactly like our mother, except she was a blonde and we were brunettes. Such was the total and complete dominance of my mother over every aspect of our lives that her tepid, Nordic genes beat my Italian father's dark, muscular DNA into submission and programmed nearly every physical aspect of my brother and me. Eric and I had blue eyes and delicate facial features, and we were built along the long, lean lines of our Scandinavian ancestors. As a result, Eric looked almost too pretty, and women often made the terrible mistake of mistaking his beauty for sensitivity.

"Anyway," my mother said, "Tricia told me that you're not living with her anymore. Why didn't you tell me you moved out? Not that I blame you. I don't know how you managed to live with Tricia and Anne in all that filth as long as you did."

"Mom, how many times have I told you never to believe a word Tricia says," I said, making a mental note to kill Tricia. "I've just been spending a lot of time at my friend's house."

"The one who answered the phone? Is her name Jean? Tricia said she doesn't like her body language, whatever that means. What's her last name?"

"Peterson," I said.

"Hmmm. What kind of name is that?" she asked. What she was really asking was whether Peterson was spelled with the Danish "sen" or the Swedish "son."

"Jean, are you Scandinavian?" I asked.

"What?" she said, looking up from the newspaper with irritation. She had lost interest in the call when it became clear I was not going to initiate a meeting between her and my parents. Ever since we got together, Jean was determined to meet my parents. I was reluctant because I knew that the combination of Jean's need to ingratiate herself with authority figures and my mother's need to be disapproving and aloof would end in despair. And, several weeks later, when they finally did meet, I was proved right. As the evening progressed badly and Jean realized that her charm offensive was not working, she simply stopped making an effort. It was like watching air being let out of a balloon. My mother was only superficially friendly and it could take years for her to warm up to people. As much as she groused about Tricia, I knew that my mother secretly respected Tricia for not trying to impress her.

"What's your nationality?" I asked.

"I don't know. English? German?" Jean said. "I don't know."

"Well, the good news is that she's not Swedish," I told my mother, pointedly ignoring the German possibility.

"That is good news," she said. "I've got my hands full with them and their hysterical punctuation. Okay, honey, don't forget about bridge on Wednesday." We played bridge every Wednesday at the Scandinavian Club. I never forgot.

"Wednesday," she said, again. "Now don't forget. Wednesday. Write it down somewhere."

"Okay," I said. "I'll see you on Thursday."

"No, Wednesday!"

* * * * * * * *

In August, Mrs. Balukis, the old Greek woman who owned the two-flat Tricia, Anne and I lived in, dropped dead of a heart attack while chasing one of Anne's animals out of her tomato beds. At her wake, her son, Nico, offered to sell the building to us. Tricia and Anne jumped at the offer, but I said I'd have to discuss it with Jean first.

"Why?" Tricia asked, genuinely baffled.

"Because she's, you know, my partner," I said, stumbling over the word "partner." I had never used that word before to describe a girlfriend. And now I said it carefully, like it was a tricky French word that could translate into something benign or really terrible depending on where you placed the accent.

"Well, we've got to act fast or else he's going to put it on the market," she said, threateningly. Tricia knew as well as I did that Nico Balukis did nothing fast. He would probably be happy to sign the deed over to us at no cost just to save him the trouble of getting dressed to go to the closing.

"And one other thing—and this is non-negotiable," she said. "Jean is not part of this deal. It's just the three of us. I'm not purchasing any property with that hologram you call a girlfriend. Sorry, I meant to say that hologram you call a partner."

That night, instead of telling Jean about the two-flat, I shook her rent bill and called it outrageous. She was swimming in debt, and at thirty-seven years old she owned little more than a sports car and some uncomfortable furniture.

"You should buy a place if for no other reason than it might make you stop spending money foolishly," I said.

"Are you proposing?" she asked.

I thought about it a minute. "I guess I am."

Our relationship began to devolve the moment we started shopping for a condo. Our tastes were so dissimilar—I liked vintage buildings in bad neighborhoods that stood a good chance of appreciating and she liked anything new, soulless and overpriced. After weeks of searching, we found a place that neither of us hated. It was a gut rehab of a charming old building. We signed the contract on the spot, and set our closing date for October.

In the next two months, as summer set into a cold and rainy fall, I saw less and less of Jean. She stayed out late, rarely bothering to make excuses for her inattention. I was so busy preparing for the move that I pretended not to notice. When I did see her, she was uncharacteristically irritable and impatient. She got into arguments with our condo developer and she threatened to cancel the contract if he didn't cave into her silly demands. As an attorney who specialized in real estate, I had witnessed this type of behavior on many occasions. It was the way clients acted when they didn't want to go through with a purchase. These clients would reschedule the closing date countless times. They'd attempt to back out of the deal at the final walk-thru. I'd soothe them and gently push them through the process until they signed the final papers, even though I knew that if they thought they were making a mistake, they probably were.

* * * * * * * *

The night before our final walk-thru, two days before we were scheduled to move into the condo, we went to a party at Susan and Sandy's home. Susan and Sandy were one of those high-powered lesbian couples who are paraded before the community as the hope of the future. In the mid 1990's, they served as the covergirls for a national news magazine story that heralded the arrival of "lesbian chic." When they sold their brownstone in Andersonville and moved to a bungalow in suburban Oak Park, they appeared in the mainstream press, flashing commitment rings and stressing the importance of graceful suburban living. And when they flew to China to adopt a baby, it set off a wave of gay adoptions, so many that the Chinese Embassy in Chicago added staff just to handle the influx of applications. Over the years, they blended into a single, glamorous unit: SallyandSusan. I could never remember who was Sally and who was Susan, so I referred to them collectively as the Ss.

When Jean and I arrived at their home, S#1 opened the door. Her hair looked like it hadn't been washed in days and a soiled bib was slung over her shoulder. Since adopting the baby, the Ss had embraced the lesser aspects of domestic drudgery with the same passion they had once adopted the swinging life of the lesbian elite. They competed with each other over who was more weary and miserable.

S #1 greeted us by stifling a massive yawn. "I haven't slept since last Tuesday," she said. S#2 called out from the kitchen that she hadn't slept since last Saturday. Jean and I snuck off to the basement as they engaged in a whining session about who was more exhausted.

The room was packed with women who were all focused on the World Series game, which was blaring from an enormous TV at the far end of the room. Jean paused at the bottom of the stairs and the crowd magically sensed her presence, turning in unison to welcome her. She swam into the sea of people and I happily walked behind the bar. Playing bartender allowed me to do something other than pretend that I knew what the hell a batting average was.

Jean's friends were divided into two groups. The core section was made up of Jean and a few other women. An outer group rotated around the core like satellites. These were the girlfriends and the wannabe girlfriends. They clung to the outer reaches of the core group's orbit, straining to hear conversations, laughing too loudly, casting suspicious looks at one another. A study of their team portraits would show there was good reason for concern. At first glance, it looked as if the same team played together for softball, volleyball, flag football, and basketball. But on closer inspection, you'd see that one blonde had replaced another in the lineup. The photos reminded me of the ones taken of the ruling regime during the days of Soviet Russia. One day a cabinet minister would be in the picture, and the next he would be gone. Airbrushed into his place was a new minister, who looked just as frightened and powerless as his predecessor. Jean and Michelle were always in the pictures, though. Standing at one end of the back row, Jean blasted her best sales rep smile. Michelle anchored the other end, seething at the photographer.

A few minutes after I took my position behind the Ss' bar, Cathy grabbed a stool and asked me to get her a beer. Cathy was the oldest member of the group. She was pushing forty, but she dressed and acted like a twelve-year-old. There was a frost warning that day, yet she wore a thin tee-shirt that revealed her bare midriff and a bellybutton piercing. The fact that she insisted on dating women in their early 20's ensured that she always had a tale of woe. Her newest girlfriend, Tabitha, a sophomore at Loyola, was sharing a loveseat with Mary Margaret, a loud-mouthed rich girl who made a sport out of stealing her friend's girlfriends. Cathy looked across the room at them miserably.

"I'm thinking about asking Tabitha to move in with me," Cathy said, absently stabbing a straw into her beer.

"How long have you been dating her?" I asked.

"Three weeks," she said with a sigh.

I opened a bottle of wine and looked around the room for Cindy, Michelle's girlfriend. Cindy had as much interest in sports as I did, so we'd often find ourselves splitting a bottle of wine at parties and gossiping. Cindy, the envied recipient of Michelle's infrequent smiles, was a pretty redhead who had been with Michelle for years.

As I searched the room for Cindy, I spotted Jean and Michelle huddled in a corner. Jean was standing with her back against the wall, nodding seriously at Michelle, who was whispering with intensity. Michelle always looked intense, like she was a general preparing to send some poor young soldier off to certain death.

"Where's Cindy?" I asked Cathy. She spit out a mouthful of beer and flailed her arms about her head, too excited to speak.

"Oh, my God!" she said. "Haven't you heard? Cindy and Michelle broke up!"

"You're kidding?" I said. "That's big news. Is there another woman?"

"There's got to be," Cathy said, leaning into me conspiratorially. "No one leaves just to leave. Know what I mean?" I glanced across the room. Michelle and Jean were still standing in the corner, but the atmosphere around them had lightened. Jean was holding a handful of pretzels and Michelle plucked one from her palm and studied it like it was an algebra problem. Then Michelle nodded her head in the direction of the stairs. I walk out from behind the bar to follow them, but before I could S#1 staggered up to the bar. She grabbed me by the shoulder and sat down on a barstool.

"I've got such a headache," she said. She was holding a cold compress to her forehead. "Can you believe that we're going to do this again? Are we crazy?" S#2 was pregnant with their second child. They decided that adopting foreign infants was passe, so they chose to go the insemination route. After the baby was born, S#1 would have to adopt the baby to be considered one of the legal parents. I was handling the legal work for the adoption.

"Do you want a drink?" I said, watching Jean and Michelle disappear upstairs.

"God, yes, but put it in one of those plastic cups. If Susan knows I'm drinking there will be hell to pay," she said.

"So, did you hear that Jean and I are moving into our new condo on Monday?" I said as I put the cup below the bar's surface and poured vodka into it.

"Condo?" she said. "I thought you were buying a two-flat with your friends."

I handed her the drink. "No, my friends—the ones I've been living with—have bought a two-flat. They're already living in it. Jean and I are buying a condo."

"Huh. Really?" she said, taking a thoughtful sip of her drink. "That's funny because Jean just told me..." Before she could finish her sentence, S #2 screamed from upstairs. There was a potty training emergency unfolding in the bathroom. "Christ, hold on to this," S#1 said, taking a deep gulp from the cup and then handing it back to me. She yelled something incomprehensible in response to S#2's mounting panic and wearily began climbing the stairs. She stopped briefly to shake her head in despair at Jean and Michelle, who were heading back downstairs.

"What was that all about?" Jean asked, leaning against the bar and popping a handful of nuts into her mouth.

"Crisis at Toddler Central," I said. I reached over to smooth a strand of hair from her forehead. She pushed my hand away.

"Speaking of crises," she said, "Michelle broke up with Cindy."

"Yeah, I just heard. What happened?"

"Oh, it's a long story," she said with a chuckle, as if she couldn't be less interested.

"Michelle is feeling terrible and she wants to talk, so we're going for a ride."

"I refuse on moral grounds to set foot in Michelle's Hummer," I said self-righteously. Among Michelle's many faults was her fondness for gas guzzling vehicles.

Jean cocked her head at me as if I had answered her in Arabic. "No, I mean Michelle and I are going for a ride. I'll meet you at home later, Okay?"

"Okay," I said, glancing at Michelle. She was standing in front of the TV screaming at an umpire, who apparently had just done something terrible. She didn't look too broken up to me. "Don't stay out too late. We've got the walk-thru at nine and then we have to finish packing." I had completed my packing weeks before, but Jean had barely started. We had an argument a few days before about her refusal to prepare for the move. In mid-fight, she tossed a few dishtowels into a box before storming out of her apartment.

* * * * * * * *

Jean called me later that evening to tell me that she was spending the night at Michelle's and that she'd be home first thing in the morning. She called in the morning and said she'd meet me at the walk-thru. She called while I was standing in the empty living room of our new condo to tell me that she didn't want to buy it.

"You're having an affair with Michelle," I said flatly like I'd known it all along. But I never even suspected it until that moment. So, on top of everything else, I felt like a moron.

Jean stuttered a denial, but then she whispered, "I'm sorry." I almost felt bad for her. The terrible thing about loving someone is that you can't hate them, even when you want to. I breathed heavily into the phone, trying to get my bearings. My brain was pounding in my skull like it wanted to bust out.

* * * * * * * *

Tricia and Anne moved into the second floor apartment shortly after buying the two-flat. When I arrived they were in the kitchen, drinking coffee and reading the paper. Tricia was sitting in the window seat in her pajamas. Her mannish feet were propped up on the table. Anne was bending over one of the dogs, talking to it in loving gibberish. The apartment hadn't changed in over fifty years. The wallpaper was peeling off the walls and the kitchen still had its original stove and appliances. The kitchen reeked of the olive oil that Mrs. Balukis used to cook everything from eggs to layer cakes.

"There she is, the happy home owner," Tricia said sarcastically.

"Have you rented out the first floor, yet?" I asked. I collapsed next to Tricia and engaged in a bout of athletic sobbing that left me exhausted and wilted against Tricia's bosom.

"Promise me something," I said to Tricia after I finished choking out the story of my betrayal. Tricia was wrapped around me as tightly as a snake.

"You want me to kill her? Sure, no problem. Gladly," she said, kissing my hair.

"Let's settle her toe case as soon as possible. I know how much you want to bring it to trial, but promise me that you'll do everything in your power to settle it."

"Don't worry about a thing," she said. "I'll take care of everything."

CHAPTER 4

A few weeks after my date with Claire Larsson, I woke on a Saturday morning determined to unpack the boxes that filled my apartment. I'd been living on the first floor of Tricia and Anne's two-flat for over six months and most of my belongings were still stuffed into boxes I'd packed for the aborted move to the condo. For the first several months after the breakup, I was simply too depressed to unpack. I'd walk into the apartment mentally exhausted from the double murder fantasies that played in my head on a continuous loop and I'd be greeted by towers of heaving cardboard that looked as sad as I felt. I was an overly ambitious packer, so the boxes were stuffed beyond capacity, which caused their walls to buckle and sag. Occasionally, the contents of a box would shift its weight, causing the cardboard to sigh, and giving the impression that it was expressing sympathy in that passive way that inanimate objects have of showing their emotions. Such was the state of my despair that I was thrilled that the cardboard had taken my side in the divorce.

As the months dragged on, depriving myself of the basic tools of civilization became something of a sport. I was amazed at how little I needed to survive. My china and kitchen utensils were buried in one of the boxes, so I ate my meals standing over the sink. Since I didn't have access to knives and forks, I'd rip apart meat with my teeth and eat cold pasta with my fingers, dropping it into my mouth strand by strand like I was feeding worms to a baby bird. I used only one bath towel, which was so threadbare and coarse it did more harm than good, and I was left to shiver myself dry after a shower.

The boxes were crammed with tchtockes, photos, and objects d'art that I once thought I couldn't live without. Ironically, one of my longest running battles with Jean was whether I'd be allowed to introduce my sentimental clutter into our living space. It took our breakup to make me realize that I could get by with little more than a warm place to sleep and my sanity.

I started unpacking on the night of the disastrous date with Claire Larrson. When we returned to the two-flat that night, Tricia insisted that we reenact the date for Anne using the finger puppets they had given me for my birthday. (The set included only three puppets, so it was understood that Bunny would not be represented in the melodrama). The puppets were buried in one of the boxes. We each grabbed a box and dumped its contents on the floor. The search ended when Tricia plucked several love letters out of the rubble. We spent the rest of the evening listening to Tricia's dramatic interpretations of Jean's love letters, complete with her analysis of how Jean's misspellings and odd use of metaphors revealed an obvious chemical imbalance.

After that night, I got into the habit of unpacking one box a day, slowly letting my belongings drift back into my life so I wasn't startled by a flood of memories. On that Saturday morning, though, I woke at dawn overcome with the desire to get my life back in order in a hurry. I jumped out of bed and marched with purpose to the living room, where the boxes awaited me in wobbly towers.

As I walked down the dark hall, Norm bumped cautiously against my legs. He had no idea what this burst of energy would mean for him. I gave him a reassuring pat on the head before tearing into the first box. Just under the cardboard flap was an outrageously expensive outfit I'd bought the week before the breakup with Jean.

The clothes came from a fussy boutique near Jean's apartment. I had walked past the shop dozens of times and never saw any customers in it. A man was usually in the window, though, madly stuffing mannequins into unbelievably complicated clothing and then bending them into highly suggestive poses. I often wondered how the shop stayed in business and what motivated the man to put so much energy into window displays that appealed only to sadists and the colorblind, a small segment of the population even in this neighborhood. On that day, I happened to pause outside the shop's window as the man was outfitting one of the male mannequins in what appeared to be a horse harness. I followed his movements in the unfocused fashion of a sleepwalker. Since Jean and I signed the contract on the condo, I found myself wandering around in a trancelike state. I would be thinking about how Jean hadn't come home until two in the morning the night before and a voice in the reptilian part of my brain would be screaming to engage my fight or flight response. But an even louder voice—the voice of denial—would order all logic centers to shut down and I'd be left staring dumbly at a point in the horizon until my mind felt it was safe to reactivate.

The man turned toward the street and lit a cigarette. I was so lost in muddled thought that it took me a minute to realize that he was waving at me. He motioned me into the store with irritation, as if he had been waiting for me for hours. I knew that if I walked into the store I'd buy something just to be polite. But it didn't seem right to walk away at this point. An hour later, I left the shop with a five-hundred-dollar pair of suede slacks and a two-hundred-dollar leopard spotted silk blouse, an extravagance I could ill-afford while facing down a thirty-year mortgage.

I had never worn the clothes and they still had their price tags on when I removed them from the box and laid them on my bed. I stared at the outfit for a few moments, wondering if I'd have the nerve to wear it out that night to Minsk, a new lesbian dance bar. Carmen called earlier that week and invited Tricia, Anne and me to join her there. It would be my first time in a lesbian bar since the breakup and I was tempted to wear something daring to put the world on notice that I was no longer taking guff from anyone.

* * * * * * * *

It took me most of the day to unpack. When I was done, I turned on a Doris Day CD, took a shower, and poured a glass of wine. I hadn't had a drink since the date with Claire and the wine went straight to my head. The wine, coupled with Doris Day's plucky good cheer, gave me the courage I needed to try on the suede slacks. After I slipped into them and put on the blouse, I walked to the mirror with great hesitation, approaching it like it was a rabid animal. Apart from catching a quick glimpse of myself in the bathroom mirror when I brushed my teeth, I really hadn't looked at myself since the breakup with Jean. I was scared to see what type of damage all those sleepless nights and crying jags had done to me. I closed my eyes tightly. When I finally squeezed my eyes open, I hardly recognized myself.

I'd always been slender, but now I had the hungry, annoyed look of runway models and heroin addicts. The animal print made me look dangerous and feral, and the suede suggested that I might be demanding in bed. I ran my hands down my face. It was hollow in all the right places, and my eyes were no longer puffy thanks to an extended period without liquor or tears. The opening notes of "Everybody Loves a Lover" came bouncing out of the stereo and I sang along in front of the mirror, swaying my body in rhythm, stopping suddenly to catch myself at different angles. It reminded me of the heady feeling of self-recognition when I first realized I was gay. In those days, I'd spend hours staring at myself feeling as if I'd never seen myself before.

A frantic knocking at the door interrupted my self-revelry. A cascade of pounding followed several sharp knocks. It sounded like someone trying to escape a coffin.

"Turn off that goddamn Judy Garland and open the door." It was Tricia. She thought any singer who hit her peak before 1960 was Judy Garland. I opened the door and leaned against it languidly in a pose that I hoped suggested Rita Hayworth in *Gilda*.

Tricia took a step back into the foyer and gave me the once over. "Oooh, let me take a look at you, you sexy thing." I twirled into the living room and tried a few of my new modeling poses on her. She picked up my glass of wine from the coffee table and nodded at me in approval. As she took a sip of wine, she surveyed the living room. The boxes were gone and my belongings were more or less in place. The shelves along the mantel were filled with books, the walls were hung with the folk art I collected, and the card table I had been using as an all-purpose dining set, ironing board, and mail basket was folded behind the couch.

"Well, haven't you been a busy beaver," she said. "When I saw all those cardboard boxes piled up in the backyard, I thought Anne had invited some of her hobos to set up housekeeping in the garden." Anne insisted that we call the homeless hobos because the word carried a romantic cache of riding the rails, eating beans from a can, and signing songs of freedom.

I brushed past her and walked into the bedroom to admire myself in the mirror again. "I think I'm attracted to myself," I said, running my hands down my torso.

"Well, just remember to take the relationship slowly. No sleeping with yourself on the first date." She drained the drink and then sloshed more wine into the glass.

"Starting a little early?" I said.

"Early for what?" she asked.

"We're going to that new bar tonight," I said. We had discussed Minsk several times during the week, but Tricia refused to commit to going. She tried to give the impression that she was juggling several invitations, waiting for the best offer. However, we both knew that she couldn't stand the idea that her friends might manage to have a good time without her.

"Minsk," she said with a sniff of disdain. "Only a lesbian would name a bar after the capital of Belarus. The boys have bars named Berlin and Milan, and we get a gloomy Eastern European outpost."

"Isn't there a limerick about the man from Minsk?" I asked. I unbuttoned the top buttons of the blouse. But when I saw that my bra was exposed, I rebuttoned them.

"You're thinking of the man from Nantucket," Tricia said, dreamily twirling the wine glass. She was standing behind me, cocking her head at her reflection in the mirror. "I've always admired the man from Nantucket. He is such a scamp." She picked up Norm and draped him over her shoulder. She used her free hand to pat his rump, which caused him to drool with pleasure down her back.

"We've got to pick up Anne at The Depression in an hour, so you'd better get dressed. Or is that what you're wearing?" She was dressed in black stretch pants and a pink sweatshirt with a teddy bear on it. Any other adult would look like an idiot in this getup, but Tricia could pull off wearing the most ridiculous clothes. The secret, she said, was to act like whatever you're wearing is sable.

"I'm not going," she said. Norm jumped off her shoulder and Tricia stretched out on the bed. "I've got a date."

I walked to the closet and stepped into a pair of shoes that I bought on a shopping expedition with my mother. They were a compromise. She insisted I get Cole Hann pumps and I wanted loafers. So, we settled for clogs. "I didn't realize Stuart Weitzman made orthopedic shoes," she said with a sigh when I handed the clerk my credit card.

"You're spending an awful lot of time with Bunny," I said. "What happened to all those women you were going to date?"

"First of all, who said I'm going out with Bunny tonight?" she said, rising up on her elbows with great indignation. Then she waved the wine glass dismissively. "Okay, so I'm going out with Bunny. Big deal. I just have to get her out of my system, like a virus. I give it another two weeks. And then you'd better watch out, sister. I'm going to be the poster child for promiscuity." The proclamation drained her and she collapsed back on the bed.

"Do you think Annie suspects anything about Bun?" Tricia asked.

"She's not an idiot," I said. "But she hasn't said anything to me." I acted like I knew more than I was revealing just to drive Tricia crazy. But the truth was that I had no idea what Anne knew or didn't know. In fact, Anne had never mentioned the alleged agreement to have an open relationship. As far as I knew, this was all something cooked up by Tricia to justify her affair with Bunny. The last time they broke up, Tricia announced to her friends that her relationship with Anne was over weeks before she bothered to tell Anne.

"There's another reason I decided not to go tonight," she said. She got off the bed and placed both of her hands on my shoulders. "If I'm not there, Anne will feel free to meet women. And you should encourage her to do it. Don't feel like you're betraying me." She gave me the same lecture every time they broke up. I was to urge Anne to date other woman, because she needed to move on. I was to remind Anne that it would be virtually impossible to meet someone as wonderful as Tricia, but she must try.

"I'm going to tell her to ask out the new chef at The Depression," I said, shaking Tricia's hands off me. I didn't want her sweaty palms to stain the shirt. "She's really cute."

She looked at me in alarm. "Is Anne interested in her?"

"Well, if she isn't, she should be. That girl is h-o-t."

Tricia tapped the wine glass against her front teeth for a moment, wondering whether to take me seriously. "You are such an asshole," she concluded.

"Yes, but a sexy asshole," I said. "Maybe Annie will want to date me."

"God help her," Tricia said. She unbuttoned the top buttons of my blouse.

"But now you can see my bra," I said, looking down into my cleavage, which thankfully wasn't a victim of my recent weight loss.

"That's the point," she said with a lascivious wink, and she bounded out of the apartment and up the stairs to prepare for her date with Bunny.

I lounged around the apartment for the next hour, flipping through magazines and darting into the bedroom for quick confirmation that I still looked fetching. As I left the house, I caught sight of myself in the darkened window of the front door. The clothes that had seemed so hip and stylish inside now looked like a ridiculous costume—something an aging divorcee would wear to a singles bar to attract fading businessmen. I ran back inside, stripped off the clothes and put on jeans, a sweater, and loafers. Then I hailed a cab and went to The Depression to meet Anne.

* * * * * * * *

When I arrived at The Depression, the restaurant was packed with the late dinner crowd. It was hard to tell the homeless from the paying customers. The homeless tended to dress up for the occasion and the paying clientele dressed down.

I walked into the kitchen and found Anne bending over a recipe with Claudia, the cute new cook. They were standing shoulder to shoulder, nodding at the list of ingredients. Anne had changed out of her chef whites and was wearing jeans, a green paisley blouse, and black clunky shoes, which could be considered formal wear on her.

"City health inspector," I announced, which is what I always said when I entered the kitchen. It never failed to get a laugh from the dishwashers.

Anne leaned against the counter and shook her head fondly. She had brushed her wild mane of hair into submission and I detected a hint of lip-gloss. Anne was naturally beautiful in the earthy, solid way of women who want to nourish you. But she hid her figure under loose clothing and her face behind her hair. I wondered if her careful grooming tonight was for Claudia's benefit. I came close to complimenting her, but if I offered her anything other than a friendly insult, she would think I was up to something.

Anne grabbed her coat, a moth-bitten overcoat she'd worn since I first met her almost ten years before, and we left the restaurant. It was April, but there was still a bitter wind blowing off the lake. I hunkered down into my coat, hoping that Anne would take the hint and suggest we get a cab. But I could tell by the way she lit another cigarette with her big, ruddy hands that she was looking forward to the long walk to the bar. She grew up in northern Michigan and had never lost her rugged, pioneering spirit, and she assumed everyone shared her love for miserable weather and harsh conditions.

I had known Anne almost as long as I'd known Tricia, but Anne and I rarely spent time alone together. When we were with Tricia, the three of us shared an easy camaraderie and genuine affection that was obvious even through our constant volley of insults and teasing. But when it was just the two of us, Anne and I were sometimes awkward and shy with each other. Tricia was such an overwhelming life force that when she wasn't present it was like the sun had fled to another galaxy and Anne and I were friendly planets left bobbing in space with no common star to worship. Tonight I was determined not to bring up Tricia's name. But there were very few areas of our lives that Tricia didn't dominate. We walked in silence for a few minutes until I thought of a Tricia-free topic for discussion.

"So, how's business?" I asked.

"Heavy on the hobos," Anne said. Although Anne started the restaurant as a charitable enterprise, now that she was making money she found herself lured by the sway of capitalism. "I'm thinking about limiting hobo seating from lunch until five. That way they get fed and get out of the restaurant before the dinner rush."

"That new cook is awfully cute," I said, playfully bumping into Anne and pushing her off the sidewalk.

She lit another cigarette and blew smoke in my face. "I've had my fill of cute," she said. "I suppose Tricia has told you about our 'open relationship.'"

"Yeah, how's that going?"

"Actually, it's going pretty well. I've gone out with a few women."

"You've been dating?"

"Sure, that's the point, isn't it? I know Tricia thinks that the open part of the relationship applies only to her, but I've decided to call her bluff."

"Well, good for you," I said with a bit too much gusto. Anne scoffed at displays of enthusiasm directed at anything other than a good meal or a well-behaved pet.

She shrugged. "So, who's coming to this shindig?"

"Carmen will probably have her usual harem of freaks and losers. Apart from that, just us, I guess."

"I invited Poppy, too," Anne said. She was referring to Pam, the catcher on our softball team. Anne gave her the nickname Poppy after we learned she was a minor soda pop heiress. Poppy's family owned a brand of soda that was popular in the World War II years, but was later bullied off grocery shelves by Coke and Pepsi. The company found a niche market with its grape, orange, and strawberry sodas, which were favorites of senior citizens with failing tastebuds and drug addicts who were attracted to the high sugar content. You could still find the soda at discount markets that specialized in off-brands, and many pizza places offered a free six-pack of the flat cola with the delivery of a pizza.

"We've been hanging out lately," Anne said. "Did you know she went to Julliard? She's an oboist. But she couldn't make a living as a musician, so she went back to school and got a computer degree." Poppy was a klutz. I couldn't imagine her tying her own shoes let alone playing the oboe. But she did look the part of a classical musician. She had long, wavy hair, ethereal facial features, and a calm manner that suggested that her inner life was choreographed by Mozart.

"It seems like everyone who works with computers was a failure at some other profession," I said.

"She's installing a computer at the restaurant to help me keep track of supplies and my books," Anne said. "And we're getting a new cash register, too. It will actually tell you how much change to give out. No more counting on my fingers."

"You're going to use a computer? Welcome to the Twentieth Century."

"It's the Twenty-First Century."

"Well, let's ease you into the last century first before we introduce you to this century. We don't want you to get the bends."

* * * * * * * *

We arrived at the bar at nine o'clock. It was dangerously situated between two straight sports bars. I imagined there would be nothing but trouble when the lesbians and straight boys met on the street at closing time. Although it was much too early for Jean and her friends to be out, I felt a surge of panic. This was exactly the type of trendy spot that attracted them like mosquitoes to a bug zapper.

I hadn't seen Jean since she stood me up at the condo. I had spoken to her, though. The night of the walk-thru at the condo, she left a message explaining that she wasn't ready to buy property yet and begging me to call her. I returned her call about a week later. When I heard her voice, I was struck dumb by what felt like a hammer blow to my heart. She said hello three times before I was finally able to speak.

"Jean." It was all I could muster.

"Oh, Julia. Julia," she sobbed. "God, you must hate me. I hate me. Where are you? Are you at the condo?"

How like her to assume that I would go ahead with the purchase of the condo and clean up her mess for her. Miraculously, Diane, our realtor, and Tricia had gotten me out of the contract. The developers wouldn't budge at first, but they were soon worn down by the tag-team craziness of Tricia and Diane and they finally agreed to rip up the contract and return my earnest money.

I told Jean that I had gotten out of the contract and that I was living with friends, but I didn't say which ones. As if she couldn't figure that out.

"Oh," she said sadly. "I'll bet Tricia and Anne hate me." There was nothing that bothered Jean more than knowing that people didn't like her.

I was silent for a moment, debating whether I should make her feel worse than she already did. Finally, I said, "Yes, they hate you." I couldn't believe how much joy it gave me to tell her that. I was tempted to tell her that my parents hated her, too, but I decided to save that for another conversation.

"Well, if this is so painful for you and Tricia, maybe I should find another law firm to handle my lawsuit." Ever since Jean left me, I had been trying to think of a way to refer Jean's toe case to another attorney without breaking Tricia's heart. But now, hearing this threat from Jean, I was determined to keep the case.

"You signed a retainer agreement with us," I said coldly. She could cancel the agreement at any time, but I wasn't going to tell her that.

She laughed lightly. "I don't want anyone else to handle it. I just don't want to cause you any pain."

Too late for that, I said to myself. "Tricia will be working with you exclusively. You won't have to see me at all."

"What if I want to see you?" she said, seductively. The nerve of her! And it almost worked. I felt myself melting. So, I slapped myself in the face, hard.

"I suggest you clear that with Michelle," I said, and I hung up the phone.

* * * * * * * *

When Anne and I entered the bar, we found Carmen seated at a table chatting with two women from Ohio. She had met them only five minutes before our arrival, but they were already fast friends.

"Now we have a place to stay when we're in Ohio," Carmen trilled.

"When are we ever in Ohio?" Anne asked.

"Now we have a reason to go there," Carmen said, always looking on the bright side.

The bar had a schizophrenic feel to it. The first floor had a dance floor with painfully loud industrial music blasting from the speakers. The second floor featured two pool tables and a jukebox featuring sentimental pop music. The music from each floor fought for dominance. It was like the dueling songs were shouting at each other to shut up. We got drinks on the first floor, which was empty except for the bartenders, each of whom had a more severe haircut than the next. There were about a dozen people on the second floor, playing pool and spending far too much time studying a Celine Dion CD on the jukebox for my comfort. I slammed down a few quarters on the pool table and challenged two angry looking women to a match.

After about an hour, the bar was filling up and Anne and I were still holding the table. I had grown bored with the game and tried to convince Carmen to take my place, but she was having too much fun buzzing around the bar like a humming bird, flirting with girls. Just when I was about to throw a game to liberate myself from the table, Poppy arrived and I shoved my cue at her before she had a chance to protest.

I grabbed Carmen and we raced downstairs to the dance floor. An overly loud song with incomprehensible lyrics was blaring out of the sound system, causing the floor to shake. It was like they were playing the music so that deaf people could feel the rhythm through their feet. I began moving my body in a way that I hoped wouldn't embarrass me. I had zero interest in dancing. It seemed a waste of time at best and an exercise in abject humiliation at worse. However, I did recognize its value as an opportunity to rub indiscriminately against attractive strangers. Carmen and I took turns pushing each other into cute women on the dance floor and bumping against them until they caught on to our antics and moved away from us.

Carmen and I made our way back upstairs to find Anne and Poppy sitting together on a ratty love seat chuckling over something. "We lost the table," Anne said lightly. What she meant was that Poppy had lost the table. Poppy shrugged haplessly.

Carmen tapped my shoulder and whispered, "Hey, Julia! That woman sitting at the bar is staring at you."

I glanced in the direction of the bar and was overwhelmed by a burst of mauve. The woman in question had a certain glossy prettiness—like the girlfriend of a college football star. Not exactly my type, but someone who might be game for a lighthearted romp. But then I noticed that her face was buried in a margarita glass and she was sobbing.

"She's crying," I said watching as the tears streamed down her face, leaving tracks in her makeup before they plopped into her cocktail.

"Perfect!" said Carmen. "She's vulnerable. Go get her."

"I'm not going to hit on a woman who's having a nervous breakdown."

"But she's cute!" said Carmen. "Buy her a drink."

A few minutes later I watched as the bartender handed the woman a cocktail and then nodded in my direction. At the same time, Anne walked back from the bar with a few drinks. She smirked as she pushed a beer into my hand.

"You didn't," I said to Anne.

"Oh, yes, I did," she said with a firm nod. Anne had ordered the crying woman a drink and told the bartender it was from me. The woman at the bar waved weakly. I glared at Anne and she burst out laughing.

I took a sip of beer and walked to the bar.

"Thanks for the drink," the woman said.

"You looked like you could use one," I said.

She started weeping again. "My ex is here with her new girlfriend." She pointed to a strapping woman with a lot of hair who looked like her makeup— heavy on the blue eye shadow and liquid blush—had been applied by a high school girl.

"Want to make your girlfriend jealous?" I asked

She gulped down the rest of her drink and we went to the dance floor. A slow song came on and she wrapped her arms around me. Midway through the song, she kissed me. It wasn't exciting, but it was consoling in the same way you'd take comfort in curling up next to someone for warmth in an avalanche.

At the end of the song, Anne signaled that it was time to leave.
Carmen was flirting with one of women from Ohio. She used a
fisherman's gesture to suggest that she was reeling in a fish on the
hook, so Poppy, Anne and I left without her. As we were walking
out of the bar, the weeping woman ran out after us and shoved
something into my hand. She gave me a quick kiss and skipped
back up the stairs to the bar.

I unfolded a soggy cocktail napkin. I laughed and danced it in
front of Anne's face as if it were a pair of silk panties.

"Gimme that," she said, snatching the napkin from me. The scrawl
on the napkin read: "Andrea: 819-6558; Dinner?!!?!!"

"Any person who punctuates a cocktail napkin with anything
more exotic than a comma is a fool," said Anne.

But I didn't care. I grabbed the napkin and Anne and Poppy
chased me down the street, until we were so winded even Anne
agreed it would be a good idea to take a cab home.

CHAPTER 5

A few days after we met at Minsk, Andrea and I went to dinner. Andrea spent most of the evening reciting a monologue of despair about her failed relationship with Bridget, a Chicago cop. She was so wrapped up in her own misery that she was oblivious to the fact that there was a woman sitting across the table from her, nodding with empathy and using her best first-date table manners. After the meal, as we stood outside the restaurant and I mumbled my good-byes, Andrea woke from her stupor and threw herself at me with such force that I almost tumbled onto the sidewalk. She kissed me madly for several minutes, leaving me baffled and disheveled.

The following Saturday, Andrea invited me to a party. When she arrived to pick me up, she was giddy. There was a certain intensity about her manic good cheer that suggested something was terribly wrong—like she had murdered Bridget and the corpse was stuffed in the trunk of the car.

"So, who will be at this party?" I asked

"Friends of Bridget," she said.

"Bridget? Your ex-girlfriend Bridget? The one who tried to stuff your head into an oven before she left you for another woman? The Chicago cop Bridget?"

"Mmmm," she said, tossing her cotton candy hair as she darted maniacally in and out of traffic.

"Are you sure we're invited to this party?" I had heard every detail of her split up with Bridget. It was one of those spectacularly nasty breakups that make police blotters so much fun to read. I couldn't imagine any circumstances in which Bridget or her friends would nod hello to Andrea let alone invite her to a party.

"Huh?" she said, checking her makeup in the rearview mirror. She had on so much kohl eyeliner that she looked like the love child of Princess Diana and a raccoon. "Oh, yeah. Of course we are."

When we arrived at the party, a stocky woman wearing a sweatshirt that read "Don't bring a knife to a gun fight" opened the door. She was holding a beer and howling with laughter at a comment shouted out by a member of the raucous crew crammed inside the seedy brick ranch. When she saw Andrea, her happy expression collapsed into a mask of distaste. After scowling at us for a full minute, she reluctantly stepped aside and let us in.

"Is Bridget here?" Andrea asked while scanning the room, which was filled with beefy female cops.

A woman as big as a refrigerator box let out a menacing snort. She gulped down a fistful of M&Ms and pulled her massive frame out of a Lazy Boy. The room fell silent as the crowd watched her lumber to Andrea.

"She...ain't...here," the Box said, jabbing her finger in Andrea's chest to underscore each word. Andrea nervously lit a cigarette and fled the room, leaving me to deal with the law.

The Box, moving as slowly as a mountain, turned toward me. I waved at her meekly. "Who are you?" she demanded.

"Tricia Polanski," I squeaked bravely. I could see the cogs turning heavily in the Box's mind, cranking open her memory bank, and dropping Tricia's name in with a thud. This gave me the opportunity to slink off to the bathroom. I hid there until Andrea knocked on the door and told me in a hurried whisper that it was time to leave.

* * * * * * * *

The next Monday at work, I spilled out the story to Tricia. I stressed that I could have been killed! Killed! But she was not impressed.

"Did you sleep with her?" Tricia asked.

"Andrea? No, of course not. She's obviously still in love with her ex-girlfriend. Why would I sleep with her?"

"For physical pleasure," Tricia said as if it was the most obvious thing in the world.

It was the first spring-like day of the year and we were sitting on the wide, oak windowsill in my office, dangling our feet over the ledge. One of the many appealing features of the old building was that it was built at a time when human life was considered very cheap. Back in those days, architects weren't hampered by pesky safety codes, and so they didn't have to hermetically seal buildings. As a result, people were free to fling themselves out windows anytime the stock market crashed or a relationship turned sour.

Although the temperature had barely inched into the 50s, people on the sidewalk below were pretending it was beach weather, trying not to shiver as they popped into coffee shops to pick up breakfast in shirtsleeves and sandals. Chicagoans know too well from sad personal experience that warm weather in April is merely a Trojan horse sent by Mother Nature to give a false sense of security before she hits the city with a final, vicious blast of winter. The phony warmth created a mood of collective fatalism. Sort of like Paris just before the Nazis invaded. You know something terrible is about to happen so why not shirk your responsibilities, drink too much champagne, and fall in love with the wrong person?

Most real estate transactions happen in the spring, so it was my busiest time of year at work. Yet, instead of attacking the pile of contracts on my desk, I was spending the morning watching Tricia throw spitballs at people sixteen stories below. She was methodically wadding tiny bits of legal paper in her palms, soaking them in saliva and then carefully aiming them at unsuspecting pedestrians. The spitballs were too small to feel, so people wouldn't realize they had been hit until much later, when they would shake spitballs from their hair and clothes. Tricia hoped that when they found the spitballs, her victims would spend a moment considering why they had been targeted. "People all across the city will be thinking about me today, even if it's only in the abstract. It makes me feel like God," she said when she launched the campaign.

"All I'm saying, Julia, is that if you had a physical release on occasion you wouldn't be so quick to jump into a relationship with every woman you meet," Tricia said. She held onto my arm for balance and leaned backwards, grabbing a legal pad off my desk. She ripped a handful of paper from the pad and tore it into small scraps. Then she tossed the yellow scraps in the air, showering pedestrians with confetti. Several people looked up at us in confusion. Tricia waved gaily at them and I jumped back into the office.

"I can't have sex with someone I don't care about," I said.

"Men do it all the time," she said, climbing off the window. "It's much more enlightened than equating sex with love."

"Yes, and we both know how enlightened you are. The only person you're sleeping with is Bunny, and God only knows why you love her, but you do."

"That's not true!"

"Are you sleeping with someone other than Bunny?"

"No, I mean, I'm not in love with Bun. I'm obsessed with her. There's a difference."

Tricia flopped into a chair near my desk. "Okay, let's get back to the business at hand. How far have you two gone?"

"Just kissing."

"Oh, Julia!" Tricia cried.

"I haven't felt compelled to go any farther. She's a bad kisser, and that doesn't bode well for the rest of her sexual skill set." Andrea's tongue darted in and out of my mouth with such force that I feared it might cause enough friction to start a fire.

Tricia pounded her fists on my desk in outrage. "Bad kisser! Julia, why are you even wasting my time? There is nothing that can be done with a bad kisser. Nothing. Kissing can't be taught. It comes from the soul. Bad soul equals bad kisser. Get rid of her. I spent my entire early 20's trying to reform a bad kisser and it got me nothing but heartache and chapped lips."

Tricia pulled herself out of the chair and picked up a contract from the top of the pile on my desk. She studied it for a few seconds. "I don't know why you like real estate work. It's so dreary." She slapped the contract back on the desk and suddenly became officious. "Okay, I don't have anymore time to screw around with you today." As if it was my idea to waste the morning throwing spitballs at strangers.

"No, don't leave, please," I begged, reaching my arms out to her as she walked out of the office. I began the morning fully motivated to tackle the work on my desk. But spring fever had since taken hold of me and drained me of any ambition. "Let's talk about kissing, sex, Bunny—anything so I don't have to review these contracts." But she dismissed me with a curt wave of the hand and sailed out of the office. I leaned back in my chair and sighed deeply at the mountain of papers in my in-box.

* * * * * * * *

I wish I could say that I became a lawyer because I had some burning desire to see justice served. But the truth was that I went to law school for the same reason most people do: I didn't know what else to do with my life. I graduated college with a major in geography, a degree guaranteed to get me nowhere in life. So, my career choices were limited to going to law school or working at my father's construction company.

Law school was more fun than I expected it to be. It was filled with rudderless students like me, so it was just an extension of college, complete with keg parties, easy friendships, and lots of napping. Shortly after starting at Darrow, I began dating a law student, a marriage-minded boy with an irritating fondness for my parents. The relationship fell apart at the end of my first year, when Matt caught me kissing our contracts professor, Delia Bergen.

Delia was a no-nonsense partner in a big law firm. She had a

Waspy prettiness, a helmet of blonde hair, and an uninspiring marriage. The moment she walked into the lecture hall and demonstrated her keen intelligence and a cool indifference to her students, I was smitten. I dedicated myself to pursuing her, which culminated in a few tortured kisses before summer break, which was when she stopped returning my calls.

Up until that point, I had never kissed a woman. I had had several emotionally fraught relationships with women in college, but they amounted to little more than intense late-night, beer-fueled conversations about how much we admired each other's breasts. After recovering from the experience with Delia, I carefully dipped my toe into gay waters. I lurked outside of lesbian bars, trying to work up the courage to enter. When I finally did, I sat at the bar with my back to the crowd, clutching a beer bottle so tightly that I thought my forearm would shatter. When a woman approached me and asked me to dance, I ran out of the bar.

In my final year of law school, I spotted a flyer advertising a dance for the school's gay and lesbian association. Silvio, a prissy soprano in the gay association's glee club, was a member of my study group. I thought about asking him to take me to the dance, but I didn't want to be obliged to sit though another performance of his one-man *Madame Butterfly*. Instead, I stole one of his notebooks at a study session on the Friday before the dance. My plan was to deliver it to him at the dance, telling him I had just found it in the study room.

On the night of the dance, I walked to the gym where it was held, holding the notebook out prominently to advertise the fact that I was there on a mission and had absolutely no interest in kissing girls. Seconds after I bought a ticket and entered the gym, I heard someone call my name. I considered dropping the notebook and running out of the room, but before I could flee I felt a hand touch my shoulder.

"So, it's true! Your boyfriend—that Matt guy—claimed that he saw you making out with Delia Bergen, but I just wrote it off as a straight-boy fantasy." It was Tricia. She was wearing the type of wild cocktail pajamas last seen on Jacqueline Suzanne. Tricia and I had been in a few classes together, but I had never spoken to her. Everyone in school knew her by reputation, though. She was a star student who excelled because of her brilliant legal mind, love of conflict, and ability to think on her feet. People referred to her with equal measures of exasperation and respect. She started law school two years before me, but dropped out in the middle of her first year and used her student loan to finance a jaunt through the hashish capitals of Europe. She returned to school the year I started, shocking the staid student body by refusing to wear underwear and flouting the very laws we would soon be sworn to uphold.

"I've got to know something," Tricia said huskily. She had an exceptionally lively voice that made every word jump with inflection. The most mundane sentence sounded like it had stopped for a drink at a smoky jazz club before it decided to dance out of her mouth. "Have you seen Bergen with her hair mussed? Is that even possible? The rumor is that it's shellacked."

My immediate inclination was to deny everything and stick to my cover story about the lost notebook. But there was something about the way Tricia was looking at me—her eyes were alive with interest and urging me to gossip about myself—that made me want to confess my flirtation with Delia. Before I could answer, though, a woman wearing a tattered pair of jeans and a tee-shirt with several generations of faded stains approached us. She was balancing four highball glasses—one stacked on top of the other, with the top glass held in place by her chin. Yet, she was still managing to smoke a cigarette.

"Hi, baby," Tricia purred, carefully lifting two of the glasses from the woman's stack. "Julia, my advice to you is to buy drinks two at a time. In this crowd, you never know when the booze will run out. Give Julia one of your drinks, baby." Tricia took a sip from one of the cocktails and squinted at the crowd with distrust.

Baby handed me a glass. Her hands were red and callused, the hands of someone who works hard for a living. Her forearms were muscular and marred by small, discolored scars. "Burns," she said, when she saw me studying her arms. "From cooking."

"Oh, God, where are my manners?" said Tricia, suddenly realizing that she hadn't introduced me to Baby.

"You have no manners," said Baby.

"You're right about that," Tricia said, giving Baby a loud smack on the lips. "Julia, this is my honey. My love. My pumpkin. My valentine."

"I'm Anne," she said, wiping Tricia's wet kiss off her lips with the back of her hand. "And I'd appreciate it if you never address me as pumpkin again."

"So what are you hoping to accomplish here tonight, Julia?" Tricia asked, peering at me as if I was on the witness stand. "I certainly hope you're not planning on finding a girlfriend here. Just look at this crowd. There haven't been this many bourgeois in one room since the Bolsheviks stormed the White Palace."

"I told you last week that you're not allowed to use that word until you learn how to spell it," Anne said.

"Which word? Bourgeois or Bolshevik?"

"Both," said Anne, blowing a stream of smoke at Tricia in amusement.

"It's true, Julia. We were having a fight—Anne was yelling at me because I spilled some Chinese food on the counter—and I told her that I was sick and tired of her bourgeois bullshit. I find it helpful to use words of revolution in any domestic dispute. Anyway, she told me that she will no longer allow me to use words that I can't spell. And if I misspell something on the grocery list, she refuses to buy it. All because I didn't wipe up a little fried rice. As if I don't have more important things on my mind." Tricia turned toward Anne and raised her arm like she was holding a sword in a gesture of threatened revolt. "You'd better watch your step, Annie, because the proletariat is about to rise up."

"Spell proletariat," Anne said, feigning weary detachment. But I could tell by the way Anne's eyes twinkled when she looked at Tricia that she never got tired of her. She followed Tricia's every movement with the bemused intensity of a mother watching her child's first performance in a kindergarten play.

Tricia tried to bluff her way through the spelling test, but gave up after hitting the wall of vowels in "bourgeois." "Okay, so it's true. I'm a terrible speller. I have a lot of other bad qualities, too. I'm sloppy. I drink too much. But I enjoy every drop of it!" she said, raising her glass. "Speaking of drinking, let's get out of here. Annie, let's take Julia to LuLu's."

Anne blew a fat plume of smoke in my direction. "She's really not dressed for it."

I was wearing what I considered to be a smart outfit for the occasion. I had dressed in what appeared to be casual clothes. In reality, though, they were some of the most expensive items in my closet. I was wearing a linen jacket over a green cashmere crewneck sweater and a pair of trendy jeans I'd bought in Rome. I couldn't imagine any place that would reject me but accept the old rags Anne was wearing or Tricia's psychedelic getup.

"Oh, everyone there will be so drunk they won't even notice," said Tricia.

LuLu's was the oldest lesbian bar in the city. It was kept afloat by a crowd of aging barflies who had been manning the same stools since the days when lesbians were neatly divided into two distinct camps—butch and femme.

When we walked into the bar, every head swiveled in our direction. The butches, dressed in men's suits and trucker's clothes, leaned away from their beers and nodded appreciatively as Tricia sauntered by them. The femmes, their faces slathered with pancake makeup and rouge, eyed us competitively and drew closer to their butch lovers. I quickly realized why Anne said that I wasn't dressed appropriately. Although I was obviously on the femme end of the spectrum, this bar demanded that you dress the part. I should be wearing a dress, or at least something retro sexy like Tricia's crazy pantsuit.

After we settled into our first cocktail, Tricia and Anne told me the story of how they met, which quickly devolved into an argument. Tricia attempted to romanticize their history, while Anne offered parenthetical explanations of the cold hard facts of their adulterous courtship.

They first met a few years before when they were both in relationships with other women. Tricia was involved with a woman who, according to Anne, was a sociopath.

"Oh, she wasn't that bad," said Tricia.

"She had no soul," Anne said.

"Let's just say she was missing certain elements that make a person human," said Tricia.

"Yeah, like a soul," said Anne. "She was the devil."

"Let's not drag religion into this."

"Then explain her cloven hooves and her forked tongue."

"Well, I may have been dating the devil, but you were living with a woman who wore tube tops," Tricia sniffed. "Unlike you, I have some standards."

The two couples were loosely connected through a group of friends. One evening about a year before, Tricia and Anne were chatting at a party when Tricia came to the stunning discovery that she was in love with Anne.

Anne was telling me about how she had gone to the forest preserves to find some fiddlehead ferns to sauté for dinner that night, and she was so passionate about her quest that I realized immediately that I couldn t live without her. And I told her right then right in the middle of the party that I was in love with her.

"Naturally, I was rather skeptical," Anne said with studied understatement. Tricia pursued Anne relentlessly for months. She left bouquets of fiddleheads on her doorstep, ate dinner nightly at the restaurant Anne worked at, dismissed Anne's girlfriends threats to keep her distance and, in general, ignored every boundary imposed by society to keep people from hopping from one bed to another.

"Finally, I agreed to have dinner with her just to get her to stop harassing me," Anne said.

"And she fell in love with me that night," Tricia said in triumph.

"Well, let's not get carried away," said Anne, who couldn't hide her adoration of Tricia, try as she might.

By the time we stumbled out of the bar that night, we had become friends. Within a month, we were best friends. By year's end, we were family. We met at a time in our lives when we were free of the career and relationship hassles that prevent you from taking a chance on new friendships. If we had met when we were older, we probably wouldn't have made the effort to look past our many differences to forge a friendship.

We had vastly different upbringings—Anne was raised by a fanatically religious widowed mother in a small mining town near the Canadian border; Tricia's parents were factory workers from Poland who raised Tricia and her six sisters in a rough neighborhood on the south side of the city; and I grew up in comfortable oppression in a tony suburb—yet we shared a kinship closer than we did to our own siblings. We were so confident in our devotion that we could bicker, behave badly, and expose the worst sides of ourselves without fear of losing each other's love.

* * * * * * * *

After law school, Tricia was recruited by one of the largest litigation firms in the city. She accepted the job because she was promised that she'd spend most of her time in court. But she soon discovered that she was little more than a glorified paralegal, doing grunt work for attorneys who presented the cases to juries.

I started out as a public defender, a job that put me off trial work forever. Like many new lawyers, I was filled with righteous outrage at a system that would wrongly convict innocent people. But after a few months hanging around the county jail I realized that while my clients may not have been guilty of the charges against them, they were all guilty of something. Eventually, I landed at a private firm where I handled real estate contracts for corporate clients.

A few years later, Tricia convinced me to quit my job and open a practice with her. It was a stupid idea on many levels, and yet I accepted because Tricia could make a suicidal pact seem like a lark. Tricia and I had diametrically opposed business plans. I proposed a general practice that would generate most of its revenue from real estate work and estate planning. Boring, yes, but it was a plan certain to provide us with a decent income and allow us to build a solid foundation for future growth. Tricia wanted to concentrate exclusively on personal injury work, a notoriously costly and risky field of law. Tricia based her revenue projections on the slim hope that a severely injured person would crawl into our office and we'd make millions off his bad fortune. Finally, we agreed to open a general practice that would take on an occasional personal injury case when time and revenue permitted.

Tricia developed a reputation as an attorney who could get a settlement for anyone who limped into our office, whether they had a legitimate case or not. Despite her success, the situation frustrated her. She longed for a death or dismemberment, the dream of every litigation attorney. Jean's toe case was Tricia's best hope of taking a case to trial, but even Tricia acknowledged that we would be idiots to turn down a decent settlement offer. A settlement is a sure thing. A trial is a big question mark. There are so many variables involved in a trial—will you get a decent judge, will the jury like your case, will the jury understand your case, will the jury like your client, will the jury like you? It's a crapshoot that only firms with deep pockets can afford to chance.

* * * * * * * *

On the same spring day that we threw spitballs at passersby, Tricia went to lunch with Humble Al, a hugely successful litigation attorney, to discuss Jean's toe case. There was nothing humble about Al, but we gave him the nickname after we saw him in action in front of a jury. Outside the courtroom, Al was abrasive, loud, and prone to rages that caused bits of foam to form at the corners on the mouth. He ate with his hands and fondled any woman foolish enough to wander into his greedy reach. But once he stepped in front of a jury, he was gentle, modest, and quietly convincing. When we learned that he binged on carbohydrates before a trial because juries prefer chubby, unkempt attorneys to well-dressed sharks, Tricia remarked, "Sheer genius."

Humble Al operated a one-attorney firm that took up an entire floor in our building. Al employed a harem of spinster secretaries and paralegals who worshipped him and made it possible for him to work without law partners. His success allowed him to be generous with us. He regularly sent us his castoffs—small cases that he couldn't be bothered with. In return, all he asked was that we provide him with salacious details about our sex lives.

In spite of his bad manners and puerile interests, I adored Humble Al. Like most complex people, it was easy to forgive his transgressions because he was so much fun to be around. Tricia's relationship with him was more complicated. She felt competitive with Al, and resented that we relied on him for advice and support. But he was the first person she called when she needed a sounding board for a personal injury case.

Immediately after returning from her lunch meeting with Al, Tricia trotted into my office and ran circles around my desk. "Do you know what I'm doing?" she asked.

"I have no idea."

"I'm taking a victory lap. Guess what Humble Al offered? He said he'd be willing to co-counsel the toe case and pay our costs."

"You're kidding?" This was an incredible offer. Humble Al was always willing to give us advice, but he had never before volunteered to become directly involved in a case. He dealt exclusively in multi-million dollar injuries. He couldn't be bothered with the scraps and bruises we typically handled.

"This means that it's not just a good case, it's a great case," Tricia said. For the past several weeks, Tricia had been deposing witnesses in the case. It was becoming increasingly clear to both Trident Towing and Tricia that we had a very strong case. After each deposition, Tricia would burst into the office with more good news: the tow truck driver, who refused to take a breathalyzer test at the scene of the accident, had been seen at a bar less than an hour before he ran over Jean's toe; the dispatcher urged the driver to leave the scene of the accident; the truck did not meet several safety codes. The only thing we had going against us was the fact that Jean was jaywalking when she was hit and she had just left Big Martha's Bar.

"Do you want to take Al up on the offer?" I asked.

"Are you out of your mind? And pay him a third of our take? No way. We can give him a consultant's fee when we go to trial. That way it will come out of your girlfriend's share."

"You mean if we go to trial," I said. I reminded her every chance I got that I wanted her to settle the case before it went to a jury.

"Yeah, of course," she said, unconvincingly. "So, you should be going soon, right? You've got that thing at two."

"What thing?"

"The adoption. For what's their names. The blondes. The suburbanites."

"The Ss? No, that's been postponed. Some stupid social worker is giving us a hard time. Completely blindsided me." S#2 gave birth to the new baby a couple months before. As part of the adoption process, they were visited by a social worker. It's usually a formality, but this social worker submitted a damning report about the Ss and their sloppy home life. I had successfully protested the report, strongly inferring that the social worker was a homophobe, though I doubted that played any part in her report. The Ss were slobs and the best thing that could be said about their parenting skills was that they had not yet managed to kill the children. The court assigned another social worker to the case, but it pushed back the adoption by a couple months. In the meantime, I told the Ss to hire a cleaning lady.

"So, you're going to be in the office all afternoon?" Tricia asked, cautiously.

"Yep."

Tricia leaned back in her chair and shouted to Lonnie, "What the hell kind of outfit are you running here? You told me yesterday that

Julia would be at court this afternoon." Lonnie was chatting on the phone with one of her friends and didn't bother to respond. Tricia dropped her head into her hands and sighed deeply. Then she ran her fingers through her hair and looked me straight in the eyes.

"Okay, well, you're not going to like this. Jean is coming in at three," Tricia said, pausing to allow the information to sink in. Tricia promised me after the breakup that she would never meet Jean at the office. "I've got to prepare her for her deposition next week. So, why don't you get out of here? Take the afternoon off."

I glanced out the window. The weather had gotten warmer and I could hear the happy din of post-lunch pedestrians on the street below. It was a tempting idea.

"No, I'll stay. I'm not going to let her chase me out of my office."

"My big girl!" Tricia exclaimed. She jumped out of her chair, grabbed my breasts, and squeezed them as if they were horns. "Honk! Honk!" she exclaimed.

"This is exactly how rumors get started, Tricia," I said plucking her hands off my breasts. "But thanks for feeling me up. No one else is doing it these days.

"That's what friends are for," Tricia said. "Oh, one other thing. I led Jean to believe that you were going to be in the office today, just to mess with her head. Of course, at the time I said it, I didn't think you would be here. Keep your door closed, but make the occasional noise so she'll know you're in here. It will keep her on edge, which is exactly where she deserves to be."

* * * * * * *

I tried to concentrate on work but the weather and the anticipation of Jean's arrival conspired against me. I reread the same contract at least a dozen times before finally giving up on it. I spent the next hour sitting on the windowsill, trying to remain calm.

At exactly three, the office door opened and I heard Jean greet Lonnie with a booming hello. I had never known Jean to arrive anywhere on time. She spent the next several minutes chatting loudly—too loudly—with Lonnie. I took pleasure in knowing that she was doing this for my benefit. The window of my office door was frosted so I walked past it a few times so Jean could see my silhouette. Then I slammed shut a file cabinet for good measure.

Tricia kept Jean waiting for twenty minutes. Lonnie told Jean that Tricia was on a call, but I could hear Tricia playing the cheap electronic car racing game she'd bought from one of the kids in our neighborhood a few weeks before. The "bling bling" of the game sounded every few seconds through the office wall.

After Tricia finally ushered Jean into her office, Lonnie cracked open my door and whispered, "She looks like she's put on some weight, poor thing."

After Jean left the office, I picked up the phone and called Andrea. We met at Minsk after work. After God knows how many drinks, Andrea embarked on a sodden crying jag about Bridget and then asked me to go home with her. We had joyless sex that ended when I raced to the bathroom to vomit. I woke early the next morning feeling as if someone was slamming an ice pick into my brain. I slipped into my clothes and went home without saying goodbye.

CHAPTER 6

I didn't bother going into work the day after I had sex with Andrea. Instead, I spent the morning at home napping and indulging in comfort foods and bad television. Once my brain was no longer busy fighting the hangover, I expected it to take up the issue of my shocking behavior the night before. But it simply yawned and shrugged with indifference. Buoyed by the absence of shame, I decided to take advantage of the warm weather and go for a walk on the beach.

On the way to the beach, I stopped at Malaise, the neighborhood coffeehouse. I generally avoided this place because Malaise lived up to it name in every respect. The staff was disenchanted and glum and they bitterly resented the fact that they had to stop scribbling nonsense in their journals to wait on your sorry ass.

I stood at the counter for several minutes before a stick figure with a buzz cut and a minefield of facial piercings finally approached me. After I placed my order, she groaned when she lifted a paper cup, as if the action was draining the last of her life force. In retaliation, I rapidly tapped my fingernails on the counter, a gesture I picked up from my mother, who used it effectively to intimidate poky clerks, bridge opponents, and my father. My impatience was lost on Miss Anemia, who was like a superhero armed with spectacular powers of passive-aggression, which she used to defy all laws of motion and civility. When she finally shuffled over with my coffee, I handed her a ten-dollar bill and told her to keep the change, hoping she'd use it to buy herself some multi-vitamins.

The beach was deserted when I arrived. There were only a few squawking terns and a couple of teenagers making the graceful transition from recreational to habitual drug use. In the distance I saw Faith, one of the neighborhood dog walkers. Like most people who spend too much time with animals, she was slightly mad and had unconventional views on hygiene. She was fond of saying things like "a little urine never hurt anyone," which was one of many reasons why people kept their distance. Faith's dogs were a pack of jumping, snapping ruffians, whose noses were always places where they didn't belong. I usually gave them a wide berth, especially on days like today when the beach had turned to mud and the dogs were cheerfully rolling in the slop. Before I could escape detection, though, Faith waved me over.

"Hey, kiddo. I've got something for you." She reached into the pocket of her filthy slicker and pulled out a sheet of wrinkled paper. It advertised a sit-in that night to protest evictions at one of the apartment buildings located just off the beach. People in the neighborhood were always taking to the streets over some issue: parking tickets, leash laws, and anything else that smacked of oppression from "the man."

"They're evicting all the people who live in this building," said Faith. I knew the building well. It was filled with junkies, squatters, and gang members who spent their time hanging out on the corner, using powerful adjectives to describe the breasts of any woman who walked by them.

"Good riddance," I said under my breath.

"They're all on welfare, so they're screwed," Faith said. "Where are they supposed to move? The suburbs?"

The building, like most of the apartment buildings in the neighborhood, was dilapidated but stately. These buildings were built in the 1920's for wealthy families who wanted a lakeside escape from the sweltering downtown, which was dominated at the time by smells of the nearby stockyards. Although the apartments were badly damaged from generations of disreputable renters, the structures themselves were solid and retained much of their original charm, including sprawling floor plans, gorgeous woodwork, and interesting courtyards.

"What are they going to do with the building?" I asked.

"Condos, probably. Just what this city needs. More condos," she said with a world-weary sigh. "Fat cats are buying up all the buildings on the lakefront."

I nodded my head to demonstrate my mutual liberal outrage. But as I strolled back home and gazed at the muscular skyline of brick and stone, I mentally calculated what it would cost to buy one of the buildings and convert it into condos. Gentrification was moving northward at a rapid pace. It reminded me of that scene in *The Ten Commandments* where a fog slips under the door of the Pharaoh's palace bringing death to the first-borne Egyptian sons. Except this modern-day plague of real estate speculation was bringing prosperity to anyone who could afford a down payment. I silently cursed Tricia for tying up all my money in our law practice.

* * * * * * * *

A few hours later I was headed to the suburbs to play bridge with my parents. My parent's house was a hulking Victorian that sat on the banks of a toxic river that lazily wound its way through town. When my parents bought the house, it was barely standing after years of benign neglect. When they first saw it, my father declared, "What this place needs is a fire." For my mother, though, it was love at first sight. She liked nothing better than a challenge, a fact she reminded me of every time she dragged me on a shopping trip. She worked my father like a slave until the house finally met her vision. As a result, my childhood was a haze of sheetrock dust, scaffolds, and rehab-induced shouting matches between my parents.

My heart stirred when I spotted its massive frame looming behind the old-growth trees that lined the street. Even though I had not lived in the house for years, I still considered it my home. And part of me couldn't quite believe that I had moved out of it for good. I was pleasantly haunted by the thought that I'd eventually give up my adventures in the adult world and crawl back into my childhood bed, returning to a comfortable life under my mother's thumb.

I pulled into the driveway and got out of the car. It was a warm, humid spring evening. The muggy air was filled with the neighborhood smells of gas grills, chlorine, gin, compost and the river, which for all its murky charms often reeked of rotting fish and industrial waste. Over the distant whine of lawn mowers, I could hear a bunch of little kids happily shrieking through a game of capture the flag.

When I walked into the kitchen, my mother was washing the dinner dishes. They had a dishwasher, but I'd never known her to use it. She had a phone wedged between her shoulder and her ear and she was sternly issuing orders into the phone. I attempted to brush past her and find a quiet place to hide until my parents were ready to leave for our bridge game, but she grabbed me by my neck and ended her phone conversation. "My daughter just arrived and she's already trying to sneak away, so I've got to go. But just remember what I told you. You can do what you like, but if you don't heed my warnings there will be dire consequences."

"Planning a mob hit, Mom?" I asked after she hung up the

phone.

"Oh, that was Dagmar. She's into her seed catalogs and, as usual, she's making a terrible mess of things," she said with a happy sigh. She pushed a lock of blonde hair back into its careful architecture. "She's insisting on planting monkey flowers. In this climate? Ha! Good luck!" My mother had transformed the yard from a river swamp into a rolling series of impressive gardens that looked like a mini Tivoli. From spring until fall she would spend all day in the yard, planting, weeding, and dispensing unyielding advice to anyone who happened to stop by to admire her efforts.

She handed me a dish to dry and watched me carefully to make sure I didn't leave any streaks on it. I could feel her eyes boring into me as she ran them from my hands up my body to my face. She was silent, which was never a good sign. Any pause in conversation was usually followed by a critical appraisal of my appearance. My mother was always perfectly coifed and dressed, even in her gardening togs. Her controlled beauty and innate elegance added to her powers of intimidation and she made it clear that I had never lived up to her demanding standards, a fact that she blamed on the louche influence of the Italian side of the family.

"Are you doing something different with your hair?" she asked finally.

"No, it's the same as always."

"Huh," she said like a skeptical detective. She circled me and studied my whole person. "There's something different about you."

It would be just like her to key into the fact that I had had loveless sex the night before. So I revealed a little information to throw her off the scent. "I'm hungover."

"That explains the bags under your eyes," she said in triumph. Nothing gave her as much pleasure as bullying her children into submission. "Have some of this. Hair of the dog." She handed me her highball glass. One of my mother's more admirable qualities was her generous views on alcohol. Her refrigerator was filled with lemons stripped of their skins, a telltale sign of a dedicated vodka-with-a-twist drinker.

I took the glass from my mother and sniffed the drink cautiously. It smelled like a combination of rubber cement and exhaust fumes.

"Jesus, what is this?"

"Oh, grow up. It's aquavit and it's wonderful." To prove her point, she ripped the glass from my hand, slugged back the disgusting liquid and poured another glass. My mother's delicate features and willowy frame often made people underestimate her hardiness. She had limitless energy and a sturdy constitution inherited from her parents, stout Danish farmers.

"You'd better go easy on that," I said. "We've got to play bridge in an hour."

"Listen, with your father as my bridge partner, a good stiff drink is the only way I'll make it through the night without killing him."

My father lumbered up from the basement, wiping sleep from his eyes. My dad spent most of his time in the basement, which my mother referred to as "the hole." The basement was unfinished and dank. It flooded every spring and always smelled like dirty socks. Its only redeeming feature was that it was the one spot in the house that my mother did not dominate. So, it was the perfect place to escape her. My dad would announce he was going to the basement to work on a "project" and wouldn't be seen again for hours. What he did down there was a family mystery no one was anxious to solve.

My dad grabbed me in a bear hug and squeezed me until I squealed. He was built like a chunk of sidewalk and cast a threatening shadow. He spent his youth getting into bar brawls and playing professional football, "before there was any money in it" my mother was always quick to remind us. But that was long before he met his match—my mother, who reduced him from a tough, urban warrior to a henpecked, sentimentalist who fretted compulsively about the happiness and safety of his family.

When I finally squirmed out of his grasp, he held me at arm's length and sniffed the air around me. "Have you been drinking?" he asked.

"Mom forced it on me." He spun around and glared at her. For a man of his girth, he was surprisingly quick, especially when he was angry. He had warned my mother repeatedly that while it was obvious she was going to hell, she wasn't going to take his children down with her.

"Tattletale," my mother said, squinting hard at me while she rebelliously splashed more aquavit into her glass.

"What the hell is wrong with you?" he asked, a question he asked her several times a day. Yet, for as much as she irritated him, my dad also couldn't get over the fact that this beautiful ice queen was his wife. My mother dumped her fiancé, a handsome medical student, for my father, a second-generation Sicilian whose only ambition was to make enough money to buy season tickets to the Bears games. I often wanted to ask my mom what led her to make this improbable choice, but I suspected that it had something to do with sex, and I didn't want to travel down that disturbing path.

"Did you know that your daughter is hungover?" my mother said, cagily redirecting my father's attention toward me.

"Where's Eric?" I asked, quickly changing the subject before my father could focus the full force of his disappointment on me. I felt slightly traitorous for bringing up Eric's name. Unlike many siblings who fight for their parents' attention, Eric and I were constantly trying to deflect their interest. Sometimes the only way to do that was to push the spotlight in the direction of your sibling.

"Good question," my mother said, taking the bait. My brother lived in the boathouse in back of the house. When we were kids, the boathouse was little more than a shack. After Eric graduated college and began working for my dad, he converted it into a bachelor pad and a hangout for his sports-obsessed friends. When they weren't inside watching ESPN or playing air hockey or foosball, they were in the yard playing whiffle ball with the little kids in the neighborhood. Eric's lifestyle hadn't changed much since he was in kindergarten except that he added cigars and girls to the mix.

My mother pushed a button on an intercom that was connected to the boathouse. "Eric, I need you in the house, pronto."

After a few seconds, my brother responded. "Who is this?"

"You heard me, mister. Dinner is ready. It's more than ready. Dinner is over."

"I'm sorry. I didn't catch your name." I could hear the telltale clicks of foosball in the background. In the distance, one of his idiot friends yelled "goal." "Shit," said my brother. "Goddamn it. I called timeout. Timeout!"

I reached past my mother and pushed the intercom button. "Eric, get in here or I'll never get them out of the house for bridge."

A few minutes later, my brother strolled through the back door. He was wearing old jeans and a faded tee-shirt, but he still managed to look glamorous. Eric was the daughter my mother always wanted. They both loved to shop, wear expensive clothes, and pamper themselves.

Eric glanced around the kitchen, which was immaculately clean and absent of any evidence of dinner. "You ate without me?" he asked in disbelief. He was accustomed to having the world bow at his feet and it never failed to surprise him that the universe did not revolve around him. "I told you I'd be right in."

"You told me that an hour ago. The kitchen is closed. You're going to have to serve yourself. I don't have all day to wait on you," my mother said. As she said this, she opened the refrigerator and pulled out containers of the leftovers she had packed away moments before. She arranged a plate of food and placed it before Eric.

Eric looked at the food and curled his lip in displeasure. "Pork roast again?" he asked glumly. "Hey, Dad, how about getting us a couple of beef sandwiches?"

My father's eyes lit up at the mention of food. He reached for his car keys but my mother slapped them out of his hands. "Not so fast, tubby," she said. "You're on a diet." My mother rode my father relentlessly about his weight. She'd put him on strict diets, but as soon as he was out of her radar he'd gorge himself on the type of meals that require a two-hour nap afterward.

"How you doing, counselor?" Eric asked, not looking up from his plate.

"Apparently, I'm not doing as well as you," I said. "Mom says that you are on the verge of matrimony with a woman who may or may not be a stripper." I could no more picture my brother married as I could imagine him living on Mars. On the rare occasions when he did stumble into a relationship, it was always with a woman who was far too similar to him—stunningly beautiful, selfish, and moody—which doomed the relationship from the start.

"Now that's just libel," my mother said. "All I said was that your brother is dating someone. We haven't met her, of course, so I was left to make my own assumptions." My dad stood behind Eric like a vulture, waiting to scavenge food that Eric left on his plate. My mother caught onto my dad's agenda immediately and shooed him upstairs to dress for bridge. A minute later, she decided that he couldn't be trusted to choose his own clothes and she followed him to the bedroom, yelling orders as she climbed the stairs.

As soon as my mother was out of the room, Eric leaned back in his chair and cradled his hands against the back of his head. "Have you heard of any decent deals on property? I've got some money that I have to invest, so I'm looking for buildings." My brother had grown wealthy working for my father, and he made my parents rich in the process. Eric didn't know anything about the construction trade, and any time he picked up a hammer someone got hurt, but he had a genius for making money.

"Almost all of my work is in the city, so I don't know what's going on in the suburbs." I collected Eric's plate and utensils and carried them to the sink. My mother didn't trust me to wash dishes, so I rinsed off the food and stacked them in the sink.

"But that's where I want to buy—in the city," he said casually. I was so surprised that I dropped a fork I was holding. Eric couldn't understand why anyone would choose to live in the city. As far as he was concerned, urban living had not changed much since the early 1900's. Condos were no better than tenement houses and were teeming with pestilence, cholera and ethnic riffraff.

To test his commitment, I told him about the apartment buildings on the lakefront in my neighborhood. I expected him to dismiss the idea because he hated Rogers Park. The first time he visited me at the two-flat he looked out the window at a gaggle of homeless swarming a dumpster and he broke into a chorus of "In the Ghetto."

"Sounds good," he said. "A young go-getter like me could do well as a slumlord."

The last time Eric showed any interest in the city was when he had gotten himself involved in a disastrous affair with one of the married neighbor ladies. He had failed to work out an exit strategy before embarking on the affair, and when it exploded in his face, he asked if he could live with me for a few weeks until it blew over. But, after staying one night with Anne, Tricia, and me in our menagerie, he hightailed it back home to my mother's ministrations.

"You're not involved with that married woman again, are you?" I asked. Eric pushed himself up from the table and grabbed me in a headlock.

"Never mind what I'm involved in," he said, dragging me around the room. "Just get me an appointment to see those buildings."

* * * * * * * *

My parents tried to teach my brother and me to play bridge on several occasions when we were growing up. But the lessons always ended in shouting matches and someone storming out of the room. I finally learned how to play in college after I fell in with a group of math majors who preferred the intellectual challenges of bridge to the easy delights of poker and euchre.

After Jean left me, my mother enrolled me in bridge lessons with her and my dad. Initially, it was a struggle to get into the car and drive to the suburbs for the lessons, but it soon became the highlight of my week.

The class was filled with middle-aged people who learned how to play bridge in the game's hey-day of the 1950's and '60's. The game had become considerably more sophisticated since then, and the older students argued with the teacher constantly, resisting every attempt to learn new skills. Roger, the instructor, quickly gave up on the rest of the class and concentrated all his efforts on me, his star pupil. This prompted my mother to lead the class in jeering "teacher's pet" each time Roger called on me to answer a question.

At our final class, Roger invited me to play in a competitive bridge club he operated a few miles from my parent's home. I made the mistake of bragging about the invitation to my parents on the ride home.

"Good. Your father and I will come, too," my mother said, turning the rearview mirror away from my father to apply lipstick.

"Oh, no you won't," I said. "This is a club for serious players."

"Listen, big shot. You keep forgetting that I potty trained you." She nodded her head curtly as if that settled the matter.

* * * * * * *

The bridge club was located above a discount dress shop in a strip mall. The majority of players at the club were men, most of whom had some form of social disorder. Competitive bridge was a magnet for people who lacked social skills. The game gave the illusion that you were having a social life without the demands of actual conversation.

My parents always played together at the club, bickering nonstop throughout the night. They became a cautionary tale for other married couples foolishly considering partnering with each other. My mother had excellent card sense but no patience, so she would race through the hands, putting much more value on speed than on careful play. My dad was slow and methodical, thinking out every possible scenario before laying down a card.

I didn't have a regular partner, so I played with whomever Roger matched me up with. On that night, I was paired with Sam, a cheeky septuagenarian with a taste for mischief and an eye for the ladies. He was a terrible player, but he was one of my favorite partners. Unlike most men in the club, he never lectured me if I made a mistake. He was too busy batting his eyes at me and complimenting my posture, which he claimed was as good as any librarian's.

During a break in play, I went to the snack table to graze on the treats. The table was always loaded with home-baked items from the female players whose children had left the nest and who welcomed an outlet for their cooking. I munched on an elaborate dessert bar, watching my parents' game. Melody, one of my least favorite players, was pitted against my parents. Melody was a hothead who threatened to sink into a diabetic coma anytime she was losing a hand. She took pleasure in berating her regular partner, Emily, a sweet, befuddled old lady. Tonight, though, Melody was partnered with Chuck, another unpopular member of the club.

"Where's Emily?" I asked George, a handsome bachelor in his forties. George had invited me out on several occasions, but finally stopped when I told him that he was barking up the wrong tree. There were several men around his age in the club, all slightly awkward around women. I was a prime target for their affections since I was the only woman in the club who was still ovulating.

"Emily's dead," George said. "Didn't anyone tell you?" Many of the players at the club were very old and a few died every month. Death was still a shocking concept for me, but it was nothing new to the older players, who thought of funerals as an opportunity to socialize and get a free lunch.

When my parents finished their game, they came over to the

snack table, where my dad made a beeline for the most calorie-rich end of the table.

"I hope you beat them," I said to my mother.

"Of course we did, and it's driving them crazy," she said with a chuckle. I glanced at the table and spotted Melody and Chuck arguing bitterly over who had screwed up the game. "When they sat down at the table, they were so cocky. People often underestimate your father and me. What they don't understand is that I know exactly what your father is thinking at all times, which means we always reach the correct contract."

"Did you hear that Emily died?" I asked. My mother was happily surveying the room, pretending to ignore the fact that my father was inhaling the entire snack table. She turned a blind eye to his binging when she was pleased with him.

"No, I didn't. That's too bad," my mother said mildly as if I told her that Emily had moved to Miami.

"I feel really bad about it. I liked her," I said.

My mother peered at me seriously in a way that suggested she was preparing to impart some mother-daughter advice. "Do you know what the lesson in Emily's death is?" she asked. "Do not get too attached." She said this slowly, overemphasizing each word for maximum effect.

"You gave me that same advice when I was ten years old and you caught me hugging Brutus." Brutus was our miniature schnauzer who was devoted to me until he got hit by a car.

"Yes, and I was right about that. Look what happened to that poor dog. And you were devastated."

"But if I remember correctly, you're exact words were 'Don't get too attached. We may have to eat that dog one day.'"

"Well, thank God it never came to that."

* * * * * * * *

Following the game, my father suggested we get something to eat. He always made that suggestion, and my mother usually vetoed it. But at tonight's game, she and my father came in third place, so she was feeling generous. My father pulled into a diner before she could change her mind.

After we were seated, my mother yanked the menu from my father and ordered the fruit plate for him. In retaliation, I ordered the gyros platter. When the food arrived, I pushed the gyros at my dad and distracted my mother by asking her about the most recent scandal at the Scandinavian Club. Apparently, someone had leaked information to the German Club that allowed the Germans to thwart the Scandinavians major fundraising effort—the publication of a cookbook. A few weeks before the Scandinavian cookbook was released, the Germans published their own cookbook with many of the same recipes.

"We have a spy in our midst, Julia. Someone is feeding our secrets to the Germans," my mother said, gravely. "We made almost no money from the cookbook, so now we have no choice but to put on a mother-daughter fashion show." I had just taken a sip of water and I spit it across the table at the mention of fashion show.

"No way, Mom! I still haven't recovered from the last one," I said. My mother forced me to participate in this ritualistic form of humiliation starting at age five, when I was too young to protest. The last time I was in the show was my junior year of high school, the year the Scandinavian Club mother-daughter fashion show had a 1950's theme. My mother and I emerged onto the runway in matching poodle skirts with the song "Shaboom" blasting around us. I looked beyond the footlights and saw that the front row was filled with my friends, who had somehow learned about the fashion show and were eager to instigate my social downfall. For the rest of my high school career, I couldn't walk down the hall without someone breaking into a rousing chorus of "Shaboom."

"Julia, the fashion show is the only way to raise enough money to make the repairs to the clubhouse. If we don't do it, we'll be forced to allow the Germans in," she said.

"That's ridiculous and you know it," I said. "Dad can do most of the repair work that's needed, and you can write a check to cover the rest. There isn't one member of that club who doesn't have more money than they know what to do with."

My mother sighed and placed her hand on my dad's wrist. "Tony, we have spoiled the children. It's our fault they have turned out this way. We've no one but ourselves to blame." I nodded in agreement, which only infuriated her. She narrowed her eyes and jabbed her finger at me. "Oh, you think you're so smart. Yes, I could write a check to pay for the repairs. That would be the easy thing to do, wouldn't it? But you have to make a little effort in life, Julia. Otherwise, what's the point of living? The members have committed to make the club self-sustaining. We will pull together and show that this club and our heritage are worth fighting for. And if that means putting on a mother-daughter fashion show, then so be it."

"Very moving, Mom, but I suggest you find yourself another daughter because this one is not interested in taking part in your hair-brained schemes," I said.

"I have never been so disappointed in you," she said wearily.

My mother had been so absorbed in trying to convince me to be in the fashion show that she didn't notice my dad gobbling up my gyros until he was mopping up the remaining juice with a piece of pita bread. "You are not doing your father any favors," she said, glaring at me. "He's going to weigh three hundred pounds and drop dead of a heart attack. And then I'll move in with you and make your life miserable."

The waitress dropped the check on the table and my dad reached into his pocket for his wallet. As he did, a piece of paper flew out and landed on the table. "What's that?" my mother asked, picking up the paper and unfolding it.

"I got it at the bridge club," he said. I craned my neck to read it. It was a schedule of bridge tournaments in the Midwest. The American Contract Bridge League, the governing body of competitive bridge, held tournaments throughout the year. Thousands of players gathered at these events and I had heard harrowing tales of people playing for seventy-two hours straight, slipping into bridge-induced psychosis and racking up piles of Master Points in the process.

"Maybe we can try this one in October," he said. "It's a three-day tournament for novices in Madison."

"Oh, we'll humiliate ourselves," my mother said. "But it will be in Wisconsin, so at least we won't know anyone there. We'll have to switch off playing with your father, Julia. If I played with him for three days straight it would end in murder."

CHAPTER 7

In the following weeks, the warm spring gave way to an op-
pressively hot summer. By Pride weekend, the temperature had
settled in the mid-'90's and refused to budge no matter how many
cranky people shook their fists at the relentless sun. Earlier in June,
when the weathermen started getting frantic about an advancing
low-pressure system, I crammed an old air conditioner into my
bedroom window. The machine had the breathing rhythms of a
dying man. Occasionally, it would sputter and cough, chocking out
a tepid gasp of air.

On the morning of Pride Day, I woke up covered in a slimy
layer of perspiration after a restless night's sleep. The combination of humidity and a beer hangover made me want to do little
more than take a cold shower and lie in front of the tubercular
air conditioner. But it was Pride Day, and I promised Anne I'd help
prepare for our annual brunch. So, I splashed some water on my
face and headed up the backstairs.

Tricia and Anne started hosting a brunch years before when they
had an apartment on the parade route. Now, even though we lived
miles from the parade, our friends trekked north to the two-flat
for brunch on Pride Day. Our guests usually had just enough time
to scarf down a Bloody Mary before we piled onto the train and
headed to Boy's Town to stake out a place on the parade path.

This year, though, the brunch was put in jeopardy when Tricia
and Anne both threatened to boycott it. Tricia hinted that she had
made other plans that involved Bunny and her cabal of disenchanted
performance artist friends. And Anne said she wanted to spend the
morning working at The Depression so her gay employees could

93

take the day off. But I insisted that we have the brunch, and they reluctantly agreed. I felt like a petulant child who thought she could save the marriage of her unhappy parents if she forced them to go through the motions of their regular day-to-day routines. I nurtured a dim hope that everything would return to normal out of force of habit if nothing else.

The truth was that Anne and Tricia's relationship was disintegrating rapidly. Tricia was rarely at the two-flat anymore. She would come home to sleep for a few hours and to maintain the illusion that she was still in a relationship with Anne. She was like a mogul who drops in on his various businesses every few months and throws his weight around just to remind everyone who's in charge. It was Anne's behavior, though, that was most unsettling. In the past, Anne would stoically bare Tricia's betrayal up to a point, and then all hell would break loose. This time, though, Anne didn't seem to care what Tricia was up to.

When I walked into the kitchen, Anne was sitting at the kitchen table peeling a mountain of potatoes. There was a cigarette dangling from her mouth and she was listening to a religious broadcast on the radio. Although Anne considered herself an agnostic, she still loved a good Bible story, especially those featuring the angry, vengeful God of the Old Testament. She said she could relate to that type of God because He reminded her of her mother.

"Listen to this guy," she said as I poured myself a cup of coffee. The preacher was using fiery rhetoric to encourage his congregation to celebrate Pride Day by hunting down gays and slaughtering them. "None of that turn-the-other-cheek crap."

I looked around the kitchen for a place to sit, but every chair and surface was cluttered with pots and pans, herbs, cookbooks, utensils, and stacks of newspapers. Anne and Tricia were both packrats and couldn't bear to throw anything away. Anne carefully cleaned around the stacks of junk daily, so while the apartment was chaotic it wasn't dirty. However, any home that has more than three animals living in it can't help but look and smell seedy.

"Can I help with anything?" I asked, hoping she'd say no. My kitchen skills were limited to scrambling eggs and opening soup cans.

"You can dice those onions," she said, looking at me over the rim of her glasses and pointing the knife at a bag of white onions. Clearly, this was meant as punishment for forcing her to have the brunch. I slipped off the counter, grabbed an onion and attacked it with a butcher knife. My eyes began to tear instantly.

"So, what happened to you last night?" I asked, rubbing my eyes with the back of my hand, which only made matters worse.

"Carmen and I hung out at that charity thing for hours waiting for you and Poppy to show up."

Lately, I had been pulled into the daffy trajectory of Carmen's social orbit. My evenings, which for months had been as desolate as the surface of the moon, were suddenly illuminated by Carmen's madcap energy. The night before, I escaped the oven that was my apartment and went to an outdoor charity dance with Carmen and her collection of oddball friends.

"I went to Poppy's house to pick her up, but one thing led to another and we wound up playing Battleship all night." Anne got up from the table and checked out my work on the onions. "You're cutting them way too thick. Dice them. Do you know the definition of dicing?" She knew damned well I didn't know any such definition. She grabbed the knife from me and expertly chopped the onions. When she finished, she yawned and returned to the potatoes. "I didn't get home until three," she said.

"You look surprisingly fetching for having no sleep," I said. In the past, Anne's troubles with Tricia diminished her, causing her to look wane and haggard. But lately she looked bonny, as if an inner light was shining out of her pores.

"I've been going to the gym. It's amazing how exercise makes you want to sleep less. You'd think it would have just the opposite effect," she said. She was concentrating on the potatoes so she didn't see my mouth go slack with surprise.

"You're working out? You're going to a gym? Have you also become a Republican when I wasn't looking?" The only exercise Anne believed in was taking long, arduous walks and lifting fifty-pound slabs of meat from the freezer at The Depression.

"What's next?" I asked, slumping against the wall in amazement. "Giving up cigarettes?"

"Oh, let's not go overboard," she said, taking an extended drag of her cigarette. "But I have cut down on alcohol. I've been trying to limit myself to one glass of wine a night. Granted, it's a very large glass. It's the size of a vase. But still... ."

I was rattled by this information. Too much change at once made me nervous. I was like a cat that walks into a room and finds all the furniture has been rearranged and responds to the crisis by peeing on everything. I pushed myself off the wall and started to walk out of the kitchen.

"Where are you going?" Anne asked.

"To get Tricia. I need outside verification."

"Tricia's not here," Anne said, dropping the cut potatoes into a frying pan.

"She's not in bed?" I asked. It was customary for Tricia to sleep through the preparation work on Pride Day and then claim credit for the meal when our guests arrived. While I did little more than watch Anne do all the work, at least I went to the effort of keeping her company.

"She may be in bed. But she's not in our bed," Anne said. One of the rules of their open relationship was that they had to sleep at home. Tricia had tested those boundaries over the past few weeks, staggering in just before dawn and taking a short nap before leaving again. But this was the first time she hadn't bothered to come home at all.

"Are you worried?" I asked, cautiously.

"About what? Am I worried that she's dead? No. Am I worried that she's been sold into white slavery? That's more of a fantasy than a worry," Anne said, bending over to remove scones from the oven. "Am I worried that this relationship is over? Honestly, Julia, I don't know the answer to that. In so many ways it would be such a relief if it was." She slipped the scones off the pan and into a basket. I rarely saw Anne show emotion to anything that did not walk on four legs, so I couldn't tell if she really was through with Tricia or if she was disguising her pain with indifference.

"Tricia isn't coming to the brunch," Anne said, mildly.

"But she promised!" I said with an uncomfortable level of passion.

"She called this morning and said she went to a party last night and passed out on someone's couch. Emphasis on the vagaries of the pronoun," Anne said with a chuckle. "She's not even trying to lie creatively anymore. Anyway, she's going to stay at the nameless couch-owner's house this morning and then meet us at the parade."

I stood silently in the middle of the kitchen. I was tempted to tell Anne about Bunny just to punish Tricia. But that would only hurt Anne. Finally, because I couldn't think of anything better to do, I picked up a crumpled pack of cigarettes from the table. "Do you want me to get you more cigarettes?" I asked.

"I always want more cigarettes," she said.

As I left the kitchen, I turned to see Anne humming quietly as she sliced into a ham. She looked happier than she had in months. The thought of Anne content without Tricia gave me the first chill I felt since the heat wave hit town.

* * * * * * *

The following week, I completed the baby adoption for the Ss, who continued to retain me as their attorney after my breakup with Jean. They arrived at the county building late and irritable, dragging two bawling children, a doublewide stroller and several mangy stuffed animals that looked like they had been dipped in sewer water. S#2 was still plump from the pregnancy. Like most slender women who take up binge eating as a hobby, the weight had settled in odd pockets rather than spreading out like a blanket over her body. As a result, she looked lumpy, as if there were water balloons placed just beneath the surface of her skin. S#1 seemed to have compensated for S#2's weight gain by denying herself any nourishment. Her body, which was once as luscious as an ice cream cone, was now desiccated and slightly jaundice, as if she was suffering from some tropical wasting malady that happened to sneak its way into her bland suburban existence.

The Ss were shadows of their former glamorous selves. I couldn't help but think about how much they had changed since the day two years before when they adopted their first baby from China. At that time, the Ss were freshly domesticated and still basking in the glory that comes when two extraordinarily beautiful creatures sign a mortgage together. At that adoption, they dressed in chic all-black outfits, as if motherhood was the opening of a hot nightclub and they were among the lucky few who would be whisked past the velvet rope.

Two years of late-night feedings combined with the relentless monotony of married life had taken its toll. The Ss once had set the standard for the ideal lesbian relationship. Now they were an example of why two fundamentally selfish people were not suitable to baby-sit children, let alone own them. Although I didn't doubt that they loved their kids, I got the sense that they resented them for not taking over the running of the household so they could return to their old, jet set lifestyle. On this day, though, the Ss understood the significance of behaving like adults, and they were attempting to honor the occasion by being kind to each other through clenched-jawed civility.

Following the adoption, I helped the Ss haul the kids and their associated clutter to the elevator. The goodwill brought about by the adoption was starting to erode. As they stepped into the elevator, the Ss engaged in an ugly debate over whose turn it was to change the baby. I stood beyond the closing door, anxiously waving them off. But just as the door was about to shut, S#1 stuck her hand though the door and pried it back open.

"Hey, you haven't RSVP'd to the adoption party," she said. She leaned against the door so it wouldn't close.

"The adoption party? I'm not sure I can make it." I had no intention of going to that party, which would be rife with bad food and sad memories.

"Oh, but you have to come," S#2 said. "If it wasn't for you, we wouldn't be a family. You're responsible for all this."

I looked at the kids, who were sucking on crusty pacifiers. "I really can't claim responsibility for your happiness," I said.

"Who said anything about happiness?" asked S#1.

"We'd really like you to be there," said S#2, hoisting Ling Ling up on one hip. "And if you're worried about Jean, come early. The party starts at three so she probably won't show up until midnight."

"It doesn't matter that you're no longer with Jean. You're still our friend," said S#1. "And we expect our friends to pay homage to our children, regardless of the potential emotional costs." The Ss weren't my friends, but I was fond of them. True, they were narcissists, and their kids would need extensive therapy one day, but they meant well. They were much too self-involved to be bitchy or judgmental, and they were secure enough in their own beauty and popularity that they never felt the need to ostracize outsiders the way many of Jean's other friends did.

"Can I bring a date?" I asked, meaning Tricia.

"Oooh, who are you dating?" asked S#1. "Our life is so devoid of romance we need to live on the scraps of others."

Before I could disabuse her illusions about my rollicking romantic life, the elevator emergency buzzer sounded and they disappeared in a final fit of bickering.

* * * * * * * *

On the day of the party, Tricia appeared at my door wearing a leopard-print catsuit and high heels. I pointed out that it was an unusual choice in clothing for a yard party.

"That's why I'm wearing an animal print. Because we're going to be out in nature." She shaped her fingernails into cat claws and growled at me.

We arrived at the Ss' house shortly after the party started. As we walked down the driveway, I could hear the din of conversation floating from the backyard.

I whispered hurried instructions to Tricia as we approached the party. "Don't leave my side the entire time we're here," I said. "Don't let me drink too much. And don't let me have public sex with a stranger just to make Jean jealous."

"I'll agree to the first two, but if this party is as dull as I think it will be, you may have to have public sex just to entertain the crowd," she said. "Try thinking of others for a change, Julia."

As we entered the yard, S#1 was walking down the backstairs. She was carrying a huge dish filled to the brim with a brown, fibrous concoction. It looked like she had dumped several different types of dip into one large bowl and hoped for the best.

"Julia, thank God you're here," she said, lethargically. "Carry this to the food table. I'm about to collapse." She handed me the bowl and melted into a beach chair. Ling Ling spotted her from across the yard and ran to her in the trademark toddler stumble. She threw herself into her mother's lap, and S#1 groaned as if she had just taken an unexpected hit from a medicine ball. She explained that S#2 was in the house taking a nap with the baby. "She's decided to pretend that this party is not taking place. And she's threatening to call the police if our guests make too much noise," S#1 said, glancing up at the darkening sky. "With our luck this weather front will blow over and we won't get rained out."

Tricia and I walked into the yard, which was soggy from a weepy weather system that had been swirling above Chicago for the past week. Tricia's stiletto heels sunk several inches into the muck each time she took a step.

I felt totally exposed walking across the yard, like I was in one of those dreams where you suddenly realize that you're naked. But I was grateful for having been given the job of delivering the food to the table. I tried to think of a way to drag out the task so I wouldn't be forced to interact with the other partygoers.

I placed the bowl of mystery slop on the table and fussed with it for an inordinate amount of time, hoping that if I kept my back to the crowd no one would bother me. The table contained an odd array of food. There were desserts and snack foods but nothing with the slightest hint of substance. "This isn't food. It's accoutrement," said Tricia in not quite a whisper.

"Do you think any of it is edible?" I asked, picking up a piece of sweaty cheese that looked as if it had spent the past two days under a sun lamp.

"It depends on what your definition of edible is," she said, scowling at a bowl of soggy chips. "I'll get us drinks. At this point, free alcohol is the only compelling reason to remain at this party."

After Tricia left, I cautiously turned to face the crowd. The Ss' social circle spanned far beyond Jean's clutch of friends, and I was relieved to discover that I didn't know most of the people at the party. The only people in the crowd that I recognized were standing at the bar. They were an anxious group of women who were self-consciously fussing with their over-styled hair. These were women who lived on the fringes of Jean's social universe. They had never managed to break into the charmed inner circle and they reacted to their social failure by turning their insecurities on others. When Tricia brushed past them to get our drinks, they drew their heads together to appraise her outlandish party wear.

"I love your outfit," one of the women said to Tricia. The remark dripped of insincerity and her hateful friends barely stifled a laugh.

"Thanks!" said Tricia, not bothering to turn from the bar to acknowledge the insult. Tricia held her ground in front of the bar, expertly eyeing the bottles of alcohol. She fished out the most expensive brand of vodka, well hidden behind the off-brands, and mixed our drinks.

Tricia walked back to the food table and handed me a drink. "How long do we have to mingle with these jackals before we can leave?"

"Well, according to my mother, you have to stay at any party for at least an hour," I said, adjusting my bra strap, which kept insisting on slipping down my shoulder. A bra problem—just what I needed to deal with at this nightmare of a party.

"Want to have a contest to see who can drink the most in the next hour?" Tricia asked, raising her glass in a challenge.

"What about your promise that you wouldn't let me get drunk?" I asked.

"Well, you don't have to win the contest," she said, draining her cocktail. Suddenly, Tricia grabbed at her crotch and frantically shifted her weight from one leg to the other.

"What are you doing?" I asked, horrified, casting a glance around the yard to see if anyone was watching us.

"I have to pee," she said.

"Well, go to the bathroom, you moron," I said, slapping her hand from her crotch.

"Hey, you're the one who told me that I'm not allowed to leave your side," she said. Tricia only followed rules—or pretended to—to underscore what a great sacrifice she was making to do so.

"I'll make an exception in this case," I said, pushing her toward the house. The Ss had positioned a Port-a-Potty near the back entrance of the house to discourage people from using the indoor bathroom. But Tricia walked past the Port-a-Potty without giving it a second glance and sailed into the house, ignoring S#1's pleas that she use the outhouse instead.

As Tricia teetered up the stairs, I looked up at the sky. Heavy storm clouds were moving in, blocking the afternoon sun. It looked like S#1 would get her wish and the party would be rained out at any moment. I sighed in relief.

But just when I thought I'd escape the afternoon with little psychological damage, Jean and Michelle arrived. I looked around the yard in a panic for Tricia and spotted her sitting with a group of lesbian moms, nodding in what appeared to be sympathy as several of the mothers fought for her attention. I stared a hole in the back of her head to signal that it was time to leave, but she was oblivious to the mounting crisis.

Jean saw me from across the yard and cocked her head in bemusement. She sauntered across the yard as if she owned it.

"Well, this is a surprise," she said, beaming at me. Lonnie's observation was correct—Jean had gained weight since our breakup. Normally, I would have been thrilled to find that an ex-lover had gotten chubby in my absence. But Jean's weight gain gave the impression that she was finally so happy in a relationship that she felt secure enough to abandon her permanent diet.

"So, how are you?" Jean asked with too much concern. I was taken aback by the physical reaction I felt from her presence. I had spotted Jean and Michelle several times over the past several months, enough so that I felt I had been inoculated against them. It was like getting small doses of a virus to prevent an attack of the flu. But now, with Jean standing before me, I felt weak and was unable to look away from her—like an animal hypnotized by a predator.

"Fine," I managed to choke out.

"I've been to your office a few times to meet with Tricia, but you're never there. I hope that's not intentional."

I shook my head and looked around the yard in an attempt to break her spell. S#2 had finally appeared with the baby and she was showing her to Michelle and her friends. They all kept a distance, regarding the infant as if it was a live grenade being waved in their faces.

"Are you here with anyone?" Jean asked.

"Yes." There was a long pause.

"Who?" she said, gesturing in that way you do when you want a dimwit to complete a thought.

"Tricia."

"I'm here with friends, too," she said, making a vague gesture in the direction of Michelle. Even though the sun was nowhere in sight, Michelle was wearing reflective sunglasses, so I couldn't tell if she was looking at us. I gave her a dirty look just in case she was.

Suddenly, I felt an arm wrap around my neck. "Hi Jean, how's the toe? Any phantom pain today?" asked Tricia, squeezing my shoulder in solidarity. "Come on, Julia, it's time to go. We've got to get to *that thing*," she said with an exaggerated wink, as if I didn't know that "that thing" was code for "let's get away from Jean."

"How are the depositions going, Tricia? Do you think Trident will offer a settlement?" asked Jean.

"They'd be fools not to," Tricia said with a cackle. "Things are not going well for Trident Towing at the moment."

"And if they don't make us a settlement offer?" Jean asked.

"Then we go to trial," Tricia said.

"But that's not going to happen. They're going to make us an offer. Let's all pray that they do," I said anxiously.

"Yes, but I'm an atheist, of course," Tricia said, smiling smugly.

Before I could make another pitch for a quick settlement, the sky broke and rain poured down in buckets. Tricia and I dashed for the car. When we were inside, I slumped against the steering wheel and exhaled deeply.

"Exorcize your demons?" Tricia asked, shaking out her wet hair like a dog.

"Yeah, I think I did. And I was greatly relieved that I was able to speak to Jean in full sentences and not drool on myself. It's so early, do you want to go to dinner?" And since I was feeling magnanimous, I added, "You can even invite Bunny."

"No and no. I'm meeting Anne for dinner, and I'm through with Bunny."

"Are you sure?"

"Yeah. The weirdest thing happened on Pride Day. Bun was standing in a band of sunlight and the light seemed to dim around her. Like she was sucking the energy out of the sun. That can't be good, can it?"

"No."

"And the sex isn't very good anymore."

"Maybe now that the taboo is gone it's not that exciting."

"Maybe, but I think it has something to do with her kissing. She says it's for artistic reasons, but I think she's doing it just to be difficult," Tricia said. "Anyway, that's why I've asked Anne out for dinner. I miss her. I want to get back together again."

"But you never broke up."

"Oh, you know what I mean. This open relationship stuff doesn't work," she said, gathering her hair into a thick pony tale and wrapping it on top of her head in a French twist. "When you're having sex with more than one person it's really easy to get confused about who you're with. All types of complications can ensue."

"What if Anne doesn't want to get back together again?" I asked, cautiously.

"What makes you say that?" she asked as she plucked a bobby pin from her mouth and stabbed it into her hair.

"I don't know. Maybe she's having a good time dating."

"Has she told you that?" Tricia asked, giving me a sideways glance.

"No, Tricia. I just wondered if you had sent any feelers out to her. To test the waters if she wants to end the open relationship."

"Feelers? Feelers, Julia?" she said with a laugh. "Annie and I have loved each other for over ten years, we don't have to send out feelers. I know what she's thinking before she does."

* * * * * * * *

For the remainder of the drive, Tricia entertained me with the latest installment of in-fighting among her sisters. Tricia's parents had long since retired to the Gulf Coast of Florida, but her sisters remained in the old neighborhood, nursing petty slights and settling vendettas by leaving key ingredients out of recipes. Tricia usually kept out of the fray until conflicts were near resolution, at which point she would enter the dispute, effectively ending any hope of reconciliation. She was like a Greek god who watched mortal conflicts on high, occasionally tossing a lightning bolt when things got dull. And then she wondered why her sisters resented her and generally wanted nothing to do with her.

CHAPTER 8

"Well, you are not going to believe this," Tricia said. She had just arrived at the office and was standing in the doorway. Her white cotton skirt was backlit by the late morning sun, making it transparent. She wasn't wearing underpants. "Anne wants to continue to have an open relationship." She dropped her briefcase. It hit the floor like an exclamation mark.

"Who can blame her," said Lonnie, who was sitting at her desk, filing her nails.

It was almost noon on the day after the Ss' adoption party. Tricia and I had a lunch meeting with a new client and I'd spent the past hour pacing in front of Lonnie's desk, wondering aloud whether Tricia would bother to show up for work that day. Tricia kept Lonnie and me in the dark about her movements. When we opened the practice, I posted a calendar on the wall to keep track of our appointments. But Tricia mocked my attempts to monitor her schedule, drawing question marks under each date.

I grabbed Tricia's briefcase from the floor and shoved it at her.

"What?" Tricia asked, clutching the briefcase against her chest with wide-eyed innocence. She was pretending that she had forgotten about the meeting, but I knew better. This was one of her favorite stunts—showing up moments before a meeting just to throw me into a panic.

"We've got to get out of here," I said. "We have a meeting at noon."

She glanced at her watch, which she wore strictly for decorative purposes. I never wore a watch because I didn't need one. I relied on my adrenaline, which flooded my nervous system if I wasn't at least ten minutes early for any appointment. "It's only 11:45. We've got plenty of time," Tricia said. Now she was just torturing me. "Who are we meeting?" she asked as I hustled her out the door.

"Paula Truitt," I said, impatiently, wishing there was time to buy Tricia a pair of underpants. Once, just once, I would have liked Tricia to appear at an important meeting wearing underwear.

Carmen introduced me to Paula a few weeks earlier. Although I was initially charmed by her ease with strangers and life-of-the-party personality, as the evening wore on I realized that those were the very qualities that attracted me to Jean.

Paula had leveraged her three-flat in Andersonville into a real estate empire. We were meeting that day to discuss converting several of her rental properties into condos.

"Don't you care about the bombshell I dropped on you today?" Tricia asked as we race-walked to the restaurant to meet Paula.

"What bombshell?" I asked absently. I was completely focused on the business deal with Paula. We stood to make thousands of dollars in legal fees if she agreed to let us handle her condo conversions, money we badly needed to finance Jean's toe case and Tricia's other personal injury cases.

"What bombshell? Well, that's great, Julia, just great. I've been your wet nurse for all these months since your breakup with Jean, and now I'm having a relationship crisis and you could care less." Tricia stood in the middle of the sidewalk, staring at me with indignation.

"The open relationship thing?" I asked, trying to control my irritation. "Well, Tricia, I'm sure Anne is just messing with you. After all, you're the one who wanted the open relationship in the first place, and now you are making a unilateral decision to end it. Annie probably wants to punish you for a few days. If it were me, I'd punish you for a few years. But Anne is more forgiving than I am."

"So, you don't think she's seeing anyone?" Tricia asked as we started to walk again.

"No," I said carefully. I didn't know if Anne was involved with another woman, but the combination of her new exercise regime and her inner glow certainly suggested that she might be. Tricia picked up on the hesitation in my voice and eyed me warily.

"Well, I hope she is," Tricia said with a bit too much bravado to be believable. "Now that Bun is out of the picture, I plan on becoming the biggest slut this city has ever seen." She said this loudly and several people turned to look at us.

I laughed. Sometimes Tricia forgot that I knew her so well. All this talk about sleeping around was just that—talk. The fact was that in many ways Tricia was just as conventional as I was when it came to romantic relationships. She lived by a skewed moral code that allowed her to cheat on her girlfriend without guilt, but at the same time wouldn't let her sleep with someone she wasn't in love with.

"Oh, you don't believe that I'll do it?" she asked. It would be just like her to have sex with the entire Chicago lesbian community just to prove me wrong. "I'm going to start today. How about Paula? She's single, isn't she?"

Now it was my turn to stop in my tracks. A man talking on his cell phone plowed into me and called me an idiot. "No, Tricia! Paula is a potential client. Keep your hands off her at least until after she agrees to let us represent her," I pleaded. But it was too late. We were in front of the restaurant and Tricia was using the reflection of the front window to fluff her hair.

* * * * * * * *

Under normal circumstances, Tricia would have taken an instant dislike to Paula. She had little use for people who wanted to be the center of attention because she had long ago claimed that spot for herself. But on this day, Tricia was determined to flirt with any woman who crossed her path, whether she liked the woman or not.

Fortunately, Tricia's aggressive efforts at flirtation fell flat. Paula focused her attention on me, offering Tricia only polite but curt responses to her questions. By the end of the meal, Tricia was sullenly playing with the remains of her lunch as Paula and I finalized our agreement for the condo conversions.

After lunch, Paula gave me a hug and she and Tricia exchanged tight smiles. As I watched Paula climb into a cab, I was giddy with the satisfaction of knowing where my next paycheck was coming from.

"Well, I'll see you tomorrow," I said to Tricia, snapping my briefcase shut.

"Where are you going?" she asked sharply.

"I'm self-employed! I report to no one!" I said, brightly turning one of Tricia's favorite phrases against her. Then I told her that I was driving to a real estate closing in the south suburbs and wouldn't be in the office for the rest of the day.

"Good," she said. "You can drop me off at The Mound, and pick me up later."

The Mound was a rough lesbian bar on the industrial south side of the city, the neighborhood where Tricia grew up. When she was a teenager, Tricia would cut school and spend afternoons at the bar with her first girlfriend, an alcoholic baggage handler who was

twenty years her senior. Tricia had a sentimental attachment to the
bar, and she was drawn back to it whenever she was feeling blue.
She once confessed that it was the one place in the world where
she didn't care what her hair looked like.

"Okay," I said, reluctantly. "But you'd better be ready to leave
when I pick you up."

"You are such a snob," Tricia said. But I wasn't a snob. I just liked
clean bathrooms. The one time Tricia dragged me to The Mound,
I refused to drink because I feared if I did I'd have to use the
bathroom, which sat at the end of a dank, filthy hallway, looking
as threatening and damning as the gates of hell.

* * * * * * *

When I arrived at The Mound after the real estate closing, I found
Tricia sitting on a stool, propping herself up with her elbow, and
drinking a vile-colored liquid through a thin cocktail straw.

"Well, if it isn't my good friend Julia," Tricia said with just enough
bite in her tone to make me nervous. Tricia was in full self-destruc-
tive mode. But Tricia was never satisfied to limit the destruction to
herself. She insisted on taking others down with her.

"You're drunk," I said, climbing onto a stool next to her.

"That I am, my friend. That I am," she said. "But what other choice
do I have? Look at this place. No one's here. Pathetic."

"Let's get out of here," I said to Tricia. There was just enough
sunlight peeping in through the grimy windows to thoroughly
depress me.

* * * * * * *

Tricia's binge continued all week. She didn't come into work
until late in the day, and when she was at the office, she was ill-
tempered, as if it was everyone's fault but her own that Anne had
rejected her. I tried to keep my distance, but she refused to be
ignored. Throughout the week she looked for any excuse to start
an argument and her frustration grew each time I refused to take
the bait.

On Friday morning, a massive bouquet of flowers arrived for
Tricia. The orchids looked like they had been fed red meat. They
had enormous, aggressive blossoms that seemed poised to attack.
I didn't trust them or whoever sent them.

"Should we open the card?" I asked Lonnie, as we eyed the
flowers cautiously.

"Now, do you really want to know who they're from?" asked
Lonnie, gingerly pushing aside the vase. "God only knows what

type of mess she's gotten herself into now."

Tricia arrived in the office just before noon. She was wearing sunglasses and drinking Pepto-Bismol from the bottle. She walked past Lonnie's desk without taking notice of the flowers. I grabbed the vase and followed her. When I entered her office, she was pretending to be studying something on her computer screen. But I could tell by the creaking noises coming from the old machine that it was still struggling to rouse itself to life.

"Look who's got an admirer," I said cheerily, putting the flowers on the desk and fluffing out the arrangement. Tricia glanced up from the computer and glared at the flowers as if they had just insulted her.

"Aren't you going to open the card?" I asked.

"I know who they're from," she said as she refocused on the computer screen.

"Bunny?"

Tricia peered at me over the top of the computer. "Now do you really think that Bun would send me flowers? Bunny? She's opposed to living things. Especially living things that do not support the arts."

"Then who?"

"You wouldn't approve," she said seriously. She started to pound away on the keyboard. Tricia never understood that a computer is not a manual typewriter. She landed on each key heavily, so it sounded like she was typing with hooves rather than fingers.

I plucked the card from the bouquet before Tricia could stop me. It read: See you tonight. Wear a black bra. Alice.

"Alice?" I said with a mixture of delight and disgust. "You slept with Alice?"

"I don't want to talk about it," she said, concentrating on her typing.

"No way, Tricia," I said, plopping down on a chair and stretching my legs up on Tricia's desk. "Sex with Alice demands an explanation."

Alice first came to our law firm when she was recovering from an appendix surgery that went awry. I soon realized that Alice had no intention of suing her surgeon. She was using the promise of a lawsuit as an excuse to soak up Tricia's attentions.

Tricia attempted to use Alice's infatuation to her advantage, hinting that she might reciprocate Alice's feelings if Alice agreed to file a lawsuit. I warned Tricia that she was playing a dangerous game. Tricia thought she could out-manipulate a master manipulator, but I was certain the whole thing would end badly. And I took pleasure in discovering that I was right.

"I'll tell you what happened with Alice," said Tricia, wearily rubbing her bloodshot eyes, "but you have to promise me that we will never speak of it again."

"Last night I went to Minsk with Alice," she said. "I had a lot to drink. End of story."

"So, what was it like?" I asked, inching my chair closer to Tricia's desk.

Tricia took another sip of Pepto-Bismol. "Very damp," she said. I shivered and emitted a variety of grossed-out noises. "Now she thinks I'm her girlfriend. I'm going to let her think that until I get control of her appendix." Tricia nodded her head to herself as if she really believed this was an excellent plan.

"Tricia, Tricia, Tricia," I said, shaking my head in mock disgust. "You have hit rock bottom." I had been waiting all week to tell her that. But it seemed like every time she hit rock bottom, she found new depths to sink.

She waved away my comment. "Now, I've got something to ask you," she said, leaning over her desk and glaring at me. "Anne says you're teaching a bridge class tomorrow night at Bravehearts. Why wasn't I invited?" A few weeks earlier, Carmen had volunteered me to teach a bridge class at Bravehearts, a women-only community center that was a throwback to lesbian separatist days.

"You hate playing cards," I said.

"You never invite me to anything anymore," she said, settling into an accusation that might finally spark the fight she had been hoping for all week.

"I invite you to everything, but you never go," I said.

"Well, I'm going this time," she said like a threat.

"Fine with me," I said. I walked out of her office before she could find something else to argue about.

* * * * * * * *

I arrived at Bravehearts a few hours before the bridge lesson to set up the cards and tables. Bravehearts was located in a dilapidated house that was once the hideout for a group of student radicals in the 1960's. Now the building offered free space to any organization that promoted an agenda guaranteed to irritate the religious right.

When I entered the building, two members of Bravehearts' board of directors met me at the door. These women were lesbians in the pure form—overeducated and underemployed women who regularly marched on Washington, wore haircuts that screamed out their sexual preference, and were earnestly devoted to recycling. One of the women—the tall, gangly one who looked like a scarecrow—sniffed the air around me. "You're wearing deodorant," she said with a frown. "Don't you realize that many of our members are very sensitive to odors?"

After I promised to wash off the deodorant, they led me into a large room that had stacks of folding tables and chairs. As I began setting up the room, Anne and Poppy arrived.

"What are you guys doing here?" I asked.

"Having our personal space violated," Anne said as the Bravehearts women rushed over to sniff her.

We set up the tables and dealt out the cards into prearranged hands that would help me explain the fundamentals of the game. Bridge is not a game that can be learned in a couple of hours. It can take weeks before novices understand the basics of the game and months before they feel comfortable playing. My goal was to give a simple overview of the game that wouldn't cause the women to run from the room in helpless confusion.

After we finished with the preparations, Anne, Poppy and I went to a nearby restaurant. When our hamburgers arrived Poppy told us about the time she made the mistake of bringing a meat dish to a potluck at Bravehearts. "The meat was whisked away from me and given a proper burial in the backyard. Several people wept. Then there was a short, painful ceremony where I was expelled from the lesbian community."

As she told the story, Anne gently pushed a lock of hair from Poppy's forehead. This small, intimate gesture happened so quickly that I almost missed it. My face must have revealed my surprise, because Poppy stopped speaking and nervously fidgeted with a button on her blouse. Anne stared at me steadily, daring me to confront her.

Although this was exactly what Tricia deserved, the thought of Anne dating Poppy made me nervous. I didn't know whether I should feel happy for Anne or sad for Tricia.

* * * * * * * *

When we returned to Bravehearts, the small room was filled. It was a typical Bravehearts crowd. The women were decidedly crunchy. Most looked like they could use a decent haircut and a B12 shot. Many had at least a hint of a mustache.

I'd been told that only twelve women had signed up for the class, but there were at least thirty in the room and they were being scolded by the Bravehearts' directors on their failure to pre-register for the session. It turned out that Carmen was to blame for the overcrowding.

"Oooh, I'm in so much trouble," Carmen said, giggling into her hands. "I didn't follow the rules. But Tricia is in even more trouble."

"For what?" I asked.

"The Bravehearts people made her take off her shoes because they're leather. She had a big fight with the Bravehearts women and they were going to throw her out, but then she agreed to take off her shoes and they let her stay," Carmen said.

"She just wants attention," Anne said dismissively. She nudged Poppy playfully and they took seats at a nearby card table.

Tricia was seated at a table in the back. She was talking to a pretty blonde, who was working a pair of knitting needles into a ball of yarn. Tricia's mouth was moving rapidly as she squinted hard at the Bravehearts women. The blonde was smiling in amusement, never taking her eyes off her knitting. When Tricia noticed me, she called out my name. The blonde jerked her head up and appeared to catch her breath when our eyes met. It was Claire Larsson, the woman I made cry at Shangri-la several months earlier. Claire let her eyes fall back to her knitting as I walked toward them.

"I heard you've angered the Goddesses," I said to Tricia.

"Goddamned vegetarians. This is what happens when you don't eat meat. You've got all this time on your hands to persecute others," Tricia said, snarling at the Bravehearts women.

.Claire looked up from her knitting shyly. My stomach surged. As soon as the wave of nausea passed I realized it wasn't indigestion but physical attraction that had caused my innards to jump. It had been months since I felt the tug of lust, so it was easily confused with physical distress. The last time I experienced a similar feeling was when Claire walked into our office the night of our ill-fated date.

"What are you doing here?" I asked, patting my stomach and urging it to relax.

"There's a bridge lesson here tonight," she said, laying the knitting on her lap.

"Yep. I'm the teacher," I said.

"I know," she said. She rummaged though her purse and pulled out a carefully folded piece of paper. "Your name is on the flyer." She handed me a sheet of paper that read: Learn how to play bridge with bridge master Julia DeTortelli. No men or boys over age 3 allowed.

"I'm not a bridge master," I said.

"Well, I'm sure you are much better player than I am," Claire said. She was dressed in high-suburban casual: Levis, a bright yellow tee-shirt with an embroidered daisy on it, and well-worn, chunky sandals.

"Don't let her fool you, Claire. She's a shark," Tricia said, looking over my shoulder at Anne and Poppy. "I'll let you two be alone to talk about whatever it is that you're talking about. I'm going to get something to eat." Tricia crossed the room, her feet loudly slapping the linoleum as she walked. She pointedly ignored Anne as she hovered over the food table, pretending to be interested in the sad vegetables scattered on it.

I turned my attention back to Claire. She was looking up from her knitting with an anxious smile. "Do you know how to play bridge?" I asked.

"I'll let you be the judge of that," she said with a laugh, tugging on a thick strand of hair. Her blonde hair was just dark enough to convince me that it was her natural color. It hung straight above her shoulders, and it was gently disheveled, as if she had just run their hands through it. "I play bridge every day at work."

"Nice job."

"We play at lunch. My friend Nadia taught me how to play."

"Nadia is the one who didn't win the Nobel Prize, right?"

Claire cocked her head at me. "Yes, how did you....oh, that's right, I told you."

My mind raced through the last evening we spent together. I grimaced as my brain pushed forward the memory of the failed kiss. We sighed in unison.

"That was quite a night," she said

"It certainly was," I said, shaking my head at my bad behavior. "Listen," I said, glancing around the room. "There are a lot more people here than I expected, so I'm going to need experienced players to help out with the beginners. But I've got a feeling that we're the only experienced players here."

"I'll do whatever I can to help," she said, picking up her knitting again.

"What are you knitting?" I asked.

"Oh," she said, looking down at her knitting as if it was the first time she'd ever seen it. "A scarf, I guess. I'm not really sure yet. It's something I do when I'm nervous."

"What are you nervous about?" I sat down in a chair next to her.

"Oh, nothing. Oh, everything," she said with a laugh. "I don't know anyone here."

"You know me."

"I think that's what I'm most nervous about."

"I make you nervous?" I asked, flattered. I couldn't remember the last time I made a woman nervous.

"No," she said, placing her hand on my knee and removing it quickly. "I was nervous before I saw you, but I'm not now. The last time we saw each other, it didn't end well, did it?"

"It wasn't so bad," I said. At the time it seemed dreadful, but I had been on much worse dates since then. "I'm sorry I haven't called. My life has been rather complicated lately."

She nodded and cast her eyes downward. And then it hit me. Claire had made an effort to see me that night. She came to the bridge lesson knowing I would be there. She had no idea how I would respond to her, yet she came anyway. It was an incredibly courageous act. My stomach surged again at the thought.

Just then, a ladybug landed on Claire's shirt. It crawled next to the daisy.

"Look, a ladybug," I said, reaching over to pluck the bug from her shirt. But when it crawled onto her breast, I lowered my hand. "What's the Latin name for it? Ladius buggius?"

"Coccinellidae," she said. She gently scooped up the bug and let it crawl on her arm. "That's good luck, you know. If a ladybug lands on you."

"We're going to need it tonight," I said glancing at Tricia, who was greeting Poppy with faux good cheer. She shot a glacial smile at Anne as she sat down at their table.

* * * * * * * *

The scarecrow ordered everyone to take a seat and I started the lesson. I quickly forgot my carefully prepared lesson and instead gave a muddled rendering of the rules of bridge, stressing the most complicated aspects of the game and forgetting to explain the fundamentals. I was interrupted so often that I gave up on the lesson and suggested we try to struggle through a few hands.

Utter chaos ensued. The players were so confused by the bidding system that most of the women abandoned the game well before the class ended. I ran from table to table trying to give individual instruction. In most cases, though, I simply grabbed the cards from the women and played out the hands myself.

Only Claire's table maintained some semblance of order. Claire was sitting with three women who looked like they subsisted on nothing but nuts and twigs. They were so fragile I was surprised they had the strength to hold the cards up. Claire calmly led them through bidding and playing, and by the end of the evening her group was the only one still playing the game.

* * * * * * * *

When the lesson ended, the Bravehearts leaders announced there would be a healing circle to resolve the feelings of inadequacy that resulted from the game. Everyone was invited to stay, but Tricia pulled me aside and said that we'd be doing our healing at a bar. Carmen was caught up in the drama of the evening, so she decided to stay for the healing circle. "They call it a 'womb,'" she twittered. "So there will probably be much caressing."

Claire, Tricia, Anne, Poppy and I left the building together. When we got outside, Claire tentatively walked off into the night.

"Aren't you coming with us?" I called to her retreating form. Claire turned and made a few hesitant steps in our direction.

"Yeah, come with us. Be part of the in-crowd," Tricia said.

"Well, I've always wanted to be part of the in-crowd," Claire said.

"Then you better put that knitting away," Anne said. "The in-crowd does not knit."

We drove separately to a bar near a university that was packed with students. Tricia pushed her way through the crowd and secured a table. I scooted into the booth hoping that Claire would slide in next to me. And I smiled to myself when she did. Tricia squeezed in next to Claire. Poppy and Anne sat across from us.

For the next hour, Tricia dominated the conversation. To the impartial observer, there was nothing amiss. But I knew that Tricia was up to something. Tricia had sulked her way through the bridge lesson, refusing to make eye contact with Anne and wandering away from the table when Carmen tried to coax her into concentrating on the game. But as soon as we left Bravehearts, her spirits lightened considerably. This sudden switch in mood worried me. Like a storm with uncertain winds, she could lurch out of control at any moment. And sure enough, after about an hour Tricia's manufactured giddiness started to harden.

"So, Poppy," Tricia said cheerfully. Too cheerfully. "How's your love life?" I gripped the edge of my seat and aimed a look of distress at Anne.

Poppy gulped visibly. "Oh, you know me, always a disaster."

"So, Tricia, how's yours?" Anne asked coolly.

"Are you still dating Bunny?" Claire asked, innocently stepping into the riptide swirling beneath the table.

Tricia stared defiantly at Anne and responded, "No, Claire, I'm not dating anyone. I'm in a relationship."

"With Bunny?" Anne asked.

Claire turned to me, her mouth half open in alarm. "You didn't do anything wrong," I whispered in her ear. I held my face next to hers for a moment, intoxicated by the warmth pouring from her body.

Tricia leaned back into the booth and took a deliberately long sip of her cocktail. "I know exactly what's happening here," she said acidly, looking first at Anne and then at Poppy. Poppy grew pale and Anne wrapped her arm around her protectively.

"Come on, Poppy, let's go home," Anne said. Poppy nodded a weak goodbye as they left the table.

"Home? Whose home?" Tricia yelled after them. "Better not be my home." She slammed back into her seat and turned to face me.

"So, I suppose you didn't know anything about this," Tricia said.

"About what?" I asked.

"That Anne and Poppy are lovers." She said the word "lovers" as if it were a dirty word, rolling it around on her tongue before spitting it out.

"I don't think that's been established," I said.

"Oh, bullshit," Tricia said. "Tell me, Claire, did it seem to you that they are lovers?"

"I'm sorry I said anything about Bunny," Claire said, holding her palms out in a plea for forgiveness. "I thought she was your girlfriend."

Tricia patted Claire's hands. "Thank you for caring about my feelings. Apparently, you are the only person who does," she said with a sniff of self-pity.

Tricia drained her drink and stood up. She was wobbly and she steadied herself by gripping Claire's shoulder. She hadn't had that much to drink that night, despite her valiant efforts to do so. The bar was so crowded that our waiter rarely stopped at our table. I assumed that it was the accumulation of overdrinking that week plus jealous rage that put her in an intoxicated state. "I'm leaving," she said.

"Where are you going?" I asked.

"Dancing," she said.

"You're taking a cab wherever you go," I said. She swatted away my words and stumbled from the table.

* * * * * * *

Claire and I watched Tricia leave. "Well, at least it wasn't me running out of the room this time," Claire said. I was concerned about Tricia, but not so worried that I didn't notice that Claire had not bothered to take advantage of the empty space left by Tricia. She remained plastered to my side.

"This type of thing goes on between them constantly. It will all work out," I said, not so sure that it would. "So, what have you been up to for the past few months?"

"Waiting for your call," she said seriously. Then she broke out in a grin. "I'm just kidding. I've been very involved in a project at work. I've been studying a bee that produces a toxic pheromone when it comes into contact with ants. It...oh, you don't want to hear this."

"Sure I do," I said. Claire explained the experiment, which I had a hard time following. I was too preoccupied watching her eyes, which jumped with excitement as she related the tale.

"And what have you been doing?" she asked after she told me about the experiment's findings, which basically foretold much bad news for the ant population of the world.

"Trying to get over my ex-girlfriend." I said. "And I think I've been pretty successful." Before I could elaborate, the waiter came by and asked if we wanted another drink. Before we could answer he tossed the check at us, anxious to free up the table. I wished I had ordered another round just to have an excuse to stay and talk to Claire.

"You live in Swan Pond, don't you?" She nodded. "That's near the bridge club I play in. Would you like to play together some time?"

Her eyes lit up, but then she demurred. "I don't think I'm good enough to play at a club."

"Sure you are. I'll call you next week and we can pick a date to play."

We left the restaurant and stood in front of her car shuffling our feet, both of us reluctant to end the evening. Finally, she gave me a quick hug that was really more like a shove and hopped into her car.

I watched as her car pulled away. It was an old, fuel-efficient Swedish-made car with a bumper sticker that read: I break for bumblebees.

CHAPTER 9

I called Claire the following Tuesday morning. I was still sailing from a coffee high when I reached for the phone, so I jumped up and down to exhaust my nervous energy before dialing. The noise caught Lonnie's attention.

"What are you doing in there?" Lonnie asked, scooting her chair into the doorway of my office. Once Lonnie took her seat in the morning she rarely left it. She remained planted in the chair throughout the day, expertly wheeling it from task to task. It was as if she was afflicted with a temporary case of paralysis during the weekday and needed the chair to power her movements.

"Jumping up and down," I answered.

"Why?" asked Lonnie.

"You don't want to know," I said, increasing the frequency of my jumps.

Lonnie watched me for a moment, masking her curiosity with a frown. Finally, she said, "Is this some type of gay thing?" She furrowed her brow to suggest that she was trying very hard to understand my lifestyle.

"Kind of," I said. I stopped jumping and wiped a drop of perspiration from my forehead. "I've got to call a woman for a date and I'm nervous. But I don't want to sound nervous."

"Now, what do you have to be nervous about?" Lonnie asked, peddling her chair into my office. "You're a good looking woman. You've got brains. You've got sense. You're not crazy like Tricia. So just call the girl. The worst thing that can happen is she'll say no. Or, in your case, the worst thing is that she'll say yes." She chuckled to herself and rolled back to her desk.

I sat at my desk, staring at the phone. Finally, Lonnie called out, "I don't hear any dialing going on in there." I punched in Claire's number. After several rings, Claire's voicemail clicked on and I hung up.

"Well?" Lonnie asked.

"Voicemail," I said. "I hate leaving messages. You know that." Leaving a message for a potential love interest always intensified my insecurities. I'd spend the rest of the day waiting for a return call, checking the phone line to make sure it was working, and then checking my voicemail to see if she had called while I was checking the line.

"Call her back and leave her a message," Lonnie ordered. Lonnie wouldn't have bothered to become involved in this developing drama if Tricia was in the office. But Tricia had been missing-in-action since the bridge lesson at Bravehearts, and since Lonnie wasn't tending to Tricia's constant demands she had time to meddle in my affairs. On the morning after the bridge lesson, Tricia left a message saying that she'd be out of town for at least a week. Her voice sounded scratchy and distant, but she may have intentionally called from a place with sketchy cell phone service just to give the impression she was in some lonely, dusty locale with nothing but donkeys for company.

I redialed Claire's number. As the phone rang, I was buoyed by the realization that Claire was so polite that she would return my call even if she didn't want to.

About fifteen minutes later, the phone rang. Lonnie answered it and rolled into my office. "It's Claire Larsson on line one," she said.

When I picked up the phone, Claire sounded excited and short of breath. I imagined her anxiously dialing my number, hoping that I hadn't lost interest in her in the time it took her to return my call. I smiled into the receiver.

"I'm sorry I missed your call," she said. "I was being interviewed by a reporter. We had a mishap at our educational outreach program yesterday and now the entomology department is big news." I couldn't imagine how insects could be newsworthy unless they had eaten radioactive pellets and grew to be ten times the size of humans. Anne and I once saw a movie at a sci-fi film festival based on that very premise and I had nightmares about being attacked by giant grasshoppers for weeks afterward.

Claire explained that she visited elementary schools once a month to introduce children to the wonders of the insect world. It was a propaganda campaign designed to make children think twice before squishing a beetle or setting fire to ants. That Monday, she brought a selection of bugs to a kindergarten class. As they were setting up the specimen jars, kids rushed the table causing it to topple. It was a mess. "These things happen with insects," she said. "They are evolutionarily programmed to escape. It wouldn't have been so bad, but there was a photographer there from a local newspaper. And now the Chicago newspapers have picked up the story. I've been giving interviews all morning. The general consensus at the lab is that any story that takes the focus away from our nuclear past and the kangaroo escape is good publicity."

The laboratory Claire worked for was the birthplace of atomic energy. Shortly after scientists created the first sustained atomic reaction at the University of Chicago in the 1940's, they established the lab in a suburban forest preserve. Ever since then, the lab had been caught in a web of controversy. To help soften the lab's deadly image, it opened a petting zoo on its grounds. A few years later, the zoo's kangaroo population hopped the fence and took up residence in the surrounding woods. The lab tried to keep the breakout quiet, but officials finally had to admit to the escape when hikers reported encounters with the animals. The lab quickly issued a statement that the kangaroos had been captured and returned to the zoo, but many people suspected a cover up. Residents in the neighboring towns still believed that a herd of kangaroos ran wild in the woods, and they were blamed for everything from odd weather patterns to child abductions.

"When will the story be in the papers?" I asked.

"Tomorrow," she said.

"Will the stories mention the kangaroos?"

"Every story about this place mentions the kangaroos," she said.

"Do you know the truth about the kangaroos? Are they still living in the woods?"

"That's top secret," she said with just enough flirtation in her tone to make my heart race. It was all the incentive I needed to invite her to meet me that Friday at my bridge club. It was the only night that I could be reasonably certain that my parents wouldn't show up to play. They went to my uncle's restaurant every Friday night with my father's relatives. It was the price my mother had to pay for refusing to serve Italian food in her home.

* * * * * * * *

When I arrived home from work that evening, I did something I hadn't done in months. I made a compilation music CD. The last time I made a music mix was a few weeks before my breakup with Jean. The disk contained a collection of the saccharine pop ballads Jean enjoyed. A couple days later I found it in the trunk of her car. It was surrounded by dozens of other compilations I had made for her during our relationship.

I worked on a music mix for Claire until two in the morning. It was filled with cocktail music from the 1950's and '60's, songs with lighthearted lyrics and swinging tunes that almost made you forget they were about sex and longing.

As I mixed the music, I debated whether to include one particular song. It was Ella Fitzgerald's version of Cole Porter's "Let's Do It." Its opening lyrics praised the romantic lives of insects, but I feared that the bottomline message of the song—"Let's do it/Let's fall in love"—might frighten Claire. Finally, just as I was about to give up for the night and go to bed, I dragged the song onto the playlist.

I knew that in the coming days I'd be tortured over whether to leave "Let's Do It" on the mix. I'd remix the CD dozens of times, taking the song off the playlist and then adding it back on again. After spending hours sweating over the final version, the odds were that I'd never even give the CD to Claire. But as I padded off to bed that night, I thought about how nice it was to be worried about such things again.

* * * * * * * *

On the Friday that Claire and I were to play at the bridge club, I met my brother at one of the lakefront apartment buildings that was for sale in my neighborhood. Ever since Eric asked me to look for a building, I had been scouring the listings for an available property. But real estate in the neighborhood was appreciating so rapidly that other developers snatched up the choice parcels before we had a chance to make an offer.

Our luck changed earlier that week when I ran into Gregor, a Bulgarian immigrant who owned one of the large apartment buildings on the lake. Unlike most slumlords who kept a safe distance from their hostile tenants, Gregor lived in the building he owned. He usually could be found in the courtyard, sprinkling seeds on the dead lawn and having earnest, no-win conversations with angry tenants.

On that afternoon, Gregor motioned me to him with a weary wave and asked if I knew anyone who would like to buy his building.

"I think I do," I said, trying not to sound too eager. I called my brother and we set up an appointment to see the building.

When I arrived at Gregor's building that Friday, my brother was waiting on the sidewalk with his arm draped around a tall, elegantly dressed woman. Eric was listening intently as the woman pointed with authority at the building's facade.

"Julia!" my brother exclaimed.

"Hi Julia," the woman said familiarly.

"Gretchen?" I asked. She nodded coolly. Gretchen Berger was raised in a modern mansion down the street from my parents' house. When I was in kindergarten, the Berger's bought a proud, old Victorian and bulldozed it as ladies from the village historical society gathered behind the construction barriers, pleading against demolition. In its place, the Bergers built a granite and glass monstrosity that could have served as the lair for a comic book villain.

Gretchen and I were never friends. When we were young, the social conventions of childhood forced us to invite each other to birthday parties, but that was as far as the relationship went. Gretchen was an only child, a situation regarded among her peers as freakish, like having a Siamese twin or eleven toes. She attended Montessori School, not public schools like the rest of the kids in the neighborhood, and later transferred to an exclusive day school where students were encouraged to celebrate their differences and weren't required to take P.E.

Gretchen's father was a severe character who always wore dark sunglasses that gave him the sinister appearance of a shipping tycoon. The first time I met him was at Gretchen's seventh birthday party. Mr. Berger suddenly appeared in the doorway of the living room, filling it like a bad shadow. Chrissy Taylor, who ten years later would have an affair with our high school algebra teacher, touched my arm and gasped in terror.

"Who vants ice cream?" he asked sternly in a thick German accent. We bit our lips, too frightened to accept his offer. This seemed to infuriate him and he stormed out of the room with his dark suit jacket flapping behind him like a cape.

Mrs. Berger was a broad shouldered woman who dressed in the type of striped fabrics usually reserved for upholstering lawn furniture. She was prone to making bold pronouncements about the futility of childhood, and her every action emphasized that she was not suited for a life in the provinces. Mrs. Berger's father was a diplomat and she never tired of saying that she spent her childhood in "the capitals of Europe."

"Oh, big deal," my mother would say under her breath. "Most of the capitals of Europe are cesspools. Except for Copenhagen, of course." My mother launched a cold war against the Bergers the day they razed the old Victorian. She would go out of her way to catch Mrs. Berger's eye just so she could freeze her out with a thin smile. The war was largely one sided, though. Mrs. Berger simply ignored my mother just as she ignored the other women in the neighborhood. Instead, Mrs. Berger concentrated her considerable energy in grooming her daughter to be a social outcast, encouraging her poetry writing, demanding that she "en-nun-ci-ate" every word, enrolling her in MENSA, and not allowing her to watch TV.

After Gretchen started attending day school, I rarely saw her. Occasionally, my friends and I would spot her sitting in her yard with some serious looking children and we'd throw things at them.

"What are you doing here?" I asked Gretchen.

"Your brother asked me to look at the building," she said. I stared at her blankly for a moment. "I'm an architect, Julia," she said imperially.

Gretchen still had the superior manner that made her insufferable as a child. But now her lofty self-regard made her seem confident and in command, like someone who you would gladly follow into battle. As a teenager, Gretchen was large and unglamorous, with long, mousy hair and a fondness for Laura Ashley jumpers. But she had grown into a handsome, stately woman. She was big-boned, like her mother, but slender, and she wore her hair in a crisp bob that showcased her strong, attractive facial features.

My brother wrapped his arms around Gretchen. This was the first time I had ever seen my brother display affection in public to a woman—unless you considered ordering your girlfriend to make you another sandwich a sign of affection.

"Look at this dump," my brother said gaily. "Wait 'till dad sees it. He'll keel over." My father shared my brother's low regard for my neighborhood. He couldn't understand why I wanted to live in the city after he spent years struggling to escape it.

Instinctively, I handed the price sheet directly to Gretchen. She reviewed it, nodding professionally. "It's a steal," she said to Eric.

The courtyard looked like a bomb hit it, but if you glanced beyond the mess you could see how lovely it once was. As we walked through the building, several residents looked on with a mix of hostility and hope. An elderly lady grasped my wrist and asked if we were going to buy the building and fix up the apartments. I nodded noncommittally. Most of the residents knew what we were there for, though. Their friends in neighboring buildings had lost their homes in recent months to condo developers. Now it was their turn.

* * * * * * *

After we left the building, Gretchen, Eric and I ate lunch at a local restaurant. It was an old hippie joint that had been around since the 1970's. They served only organic fare, which is rarely as flavorful as food pumped full of chemicals and antibiotics. I ate at the restaurant often because it helped ease the guilt I felt for my

lackadaisical commitment to liberal politics and the oppressed. It
was the same guilt that made me boycott certain brands of beer
and to not wear my mother's old mink-lined raincoat, even though
it was the warmest, most comfortable piece of clothing I owned,
and, as my mother liked to remind me, the animals were killed
long before I grew a social conscious.

"What's good here?" Eric asked as he scanned the menu.

"Nothing," I said.

After we ordered our food, I pulled out a calculator and esti-
mated how much money Eric would make from converting the
apartments to condos. Even under the worst-case scenario, Eric
would stand to make a fortune.

"We want you to go in on this with us," Eric said casually wrapping his arm around Gretchen.

"I'd love to, but I can't. All my money is tied up in the law practice," I said. I had some savings, but I kept the money in reserve in
case I needed it for the practice. We still were funding the costs
of Tricia's personal injury cases out-of-pocket, and I had seen my
savings dwindle to practically nothing over the years.

"I'll lend you the money to invest," Eric said.

"I can't take money from you."

"Well, the offer is there," my brother said. "Think about it."

When we finished lunch, Eric invited me to a sports bar downtown. "Gretchen has to hook up with her mom and I've got some
time to kill," he said.

Gretchen wiped her mouth with her napkin and tossed it onto
her plate. "I'm meeting my mother for dinner and then I'm taking
her friends on an architectural tour of the Loop. Do you remember
my mother, Julia? Well, she hasn't changed."

"Gretchen is giving a tour to the German Club," my brother
said, raising his eyebrows to emphasis the significance of what
he'd just said.

"The German Club? Your mom belongs to the German Club?"
I asked.

"She certainly does," Gretchen said.

"Our mother is involved in the Scandinavian Club," I said, shoot-
ing Eric a warning glance, which he chose to ignore.

"Yes, I'm well aware of that," Gretchen said with a smug little
laugh that I remembered from childhood.

"Sorry, Eric, I can't," I said. "I'm heading to the suburbs after
this."

"To see Mom and Dad?" he asked, screwing his face into a look
of displeasure.

"No, to play bridge."

"Then Gretchen can take my car and you can drive me home."

His car? No one was allowed to touch his car, much less drive it. His car was as dangerous and complicated as a nuclear submarine. I couldn't even figure out how to open its doors.

Gretchen brushed away his incredible offer with a wave of her hand. "I don't need your car. I take cabs. Julia, your brother has this crazy idea that you need a car in the city. He doesn't trust taxi drivers."

"You're taking the car," he said manfully. He was as surprised as I was when Gretchen demurred and allowed him to drop the keys into her palm.

* * * * * * * *

After we left the restaurant, Gretchen folded herself into the front seat of Eric's hot rod. He gave her last minute instructions on how to operate the thing and we climbed into my car. "Okay, what's going on between you two?" I asked as I pulled into traffic.

"I'm going to marry Gretchen, Julia," he said with a defiant nod of his head.

"Well, Eric, I expected much less from you," I reached over and patted him on the back. "Well done."

On the ride to the suburbs, Eric gave me a highly romanticized version of his courtship of Gretchen. I could only conclude that he had created this preposterous myth to cover the fact that he had run into Gretchen at a bar and a one-night stand had blossomed into love.

"Do Mom and Dad know about Gretchen?" I asked.

"I'm not telling them anything until we're engaged," he said. "I'm going to propose next month. In the meantime, it wouldn't hurt if you started working on Mom."

"What do you mean?"

"Soften her up. Drop some hints, so she's not completely shocked."

"Eric, don't take this the wrong way, but Gretchen kind of reminds me of Mom." Eric reacted as if I had slugged him. "She looks like a younger version of Mom, and she's kind of controlling and domineering, also like Mom."

"I think Gretchen looks like that actress. The one in Casablanca."

"Ingrid Bergman? Well, Mom looks like her, too. Listen, if it makes you feel any better, I once went to a therapist who accused me of wanting to sleep with Mom."

"That's disgusting."

"What's worse is that after she sprung that on me, all she wanted to talk about was Mom. She would spend all session criticizing Mom and I would stick up for her. And then I realized I was spending a lot of money to defend Mom, which was not fair at all, and so I quit therapy."

* * * * * * * *

When we pulled up to the house, Mrs. Nielsen, my parent's next-door neighbor, was out front watering her garden. She put her hand over her eyes to shield them from the sun and waved when she spotted me in the driver's seat. Up until that moment, I had no intention of going into my parents' house. I was nervous enough about the date with Claire without adding an encounter with my parents to the mix. But Mrs. Nielsen was one of my mother's chief spies and I knew she would report me if I failed to stop in to visit my parents. So, reluctantly, I went into the house.

"Well," my mother said when she saw me. "This is a surprise!" She was standing in the front foyer, adjusting an earring and patting her hair into place.

"I drove Eric home," I said, following Eric into the kitchen.

"What were you two doing together?" she asked, narrowing her eyes. My mother always suspected that Eric and I were conspiring against her and she discouraged us from spending time together.

"I took Julia to lunch to meet my girlfriend," Eric said casually, opening the refrigerator and pulling out some lunchmeat.

"Ah ha!" she said. "I knew something was up. So, who is she?"

"She's sweet and demure," I said, thinking of the two adjectives that would least describe Gretchen. "You'll hate her."

I looked up at the clock. "I gotta run."

"Where are you going? " my mother asked.

"I'm playing bridge tonight," I said, heading toward the front door.

"Tonight? This isn't bridge night," she said.

"I'm playing with a new partner," I said.

"Well, give me a few minutes to dress your father and we'll come, too, " she said. I looked at my brother for help.

"But what about dinner with the Italians?" Eric asked.

"The world will not end if your father does not get a trough of spaghetti tonight."

"Mom," I said, "it's my first time playing with this person, and I'm nervous. "

"Well, having us there will make you less nervous, " she said.

* * * * * * * *

My mother insisted that we ride to the club together in their car so she could browbeat me about my brother's girlfriend. I was in no mood to be coy, so as we pulled out of the driveway I told them about Eric's intention to marry Gretchen.

"Oh, God, my worst nightmare!" my mother said. "That mother of hers is horrible! Oh, Christ, Tony, what are we going to do?"

"We're going to go to the wedding and be nice to the girl," my dad said. My mother looked at him in horror, as if he had suggested they perform a ritual sacrifice in order to break Eric and Gretchen apart. After a moment of stunned silence, she leaned back in her seat and sighed.

"You know, it might be exactly what he deserves," she said. "If she's anything like her mother, she'll keep that brother of yours in line. He thinks I'm impossible. Just wait until he gets a load of that bunch."

* * * * * * * *

When we arrived at the club, I raced out of the car to avoid making an entrance with my parents. Claire was already seated at a table, wielding her knitting needles furiously. Several men were hovering nearby, trying to get as close to her as their social disorders would allow.

"Still working on that scarf?" I asked.

She held out a long stretch of red wool and sized it up. "I've decided that it's got bigger ambitions. I've turned this into a sleeve and now I'm working on the neckline. Do you knit?"

"No," I said. "I'm really impressed with people who know how to do things like that. I can't do anything."

"You can play bridge," Claire said. "Several people told me what a good player you are."

I glanced around to see who could be spreading these rumors and I spotted my parents enter the room. They were both out of breath from climbing the steep stairs. My mother pointed at me and they walked over. "Why did you run in here?" she asked. "You're going to give your father a heart attack." She clutched her side and caught her breath. Her posture straightened immediately when she noticed Claire.

"I'm Astrid DeTortelli." She thrust her hand at Claire.

"My parents," I said lamely.

"So, you're my daughter's new partner," my mother said.

"Bridge partner," I clarified.

Roger ordered us to take our seats. We were assigned to north-south seating, which meant we wouldn't play against my parents that night.

"Darn," my mother said. "We won't have a chance to chat. Oh, well, we'll all go out to dinner afterward."

"Oh, God, no," I thought to myself as they walked away.

Claire was an excellent player, but she didn't know the sophisticated bidding strategies I had learned in bridge class. As a result, we stumbled through the first few hands, but I quickly adjusted my bidding to fit hers and we easily bested our first several opponents. I grew hopeful that we might not finish in last place that evening. But my high spirits were crushed when Sal and Leon approached our table. Sal and Leon were my Moby Dick, my Waterloo. They weren't good players, but I always lost to them because they drove me to distraction with their annoying habits and body odor.

"Helloooo, ladies," Sal bellowed as he slammed into a chair. Sal was a big, messy man who smelled like the inside of an old gym shoe. He ate constantly while playing, unwrapping greasy napkins filled with chicken wings and potato chips. When Sal wasn't slobbering over his cards, he was boasting loudly about his brilliant card sense and lecturing his opponents on their mistakes.

Leon, a small, pudgy fellow who resembled a garden gnome, twittered girlishly and took the chair opposite Sal. Leon spoke in a high-pitched whine that pinched at my eardrums like an infection. I often had to resist the urge to pick up Leon and stuff him into a garbage can.

I braced myself against the table as they took their seats, determined not to let them rattle me. Sal opened a bottle of BigFiz orange soda and performed a nauseating routine in which he strained small dribbles of the soda over sugar cubes and then swirled it as if it was a martini before knocking it back and then blenching loudly.

I arranged my cards slowly, trying to shake off an attack of irritation so I could concentrate on my cards. Claire watched me expectantly, waiting for me to make the first bid. I had a very odd hand. Eight of the thirteen cards I held were hearts, yet I didn't have many points. Before I realized what I was doing, I made a bid that I learned in bridge class. It was one of those seemingly nonsensical bids that make people give up the game in disgust. As soon as I pulled out the bidding card, I groaned silently because I was certain that Claire wouldn't understand the bid.

Claire frowned at me in confusion, trying to figure out what the bid meant. She ran her hand through her hair in frustration and then she looked directly into my eyes. When our eyes locked, I felt an electric current surge through my body. She must have experienced the same sensation because we both jerked our heads back at the same moment. Claire's lips slowly formed into a smile. She had figured out the bid.

The intimacy of the moment was exhilarating and slightly embarrassing. I was flushed with the thought that such an intense exchange had taken place in a room full of people. Claire had climbed into my brain and read my thoughts. With just a glance we had forged a connection that took many bridge partnerships years to develop.

Claire and I finished in second place that night, a remarkable achievement for two people who had never played together before.

"Well, I think the champions deserve an ice cream sundae," my father announced.

"The girls can have ice cream. You're getting Jell-O," my mother said.

* * * * * * *

My parents were already at the diner when Claire and I arrived. My mother was whispering urgently into my father's ear as we approached the table. She stopped suddenly when she spotted us and greeted Claire with a broad smile. My dad grunted a hello. I assumed that my mother had figured out that I was interested in Claire as more than a bridge partner and she was instructing my father not to make a scene.

Claire studied the menu carefully and ordered the deluxe patty melt, which came with a bowl of soup, a salad, and a mountain of fries. My father pulled his face into an Italianate gesture to signify that he was impressed.

"I didn't have dinner," Claire said unapologetically. I felt my face go flush. It was my experience that women with healthy appetites for food had good appetites for other things, as well.

"I'll have the same thing," my dad told the waitress. Then he gave Claire a wink of commiseration.

My mother opened her mouth to scold my father, but she stopped herself and settled on a "he's a lost cause" sigh. My mother had a whole vocabulary of sighs, all of which were meant to communicate exactly how disappointed she was with her family.

"So, Claire," my mother said, picking up a roll, buttering it, and then discarding it after deciding it was inedible. "What's your last name?"

"Larsson," she said.

My mother perked up. "Oh! Is that spelled L-a-r-s-e-n?"

"No, L-a-r-s-s-o-n."

"So is that a Norwegian name?" my mother asked. I glanced at her in surprise. It was highly unusual for my mother to give someone the benefit of the doubt that they were Norwegian rather than Swedish.

"It's Swedish," Claire said.

My mother grimaced for a split second, but she recovered quickly. "What do you do for a living?" When Claire said she was an entomologist, my mother said, "Then you're a doctor? A Swede who is a doctor! Well, then, see, you can never tell."

"I knew I recognized you!" my father said. "You're the bug lady. The one in the newspapers." Earlier that week, the story of the insect escape was on the front page of both of Chicago's big daily newspapers.

"Yes, I'm afraid so," she said.

My mother, no friend to insects, jumped into the discussion to defend her liberal use of pesticides and other poisons in her garden. Claire gently told her that there were natural methods that would be more conducive to healthy plant growth.

My mother eyed her suspiciously. But then, remarkably, she exclaimed, "Okay! Sold! Come over next week and take a look at my garden and tell me what I should do. And then we'll go to the Scandinavian Club. We Scandinavians need to stick together! I'm sure my daughter has told you that Germans are trying to take over my club, and now, apparently, they are also moving in on my family."

"The subject hasn't come up, Mom," I said.

My mother slammed her hands on the table in excitement, thrilled that she had a new audience. She leaned over the table and began to tell Claire about Eric's impending nuptials, but my father interrupted her.

"Where are you from, hon?" he asked Claire. It was a benign question and yet it left me breathless. My father had always treated my girlfriends with willful disinterest. If he was forced to interact with them, he was careful not to show the slightest curiosity about their lives.

"I came here from Minnesota, but I grew up in Wisconsin," Claire said.

"We're playing in our first bridge tournament in Madison in October," my father said. "Why don't you play in it with us?"

"Oh, of course she will," my mother said, regaining control of the conversation. "But we'll have to switch partners once in a while so I stand a chance of winning a game.

* * * * * * * *

After dinner, as we stood in the parking lot, my mother made plans with Claire to visit her garden the following week. She hugged Claire goodbye and ordered me into the Town Car. As I climbed into the backseat of my parents' car, I spotted the CD that I made for Claire on the floor. I jumped out and ran to Claire's car.

She rolled down the window and I handed her the CD. "I made you a music mix." I said, panting from the jog. "To play on your drive to work. It's no big deal. It was easy to make. Really. No effort at all."

"I can't wait to listen to it," she said. I immediately regretted including "Let's Do It" in the mix, and I wondered if there was a graceful way to reclaim the disk so I could remix it.

Claire stepped out of the car and embraced me. As the hug lingered I couldn't stop my hands from running up the length of her body. I peered over her shoulder to see if my parents were watching. My mom was looking at herself in the mirror, applying lipstick and issuing a directive to my father, who wasn't paying attention to her.

CHAPTER 10

Tricia resurfaced the following Monday. She strolled into the office late in the afternoon carrying a beat-up duffle bag. It was the same bag she dragged across Europe the year she took a break from law school. She'd pull out the bag whenever she wanted to put people on notice that she could slip back into her unfettered youth anytime she pleased. It was the bag she packed whenever she left Anne. At times, the bag would mysteriously appear in prominent view to suggest that Tricia was considering walking out on the relationship again. Anne claimed that the bag was "as threatening as an inanimate object is allowed to be in civilized society."

"Hi ya," Tricia said casually, as if nothing unusual had happened since the bridge lesson at Bravehearts. She let the duffle slip from her shoulder and picked up a stack of mail. As she ripped open an envelope, she glanced around the room. "Where's Lonnie?"

"With the nuns," I said. Lonnie was Baptist, yet every year she went on a religious retreat to a Catholic convent, mainly to escape her five kids and her husband, a postman with a weakness for pork rinds and ponzi schemes. We begged her for details about the retreat, hoping to get some insight into the sexual tensions that exist among the cloistered, but Lonnie would simply cross herself elaborately and refuse to comment.

I leaned back in my chair, stretching languidly. I had been working steadily since early that morning and my in-box was empty for the first time in months. I had used the quiet of Tricia's weeklong absence to plow through the stack of tedious paperwork that always managed to find its way to the bottom of my to-do list. Each time I was tempted to give up on the drudgery, I'd coax myself back

133

to work by rewarding each completed task with copious infusions of sweets and small fantasies about Claire.

I began fantasizing about kissing Claire the morning after we played bridge at the club. I lingered in bed that morning, embracing my pillow, pretending it was Claire. Just as I placed my mouth on the pillow—revisiting my days as a demented preteen who thought humping my bedding was good training for future romance—the phone rang. When I heard Claire's voice at the other end of the line, I tossed the pillow across the room in a rush of guilt. She was calling to invite me to a work outing. The laboratory was sponsoring a trip to The Medieval Palace, a fake castle that hosted jousting competitions.

"The Medieval Palace? Isn't that the place where you have to eat with your hands?" I asked. Commercials for the place dominated late-night TV. They featured lusty waitresses balancing mugs of beer against a backdrop of deep cleavage, leotard-clad men speaking in iambic pentameter, and mildly obese suburbanites biting into turkey legs.

"Our human resource staff plans these outings because they think that none of the scientists have a life outside the lab. And, maybe they're right. The tickets sold out on the first day," she said. "But we don't have to go. We can play bridge instead."

"We can play bridge anytime," I said. "But how often do you get a chance to use the word 'codpiece' in polite conversation these days?"

The anticipation of turning my kissing fantasies into reality put me in good humor, and I welcomed Tricia back with a generosity of spirit that surprised us both. In the past, I treated her homecomings with cool disregard. She, in turn, would act wrongly maligned and victimized, limping around the office as if she had chewed her leg out of an animal trap. We'd engage in a passive-aggressive stalemate until one of us—usually Tricia, who had no stamina for tense standoffs—finally gave in and invited the other out to lunch at our favorite Greek diner, a place where the owners always flirted with us and where it was impossible to hold a grudge.

"So," I said, following Tricia into her office, "where the hell have you been?" I said this in a puckish tone that made it clear I was delighted to see her.

"Liechtenstein," Tricia answered, as if it was the most reasonable response imaginable. She flicked on her computer and bent over to rummage through the duffle bag. "I brought you a present," she said, pulling out a wrinkled paper sack and tossing it onto the desk.

As she bent over, her shirt inched up her back and I was shocked to discover that she was wearing thong underwear. Tricia didn't wear underpants often, and when she did they were always waist-high cotton briefs, the type you'd see flapping on your grandmother's laundry line. Unlike so many women who relied on their lingerie to do the heavy lifting where looking sexy was concerned, Tricia was confident enough in her innate seductive powers to leave provocative undergarments to lesser females.

"I hope it's not a thong," I said, peeking into the bag cautiously.

"Hey, it's not my fault," she said, scrunching her face in discomfort and tugging at her crotch. "I forgot to pack underwear, and this is the only type they sell in Liechtenstein. Apparently, every woman in Liechtenstein thinks she's Cher."

"Since when do you feel the need to wear underpants?"

Tricia regarded me with barely contained outrage. "You have to wear underwear on an airplane, Julia," she said, as if this was some type of official policy that everyone knew about except me. Tricia didn't abide by many rules, and the ones she did adhere to usually were ones of her own making that no one followed but herself.

I peered into the bag. It was filled with bite-sized candy in colorful wrappers. On closer inspection, I noticed that most of the candy had been eaten already and what remained were empty wrappers. I pulled out a handful of wrappers, raising my eyebrows at Tricia. "I got a little peckish on the plane," she explained with a shrug.

"I'm probably going to regret asking you this, but why were you in Liechtenstein?"

"Well, Julia, I've never been to Liechtenstein," she said, squinting at the computer screen. "Every lesbian should go to Liechtenstein once in their lives. Listen to the name: Lick-ten-stein. If lesbians were going to own their own country—God forbid—that should be the name of it."

"So, did you like Liechtenstein?" I asked.

It s no Andorra, she said. Tricia began pounding furiously on the keyboard, which effectively put an end to the discussion about Liechtenstein. The last time Tricia disappeared, it was months before she finally revealed details of her trip a two-week mescaline clouded jaunt through the interior of Mexico. The only clues she offered upon her return on that occasion were the sombrero and piñata that she brought home.

Eventually, we hung the piñata in the backyard and invited the neighborhood kids over to break it open. The result was predictably disastrous. You don t blindfold a group of eight-year-olds, hand them baseball bats, and yell Candy! and expect anything good to come of it. Within five minutes, every child was sprawled on the lawn, nursing head wounds, weeping uncontrollably and calling out for their mothers, while the piñata remained twisting gently from a tree, completely unscathed.

Tricia stopped typing and read over her work as she reached into the pile of candy. "Julia, you have to try these hazelnut things," she said, popping a chocolate into her mouth. She closed her eyes and savored the candy for a moment. "Okay, now get these goddamned things away from me," she demanded. Tricia was always commanding me to remove food from her reach. Minutes later, though, she'd beg me to return it, gobbling it down and cursing me between bites. She lurched between denouncing stick-figure movie stars who, like flowers, ate only sunlight, and embracing fad diets with evangelical fervor, following a diet for a day at most before sinking into her old, undisciplined routines and blaming her lack of willpower on her friends' inability to police her.

I swept the candy into the sack, but Tricia quickly plucked the exiled sweets from the bag and piled them protectively behind her computer screen. "Julia," she said, unwrapping a candy with deliberate concentration. "I really don't have time to chat now. I've got only fifteen minutes to prepare for that hearing."

"What hearing?" I asked. During the week that Tricia was in Liechtenstein, Lonnie and I attempted to piece together Tricia's work commitments by hunting through the scraps of paper and scribbled notes that served as her appointment diary. As far as we could tell, she had cleared her schedule of meetings and court appearances before she disappeared.

"Ummm, you know," she said absently. "For the toe case."

"Jean's case?" I asked. "I thought we agreed to a settlement over a week ago." The day before Tricia disappeared, Trident Towing offered Jean $200,000 to settle the case. If Jean accepted, it would represent the most money we had ever won in a personal injury case. Tricia agreed that it was a good offer and she promised that she would advise Jean to accept it. For the past week, I had operated under the assumption that the case had been settled. I felt relieved and, to my great annoyance, disappointed that my professional dealings with Jean were complete.

"We didn't accept the offer," Tricia said as her fingers rained down on the keyboard. "The pretrial conference is today." The pretrial conference is the last step before a trial. The judge makes a final attempt to get the parties to agree to a settlement. If they refuse, he sets a trial date.

I grabbed hold of Tricia's desk and clung to it as if I was drowning. "Tricia!" I exclaimed.

"What?" she asked with annoyance.

"What happened to the last settlement offer? The $200,000 offer?"

"I just told you. We rejected it," she said with a finality that suggested she owed me no further explanation. She punched a button on the keyboard and papers began to churn out of the printer. Tricia refused to make eye contact as she pulled herself out of the chair and yanked her shirt over her head. She crossed the room and slipped a business suit from its hanger, sniffing her armpits before putting on the blouse.

"When did you reject it?" I asked. My voice was hoarse and shrill, like something forced out of a kazoo.

"Last week," she said, glancing down at her bosom as she buttoned her blouse.

"Last week? You rejected it from Liechtenstein? Is that even legal?" I was standing behind her now. She was in front of a mirror brushing her hair in sweeping strokes. In the reflection I saw that my mouth was formed into an almost perfect "o" of surprise.

"Listen, Julia," Tricia said, spinning around and pointing the brush at me, "you asked me to keep you out of this case and that's exactly what I did. You can't just jump back in anytime you want."

Tricia rarely involved me in the day-to-day workings of personal injury cases, but she always consulted me before making any major decisions. Typically, she ignored my advice, but at least she gave me the courtesy of pretending that she cared about my opinion. Jean's toe case was different, though. Tricia rarely discussed the case, volunteering little more than a few breezy comments about Jean's wardrobe or details about her increasingly contentious relationship with Trident's attorney, Tom Mahoney.

Mahoney represented everything that's wrong with corporate attorneys and straight, white men. He was a young, entitled ass who knew too much about baseball statistics and not nearly enough about America's criminal neglect of Africa. In the early stages of the toe case, Tricia pretended to fall for Mahoney's frat-boy charms. She marveled at his skills, laughed at his jokes, and turned to him for advice on procedural matters. She lulled him into a false sense of superiority, which she whipped out from under him at the first deposition, when she excoriated the driver of the truck that ran over Jean's toe. Mahoney watched in jaw dropping horror as Tricia attacked his client, realizing too late that he had been hustled. From that day forward, the case devolved into a street battle. Both Tricia and Mahoney were determined to take the case to trial if only to humiliate each other in public.

Tricia turned her attention back to her hair and I considered my options, which seemed limited to stomping out of Tricia's office in a rage and/or weeping. At some point in our friendship, Tricia had relegated me to the role of the disapproving parent, which left her free to be the impossible child. Sometimes it seemed like she behaved badly just to force me into a position to judge her harshly. It never failed to make me feel sour and thin-lipped, and

I resented her for it.

"You should wear your hair in a bun," I said finally, resisting the urge to grab her by the shoulders and shake her senseless. "It makes you look vulnerable and lovelorn. The judge might take pity on you."

A smile slowly crossed her face and she began to pile her hair on top of her head. "Don't worry, Julia. Trident doesn't want to drag this thing out. They'll up the ante today. It will kill Mahoney, but he'll have to do it. Now," she said, twirling slowly before me, "how do I look?"

I took a step away from her and sized her up with studied seriousness. She waited patiently, knowing what I was going to say before I said it. It was the same response I gave whenever she asked me that question. It was the same thing her father told her the day he learned that Tricia had received one of the highest scores in history on the state bar exam. "Tricia, I think this bar association made a mistake," her father said, taking in Tricia's mini skirt, fishnet stockings and outrageously high heels—an outfit carefully designed to offend her parents' Old World sensibilities. "You don't look like a real lawyer. You look like a woman who needs to be defended by a real lawyer."

When I learned of the exchange, I did the only thing a good friend could do under the circumstances: I repeated her father's remark every chance I got. Sometimes the only way to take the sting out of a humiliating episode is to replay it so often that you become comfortable in its familiarity.

"Tricia," I said finally, as she stood before me, waiting for my verdict, "you don't look like a real lawyer."

"Wish me luck," Tricia said, snapping her briefcase shut and walking out of the office. "And don't eat all the candy."

* * * * * * *

I spent the remainder of the afternoon nervously waiting for a phone call from Tricia. At six-thirty, when I still hadn't heard from her, I tried to reach her on her cell phone, an act of desperation given that she turned on the phone only to order takeout.

On the bus ride home, I gnawed my thumbnail and stared out the filthy window, imagining a series of scenarios that ran from bad to worse: Tricia insulting the judge and being tossed into jail for contempt; Mahoney reaching for a revolver and gunning down everyone in a room; Tricia and Jean accepting a big settlement and running off together to a Caribbean island.

As I walked home from the bus stop, toting my briefcase like a ten-pound sack of worries, I felt a cool breeze blow off the lake, gently chilling the late summer air and heralding the onset of autumn. The breeze brushed my cheek and I was cheered instantly. Fall was my favorite time of year. Summer was too demanding, always pushing you outside and thundering its disappointment if you refused to enjoy the bonny weather. But autumn appreciated the value of napping through gray afternoons and cuddling up under a flannel blanket with a good book.

I kicked through a pile of leaves and smiled at a gang of drug dealers who were hanging out in front of a dilapidated apartment building. They nodded and muttered pleasantries. These were the same guys who had eyed me with hungry hostility when I first moved into the neighborhood. Over the years we had developed a casual camaraderie, the byproduct of cooled suspicion and fear.

I never thought I'd ever feel comfortable living in this neighborhood, with its crime, strange smells, and alarming noises. And, yet, now I considered it home. Like so many people who grew up in the suburbs, I longed for the romance of living the life of a jaded urbanite, but without the danger. Until I moved into the two-flat, I lived out my urban fantasies in trendy neighborhoods where the biggest threat to my welfare was the price of a cup of cappuccino. It wasn't until I decided to move out of the two-flat to live with Jean in upscale splendor that I realized how much I'd miss the neighborhood's diversity and edginess, and the joy of being accepted by people who once regarded me as an invader from a foreign land.

As I approached the two-flat I noticed a figure bent over on the front steps. Initially, I thought it was a gunshot victim because the person was moaning in pain, but as I drew closer I realized it was Tricia.

Tricia had her head in her hands and was sobbing with gusto. Tricia always cried generously, like a river overflowing its banks. When she was hurt, she wanted everyone to know about it.

"What's wrong," I asked, mentally clicking through my list of nightmare scenarios related to the pretrial conference.

Tricia kept her face buried in her lap as she reached up and handed me a piece of paper that was soggy and stained with tears. I glanced at the paper and immediately recognized Anne's crabbed penmanship.

"Anne's left me," Tricia sobbed. "I came home and found this taped to the refrigerator." I studied the sheet. It was an elaborate feeding schedule for the pets.

"She moved out?" I asked, staring at the note and trying to digest the news. Anne had threatened to leave Tricia dozens of times over the years, but she never followed through. It was always Tricia who left—usually with little notice and always for another woman. For a moment, I felt as if the Earth had tilted off balance. I steadied myself by placing my hand against one of the porch's decaying pillars.

"You didn't know she was going to do this?"Tricia asked, looking up at me. Her face was red and bloated, yet she looked impossibly beautiful. Tricia possessed one of those fleshy, blemish-free faces that look prettiest when wrecked with pain.

"I had no idea," I said.

"How could you not have known about it? You two have been alone all week. She must have said something about it."

I shook my head numbly.Anne and I had talked only a few times in the past week. When I told her that Tricia had left town for parts unknown,Anne shrugged off the news and said she welcomed the break. I ate dinner at The Depression twice during the week, but Anne was so busy cooking that we did little more than exchange quips as she raced in and out of the kitchen.

"Anne is leaving all the animals with me,"Tricia said. "So, I can't even have a social life because I have to stay home and tend to their bizarre dietary demands."

"Did Anne say where she's going?" I asked, flipping the sheet of paper over, searching for an explanation.

"No, but I know she's moving in with Poppy," she said, acidly.

"Oh, Tricia, I doubt that."

"Why do you doubt it?" she asked. She had stopped crying and was challenging me with her eyes.

"Do you think I know something that you don't?" I asked. "Because I don't. I'm just as surprised as you are."

"Ever since I told you about the open relationship you've been pushing Anne to get involved with other women," she said, her voice warming for a fight. "And I know why you did it. You did it to hurt me. You know how much I love Anne. You made sure she spent all that time with Poppy. You pushed them together just to spite me. Were you trying to teach me a lesson? Was this some type of morality tale you had to play out?"

"Are you out of your mind?" I asked. "Are you crazy?"

"Maybe I am," she said. "Maybe I am crazy to think that you are my best friend."

Tricia shot the remark at me like a bullet. Her eyes hardened with grim delight as I flinched at the impact of the blow. She knew there was nothing that irritated me more than having my loyalty questioned.

Tricia was a dirty fighter, a skill honed in childhood during daily, vicious squabbles with her sisters. Like most women who were raised in female-dominated households, Tricia recognized the destructive power of a well-placed verbal jab. When she was angry, she'd lash out as cruelly as a tornado. The storms were fierce but short-lived, and she'd quickly return to her sunny disposition while her victim struggled to deal with the hurtful mess of accusations and insults left in her wake.

Sometimes I'd punish Tricia following one of her blowups. I'd refuse to talk to her for a few days or demand an apology that would never come. She'd try to make amends in some half-hearted way. She'd leave a bouquet of half-dead daisies on my doorstep or bring me a container of chicken soup, as if my anger were a nasty flu that could be cured with some light nurturing. Usually, though, I didn't take our fights seriously. In fact, in many ways, I considered our battles as one of the hallmarks of our friendship. It was a tribute to our level of intimacy that we could shrug off arguments so easily. There was no one, apart from my mother, who I felt so comfortable yelling at.

"Tricia," I said through clenched teeth, trying to remain calm. "You can't believe I served as Anne's pimp. You were invited to everything that Poppy and Anne went to."

"I wasn't invited to the bridge lesson at Bravehearts," she said, wiping her nose on the sleeve of her suit.

"Because you don't like to play cards," I said in exasperation.

"I know what happened, and I know your role in it," she said. "Anne might want to pretend that you're not in the middle of this, but that's exactly where you are. Right in the middle. Pulling the strings."

I dragged the heel of my hand across my eyes wearily. There was no point in trying to reason with her when she was like this. My best defense was to keep quiet and wait for her to come to her senses. I walked up the stairs and opened the door.

"Don't you want to know what happened at the hearing to-day?" Tricia asked, almost sweetly. I turned around to look at her. In the heat of the exchange, I had forgotten about the pretrial conference.

"Trident offered us $300,000," she said.

My mouth dropped opened and I started toward her with my arms flung wide in preparation for a celebratory embrace.

"Tricia!" I exclaimed.

"We turned it down," she said, menacingly.

"You did what?" I asked, dropping my happy arms to my side.

"We turned it down," she said again.

"Are you out of your mind? Are you?" I was screaming now. A homeless man lying in the alley across the street echoed me and then laughed crazily.

"The judge set the trial date," she said. "It's on October 24, two months from today."

"You turned down $300,000 for a toe? Not even a whole toe. A half a toe!"

"She's permanently disfigured."

"There was no real pain, no disability," I yelled.

"It's a disfigurement," Tricia yelled back.

"It's a conversation piece! She uses it to pick up women! I know! It worked on me!"

"You don't believe that I can win this case, do you?" Tricia said. "You've never believed in me. That's why you're always so anxious for me to settle. Well, you know who does believe in me? Humble Al. He wants me to join his practice."

I stood on the step in front of Tricia, shaking with rage. I waited for a calm inner voice to urge me not to overact, as it usually did when Tricia baited me into a fight. But, instead, the voice grew in volume until my head vibrated rage.

"I'm leaving the partnership the day after the trial," I said with a calm finality that frightened me. "That will give me two months to inform our clients and to close the practice. And I'm moving out of the two-flat. I'll be out by the end of the week." Sometimes I hated that I was so responsible. I wanted nothing more at that moment than to walk away from Tricia and never look back.

Tricia opened her mouth to say something, but then thought better of it. She stared out at the street as I brushed past her and walked into my apartment.

I collapsed in a chair and glanced up at the ceiling. The week before, my father had plastered the cracks in the ceiling and hung an expensive, retro light fixture I had picked up at an architectural salvage store. Over the past few months, I'd made many improvements to the apartment, and I no longer considered it a transitory refuge from heartache. More and more, it was beginning to feel like my home. The day that Trident Towing offered the $200,000 settlement offer, I told Tricia and Anne that I planned to use my share of the settlement to buy a half-interest in the two-flat. Now, as I sat in my freshly painted living room, I realized with crushing exhaustion that I'd have to find a new place to live.

* * * * * * * *

Tricia and I had had many arguments over the years. But we had only one serious falling out. In that instance, though, the problem wasn't caused by a disagreement. It was caused by a kiss.

The trouble began a few months after we opened the law practice. Tricia marched into my office with a glint in her eye that suggested she was up to no-good.

"Guess what we're doing next Saturday?" she asked. "That Jessica Lange movie is filming at the Baby Doll Polka Club this weekend and they need extras who can polka. So I signed us up."

For the past week, a movie crew had been stationed a few blocks from our office. I walked past the set every morning, hoping to get a glimpse of Jessica Lange, an actress who played a central role in my fantasy life.

"Tricia, you know I don't know how to polka," I said. Tricia had tried to teach me how to polka at her sister Jan's wedding. She bullied me around the banquet hall floor, stomping on my toes and yelling out choreography, until my legs got tangled in hers and we fell against the wedding cake. Tricia kept a picture on her desk of the two of us smirking behind the lopsided cake as the angry bride and groom rushed to cut it before it toppled over.

"You'll know how to polka by Saturday," Tricia said. "Lessons begin in front of Lonnie's desk at five sharp. I'm a very demanding instructor and training will be rigorous. But, I assure you, it will be a rewarding, if painful, experience."

"No way, Tricia."

"Too late. We're already committed. It will be fun," she said, grabbing my hands and pulling me from the chair. She tried to dance me around the room, but I remained firmly rooted. "We haven't spent any time together since you started dating what's-her-name." At that time, I was involved with a woman named Margaret who came from a wealthy family and had all the quirks associated with the very rich, including a creepy relationship with her brother that required she tuck him into bed each time he visited. She had tremendous social phobias that prevented us from doing anything other than sitting in her dark apartment and discussing her inability to love.

"Not to mention," Tricia said, lifting her eyebrows provocatively, "it will give you a chance to meet the lovely Ms. Lange."

Tricia gave me my first polka lesson that evening. She was not a patient teacher. When I failed to follow her steps, she would shove me and called me names. As a result, we spent more time bickering and insulting each other than dancing.

By the end of the week, I had managed to learn the basic steps, but I performed them so rigidly that I feared my shins might splinter from the tension. Tricia had all but given up on me and I suspected that she was secretly calling her sisters, trying to convince one of them to take my place on the movie set.

On Friday, the final night of rehearsal, Tricia demanded we go to Shangri-la for a drink before the lesson. "Maybe it will loosen you up," she said grimly. We drank our cocktails as seriously as patients taking medicine for a terminal condition. Then we returned to the office for our final practice session.

Tricia pulled out the Andrew Sisters Greatest Hits and slipped it onto the CD player. As the sisters began singing "The Beer Barrel Polka," I took a deep breath and Tricia closed her eyes tightly as if bracing for bad news. Then she slapped me on the shoulder to remind me that she was in the lead. As we took our first steps, I experienced an odd sensation. My feet felt like they were freshly liberated from their limbs and they propelled me gracefully around the floor, gliding in unison with Tricia. Up until that moment, I danced with my brain rather than my body, mentally calculating each footfall as if trying to solve a difficult calculus problem with my feet. But, now, I wasn't thinking at all and I moved around the room with confidence and ease.

"You're doing it!" Tricia exclaimed. "You're the polka queen!" We picked up the pace and flew across the floor. In a burst of enthusiasm, Tricia swung me out and I tripped on Lonnie's desk, landing squarely on Tricia and pushing us both to the floor.

I lay on top of Tricia, panting and laughing with surprise and relief. After a few minutes, our laughter sputtered into contented sighing. I gazed down at Tricia until our smiles dimmed. Before I could register what was happening, I lowered my face to hers until our lips were barely touching. We remained in that almost-kissing position for a fraction of a second. Then, simultaneously, we rolled away from each other. I turned onto my back, blinking my eyes in disbelief. Tricia stood and made her way to the door.

"I've got to meet Anne," she said. "See you tomorrow morning."

I remained on the floor, staring dumbly at the ceiling, my mind swimming with confusion. I propped myself against Lonnie's desk, trying to picture what it would be like to have sex with Tricia. The image made me tremble with revulsion. I shook my head violently to erase the image of Tricia's naked body flopping against mine.

It wasn't that I found Tricia unattractive. In fact, I'd always been a little infatuated with Tricia, and she with me. There had been plenty of moments when our eyes met for just an instant too long and when our playful flirting caused others to question the nature of our relationship. But we had been friends too long to be lovers. It's against the laws of nature for passion to operate in reverse. That's why it's much more common for former lovers to become friends than the other way around.

The kiss was just one of those things that happens when two good friends briefly confuse affection with desire. Still, I could see Tricia taking this opportunity to showcase her lack of inhibitions. It wouldn't surprise me if she demanded we have sex just to prove how daring and un-provincial she was.

The following morning, Tricia was supposed to pick me up for the movie shoot but she never showed. When I arrived at work that Monday, Tricia was already in her office. She didn't mention anything about our missed polka date, and neither did I. The situation quickly chilled into a tense but polite standoff. Our casual intimacy was replaced with a mechanical professionalism that left me feeling sadder and lonelier than I ever had before. The sudden absence of her friendship made me feel as if I had had an internal organ removed—one whose value I didn't recognize until it was taken from me.

I feared that we'd never recover from the kiss, but after a few weeks, when it became obvious that the kiss would never be discussed, we slowly drifted back into our friendship. On the surface, our relationship returned to normal. But there was an underlying tension—a fault line running beneath our relationship that occasionally quivered to remind us that we weren't on solid ground.

Now, as I sat in the living room, quietly seething as I glared out at Tricia's stubborn back on the front steps, I realized that the crack in the foundation of our friendship still existed. In a final quake of anger, I felt it rupture.

I reached for the phone and called my brother. I told him that I was leaving the law practice and I would like to go into business with him. Then I asked him to alert our parents that I would be moving back home at the end of the week.

CHAPTER 11

I didn't go to work the rest of the week. Instead, I stayed home and packed. Living in semi-permanent transiency throughout my adult life had made me a fast and efficient packer. But this time it seemed like my things were heavier and less cooperative, as if they were reluctant to leave after such a short time liberated from their crates.

Tricia and I did not see each other that week, yet we still managed to communicate. She did so exclusively by slamming doors and stomping around the apartment above me. Even Tricia's most passive gestures were meant to express exactly what she was feeling. Anger had the opposite effect on me. I became silent and focused, moving through my apartment as quietly as a stingray.

That Saturday, I moved back into my childhood bedroom. It remained much as I had left it—a shrine to my troubled adolescence. The walls were plastered with mementoes from proms where I had narrowly escaped date rape and posters of pop stars who couldn't quite keep their tattered shirts buttoned. "They're so smooth," my grandmother once said, standing an inch from the wall, examining the boys' furless chests through bifocals.

I heaved a suitcase onto a chair and opened the closet. It was crammed with my mother's clothes. Years before, she converted a bedroom into a walk-in closet, but she kept this small closet in reserve for clothing she hadn't worn in decades. The clothes hung ever hopeful, still bleeding my mother's scent, waiting for the day they would return to style. I wrestled the tangle of hangers to one side, clearing about an inch of space for my clothes. As I attempted to close the door against the rush of fabric, dozens of arms reached out at me in a panic of color.

Weary from the effort, I collapsed onto my bed, a four-poster Victorian nightmare I badgered my parents into buying during a rather melodramatic period of my youth. I gazed out the window at the branches of two witchy cottonwood trees. In high school I spent countless hours staring at those same trees, planning my escape from these suburban confines and entering a world of urban elegance, complete with cocktail parties, romantic encounters with slightly shady foreigners, and no curfews. Yet, here I was, back again at an age when most of my peers had their own homes and families. When I arrived at my parents' house earlier that day, my father greeted me eagerly with reports on several of my contemporaries who had recently moved back in with their parents. I took little comfort in joining the parade of sad divorcees and failed businessmen forced to seek refuge in their childhood homes.

Even my brother had finally managed to move out. He now was living with Gretchen in her co-op in the city. The day after my mother learned of Eric's plans to marry Gretchen, she confronted Eric in a vodka-induced state of self-righteousness. The resulting argument was so ugly that no one wanted to discuss it. When I tried to pump my mother for information, she cast a sidelong glance at my father, who simply shook his head at her in disgust. Although my brother was no longer on speaking terms with my mother, he still returned home at least once a week to raid the refrigerator and drop off his laundry.

"Apparently, the freulein is too much of a big shot to cook for your brother or wash his clothes," my mother said with a sniff of satisfaction.

My mother gleefully welcomed my arrival home, mainly because my troubles with Tricia helped take attention away from her own bad behavior. As soon as I walked in the door that morning, she ushered me into the kitchen and demanded to hear about the argument with Tricia.

It was always fun to tell my mother a story. She would listen with rapt attention, asking questions about the most mundane details and repeating salient information to stress its importance. She fueled the emotional trajectory of the tale by emitting bursts of laughter, surprise, outrage, or sorrow.

I had been too busy that week to fully comprehend the force of my fury, and now I was like a teakettle releasing a scream of steam after a slow boil. As the story built to its climax, I added a few exaggerations of fact to underscore my role as the victim in the drama. When I finally finished—in a gale of accusations and vows of retribution—I glanced at my mother in triumph, expecting to find her nodding vigorously in agreement. Instead, she smiled weakly and slowly rose from the table. She picked up her teacup and took it to the sink.

My heart was still galloping from the outpouring of emotion and my mother's lack of response alarmed me. I rarely took the risk of revealing my feelings unless I was fairly certain they would be validated. Now I felt as if I had sent them charging off a steep cliff, their tiny legs paddling helplessly beneath them, treading thin air.

"Well," I snapped, "what do you think?"

She washed and rinsed the teacup methodically, slowly turning off the tap, shaking the excess water from the cup, and delicately wiping it dry before returning it to the china cabinet. Finally, she sighed meaningfully and muttered a Danish platitude that translated into "this too shall pass."

"Since when are you the voice of reason?" I asked, reeling from what felt like a slap of betrayal.

"I know you think I don't like Tricia, and, well, you're right. She's disrespectful and that outfit she wore to your father's birth-day party was highly inappropriate," she said, raising her hand to indicate that she could spend all day rattling off complaints against Tricia. "However, I do appreciate that she has been a very good friend to you, and I don't think you should be so quick to toss away a friendship."

I huffed an objection and stormed up to my bedroom. I spent the rest of the afternoon in my room, sulking and playing out one-sided arguments with Tricia and my mother, feeling that I'd never managed to escape that bedroom in all the years I had lived away from home.

* * * * * * * *

After I finished shoving my clothes into the closet, I dumped the contents of a suitcase onto my bed. There among the detritus of my recently abandoned adult life was my vibrator. It lay on my girlhood comforter as fat and pink as a frightened worm.

The vibrator had been a gift from Tricia and Anne. A few days after I moved back into the two-flat following the breakup with Jean, I found it wrapped in a lavender bow at my front door. A card attached said: "Use it!"

Occasionally, I'd remove the vibrator from my nightstand drawer, intending to put it to use. But then I'd see it, looking so alone and vulnerable, like a Barbie Doll with a provocatively shaped head who had never recovered from some bad mistakes made early in life, and I'd return it to the drawer.

As I sat on my bed, clutching the vibrator in one hand and my aching head in the other, I glanced around the room, looking for a hiding place for the vibrator. I gazed out into the backyard and spotted the sagging roof of the boathouse through a veil of foliage. Now that my brother had moved out, the boathouse was the perfect hideout for both the vibrator and me.

The boathouse sat perched on eroding stilts above the filthy river. An old rowboat bobbed in the water beneath the house, bumping the stilts in rhythmic motion. The house consisted of one barn like room with a small bathroom. Most of Eric's belongings remained in the boathouse because Gretchen had barred his collection of post-adolescent toys and Playboy chic bachelor furniture from her tasteful home. I settled into the black leather couch and flipped on the TV, which was so large it looked like it should have been soldered to a building in Times Square. Just as I was nodding off, the intercom crackled on and I was startled awake by the disembodied voice of my mother.

"Julia? Julia, are you there?"

I groaned and punched the intercom button. "Leave me alone."

"What are you doing in that filth-hole?"

"I'm moving in," I said.

"You most certainly are not. It's not safe out there. Don't forget about the serpents. The river is full of them. And if you move in there, where are we going to put your brother when he returns home?"

"He's not moving back," I said with a yawn, looking out the window, searching the oily surface of the river for snakes. I was terrified of snakes and my mother knew it.

"Oh, that relationship won't last. Mark my words. Now get dressed. Your father and I are going to dinner and you are coming with us. I don't want you moping around here by yourself."

"I have other plans."

"What plans?" she asked, not believing me.

"I'm going out with Claire."

"Claire from bridge?" my mother asked, intrigued. "She didn't mention anything about this when I saw her on Wednesday."

"From what I understand, you didn't give her much opportunity to speak at all." Claire visited the house earlier in the week to prescribe non-toxic solutions to my mother's garden pest issues. After a brief visit to the yard, my mother spirited Claire to the Scandinavian Club and nominated her for the mother-daughter fashion show committee.

"Where are you and Claire going?" she asked.

"The Medieval Palace," I said. There was a moment of silence at the other end of the intercom. I feared she was contemplating joining us.

"Well, be careful," she said, finally. "They run around with swords at that place."

* * * * * * *

Claire lived in a town on the other side of the river. When I was growing up, the area was a woodsy, swampy island that attracted people who liked to grow marijuana in their gardens and keep strange animals as pets. After I left home for college, one of the island's residents—a professional square dance caller who kept a brood of pale-eye kids and at least one rhesus monkey in his river shack—published a memoir on his early years in Appalachia. It contained just enough homey advice and tales of bestiality to make him the darling of the talk show circuit, and, suddenly, the island became rather chic.

Claire's house was on the river, almost directly across from my parents' home. As I pulled into her driveway, I could see a light from our boathouse shining across the water. Her house was a cheery yellow cottage surrounded by a lush garden of wild flowers. Hundreds of flower heads bobbed in the breeze, filling the yard with a happy burst of color. The property on this part of the island—dismissingly called "the delta"—was so low that it was flooded every spring by river water. Most yards could support only vegetation that was hardy enough to withstand the rank water. But Claire somehow managed to nurture a more delicate ecosystem in the toxic soil.

Claire was kneeling in her front yard when I arrived, plucking weeds from the garden and tossing them into the driveway. A small dog rolled ecstatically in the mud beside her. When my car rumbled up the stone driveway, Claire placed a hand on her lower back and slowly stretched off an ache. When she waved and smiled, I felt the first surge of happiness since the day Tricia returned from Liechtenstein.

The dog trotted to me and nuzzled its homely face against my leg. The animal had a shaggy white coat, a potbelly and no chin. In profile, it looked exactly like Eleanor Roosevelt. I resisted the urge to bend down and pet him. In the past, I went to great lengths to win over my girlfriends' pets, reasoning that if the animal liked me, so would its master. But the plan usually backfired. Its owner inevitably grew jealous of my close relationship with her pet, and I'd become too attached to the animal, remaining in a troubled relationship much longer than I should just because I didn't want to lose contact with the pet.

"Leave Julia alone, Flop," Claire said. The dog ignored the command and continued to demand affection until I acknowledged him with a pat on the head.

Claire bent over to slap mud off the knees of her slacks. "I'm a mess. I was standing out here, waiting for you, and I spotted a weed. One thing led to another and pretty soon I was on my knees, up to my chin in larkspur. Now I have to change, and after I spent hours trying to figure out what I should wear tonight. Oh," she said, looking up at me in alarm, "I guess I shouldn't have admitted that I spent so much time dressing for this evening."

"I had a hard time deciding what to wear, too," I said. "Honestly, how does one dress for the Crusades?" I was wearing a suede blazer over beat-up jeans and a rich silk blouse, unbuttoned just low enough to announce my intentions. I thought it gave me the overall appearance of a wealthy porn producer, circa 1978.

Claire cocked her head at me and tugged on her hair quizzically. "No, what I meant was that I probably shouldn't have let you know how much time I spent getting ready for our date."

I stared at her for a moment, dumbstruck. Women generally don't acknowledge they're on a date until the kissing starts. Claire seemed blithely unaware of this rule. She didn't understand that we were supposed to pretend that we weren't attracted to each other until well after we began ripping off each other's clothes. I knew of women who went out for months before either of them acknowledged that all those evenings spent gazing at each other at romantic restaurants were, in fact, dates.

* * * * * * * *

"Sorry this place is such a mess," Claire said, making a vague gesture to the interesting clutter that filled the home. Claire had moved into the house less than a year before, yet it looked like she had lived there all her life. The furniture emphasized comfort over style: a well-worn couch was covered with rich, hand-knit blankets; an overstuffed reading chair was paired with a wide ottoman of unmatched fabric. A large wicker basket filled with yarn and knitting needles sat next to the chair. Piles of books littered every available surface.

Flop scampered into the living room and jumped onto my lap. He promptly turned on his back and batted his eyes at me with the manipulative force of a silent screen star. When I finally gave in and stroked his belly, he cooed with pleasure.

* * * * * * * *

Claire insisted on driving. Her old Volvo coughed several times before finally rousing to life. When it did, the stereo blasted Ella

Fitzgerald's "Let's Do It." I grimaced, assuming she would be embarrassed to be caught listening to the CD I'd given her the week before. But she smiled unapologetically and turned down the volume. "I listen to this CD every day," she said. "I know the words to all the songs already."

She clutched the steering wheel with both hands as if she was scared it might fall off and sat forward in her seat, assuming the posture of a ninety-year-old woman navigating the streets of Palm Beach. As she inched down the driveway, she confessed that she learned to drive only recently.

"How recently?" I asked.

"Oh, a few months ago," she said, never taking her attention off the road.

"How did you get around before that?" I asked as the car crept down the street well under the twenty-five mile per hour speed limit. She had moved to Chicago from Duluth, a city not known for its robust public transportation system.

"My husband drove me everywhere," she said, studying the road as if it might disappear if she took her eyes off it for one second.

"You're married?" I asked, suppressing a groan.

"Yes," she said absently. Suddenly, she slammed on the brakes, causing a driver tailing us to pound his horn and swerve around us. "I mean no! I was married. I'm divorced now." She leaned back in her seat and took a deep breath. Then she cautiously pressed the gas pedal. "Didn't I mention my husband to you?"

"No," I said, grinning contritely at the tailgater as he gunned past us. "Does your ex-husband know you're gay? You are gay, right?"

"Yes to both questions," she said. "He's the first person I told."

Claire explained that she met her husband in graduate school. They were married for nearly ten years before she realized she was a lesbian. It happened the summer she was studying a honeybee colony on a goat farm in Vermont. The farm was owned by a lesbian couple who sold goat cheese and honey via mail order. One night late in the summer, one of the women got drunk on homemade cranberry wine and lunged at Claire. The commotion woke the woman's girlfriend, who blamed Claire for rousing her partner's long dormant passions, which she and the goats would have to deal with long after Claire left the farm. Claire fled that night. On the drive back to Minnesota, she reflected on the incident and realized that she had long had feelings for women. In graduate school there had been some confusing episodes with her doctoral advisor, a glamorous woman who wore flowing silk scarves, played dense piano concertos at faculty parties, and stroked her foot against Claire during dissertation meetings.

"By the time I arrived home, I realized I was a lesbian. I woke my husband and told him immediately," she said. Claire was a woman eager to own up to responsibility. I would have stayed in the marriage, hiding my secret and making my husband miserable until he had no choice but to leave me.

"Was he upset?" I asked.

"He was relieved. He had fallen in love with a pastor of a church he had been attending on the sly," she said. "Now he's married to her, but he's still my friend."

"Do you like the new wife?"

"Not especially. She has some rather alarming views on Darwin," she said sternly. Then she shot me with a look of concern. "I shouldn't be telling you this. You'll meet her eventually and I don't want you to have preconceived ideas about her. That wouldn't be fair to her."

Claire was too busy studying the road to notice that I was gawking in amazement. I couldn't believe how casually she included me in her future plans. On a first date, I wouldn't commit to the possibility of a second date, and yet Claire was already making arrangements for me to meet her ex-husband and his wife.

* * * * * * * *

"Here we are," Claire announced as we pulled up to a guardhouse outside the laboratory. As we drove down the heavily wooded drive, I spotted several school busses idling near the entrance of the main building.

"It looks like we're early," Claire said, with a sigh of relief. In a phone conversation that week, Claire confessed that she was obsessively punctual. She was always the first to show up at parties. She'd often arrive an hour ahead of time, waiting patiently in her car for the clock to tick down to the scheduled start time.

"Would you like to see where I work?" she asked.

Claire led me into one of the buildings lining the drive. Inside, I expected to see smoke seeping from under the doors or atoms crashing into each other with loud bangs, but there was nothing to suggest that anything as sinister as fission was taking place here.

Claire worked in a small wing of the building devoted to biological sciences. The walls of her office were decorated with corkboard displays of dead bugs, some so fierce looking that it appeared they could will themselves to life at any moment and attack.

"Did it hurt when they got pinned to the board?" I asked, drawing closer to her in terror.

"You drop a cotton ball of chloroform into the specimen jar first, so they don't feel a thing," she said, walking briskly into a large laboratory. A green light cast an eerie glow on giant terrariums filled with restless bugs. I picked up a jar of creatures that looked like they had the appetite and inclination to eat a kitten.

"Those guys come from the Amazon basin," she said, smiling affectionately at the beasts. "They have the most amazing reproductive system." The word "reproductive" made me twinge with delight. My body, which had been achy and exhausted from the stress of the past week, began to warm to life.

"I love all insects and most other arthropods. Although, just between you and me, I wouldn't be sad if all ticks were to disappear from the face of the Earth. But my true love are bees," she said, walking to a glass wall that protected a beehive. "Did you know that bees are the most highly evolved insects?"

"I thought that honor belonged to ants," I said. I had done some research in preparation for the date, and I was thrilled to get an opportunity to introduce my newfound knowledge into the discussion.

"The bee verses ant argument is one you'll hear at every entomology conference," she said with a sigh. "I specialize in honeybee behavior, so you can guess where I stand on the issue. Look at this. See how that bee is wiggling his behind? That's a mating dance. I'd like to see an ant try that!"

"I had no idea that the insect world was so rife with romantic intrigue," I said, trying to be flirtatious and scientific at the same time. "What's the human equivalent of a mating dance?"

"I don't suppose it's an invitation to The Medieval Palace," she said wryly, leaning provocatively against the hive's glass wall. Claire's beauty seemed even lusher against the backdrop of the hive's controlled chaos. I tentatively moved toward her, trying to forget her startled reaction to our first kiss at Shangri-la months before. Just as our lips met, the laboratory door slammed open.

"So, this must be the famous Julia."

I turned to find a small woman standing solidly with her hands planted on her hips. The woman had skin the color and texture of a used tea bag and was dressed in an elaborate suit that looked like a uniform an Eastern European dictator might wear. She spoke in a thick Russian accent that made every word sound like a command.

"I'm Nadia," she shouted.

"You're the one who didn't win the Nobel Prize," I said.

"I've lost many other things, too!" she barked. "I've lost my husband. Where is he? He was right behind me. Bernard!" She marched out of the lab, slamming the door behind her.

"She refuses to admit that she has a hearing problem. She thinks it's the rest of the world's fault for not speaking up," Claire said, warmly glancing at Nadia's wake.

I was still bewitched by our kiss, which had left me feeling pleasantly sedated. I imagined it was similar to what the bugs on Claire's wall felt when they got their first whiff of chloroform. My head bobbed drowsily toward Claire. She steadied my face in her hands and gently placed her lips against mine.

"Look at these two! Always kissing!" Nadia exclaimed as she exploded into the room. She was clutching the hand of a short, stocky man. He looked bewildered and disheveled, like a child who had just been rescued from a well. He was dressed in a confusion of checked and striped fabrics. This type of getup might look elegant and chic on a gay man or certain members of the British royal family, but on him the collision of geometric lines only added to his overall muddled demeanor.

"Julia, this is my husband, Dr. Bernard Goldman. He hasn't won a Nobel, either."

"Ladies," he said with a slight bow. "The busses will be leaving shortly. We do not want to miss the action."

"It was Bernard's suggestion that we go to the Medieval Palace. He loves the food!" Nadia exclaimed.

* * * * * * * *

The Medieval Palace was a glorified horse barn housed in a faux castle. Its bar served only a cheap, fizzy domestic beer that never failed to give me a headache, yet I gulped it down to steady my nerves, which were frayed from intense physical stimulation. Shortly after getting our drinks, a large man in a ridiculous leotard appeared and blew a horn. We entered the arena, which was separated into six colored sections, each color representing a cheering section for a certain knight. Bernard and Nadia rushed to the green section and shooed interlopers away until our group arrived.

When we took our seats, Claire introduced me to two of her colleagues. Max, who possessed the type New Testament sensitive looks that appeal to women who believe in the power of crystals, and Kelvin, a puppy-like redhead who told me to call him OK.

"OK means absolute zero on the Kelvin temperature scale," Claire explained.

"So, you refer to yourself as 'absolute zero?'" I asked.

"I have low self-esteem," he said.

The show began and we were served our first course, a bowl of vegetable soup that we had to slurp from the bowl because spoons didn't exist in the Middle Ages. Two knights rode in on horseback and began attacking each other with sharp instruments. I was well into my third beer, which is usually the amount of alcohol I need to become mildly interested in any sporting event. Bernard was already on his feet, cheering loudly when the Green Knight entered the arena on a white steed.

I craned my neck to get a better look at the Green Knight. He had a sunken chest and a hapless expression. His horse appeared to be underfed. This did not bode well for fans in the Green Knight's cheering section. I looked at Bernard with concern, hoping he wouldn't be too devastated when the Green Knight was knocked out of competition.

"Hey, Julia, what's your favorite insect?" asked Kelvin, gazing down the cleavage of the portly wench who was serving us turkey legs.

I was tempted to say honeybee just to please Claire, but I didn't want to be accused of pandering. "The beetle bomb? I don't know if that's its scientific name. My brother and I used to play with them when we were kids."

"Well, if you like beetles, you might be interested in this," he said, pulling a leaflet from his jacket. It featured a photo of a worried-looking bug with the word "Endangered" printed over its head.

"I'll bet you've heard all about endangered mammals, like the wolf and the tiger," said Kelvin. "But not many people know that there are also endangered insects. You tell someone that an insect is endangered and they say 'good.'"

Claire nodded her head while greedily munching a turkey leg, never taking her eyes off the action in the jousting ring.

"There's going to be a rally at the state capitol in October to support a measure to protect this beetle," Kelvin said. "Claire, Max and I are driving to Springfield to show our support. Want to come with us?"

Agreeing to attend the insect rally would mean that I was committing to a relationship with Claire for the next two months. I was tempted to respond with one of the gray words of consent— "Sure," or "Why not?"—words that would not firmly bind me to any obligation. I glanced at Claire. She was looking up at me expectantly. Her full lips were greasy from the turkey. There was nothing I wanted to do more at that moment than kiss her.

"Absolutely, Kelvin," I said. "I'd love to go to the rally."

* * * * * * * *

When we arrived back at Claire's home, I followed her inside without an invitation. As soon as she closed the door, I pushed her onto the couch and covered her face with kisses. Claire squirmed out from under me, and moved to the other side of the couch. "Julia, I have something to tell you," she said. I ignored her and began unbuttoning her blouse.

"Stop that," she said, laughing and slapping my hands down. "This is important."

I threw myself against the couch with the poutiness of a two-year-old. She folded her hands over mine and gave me the same look of intense understanding that caused me to wilt when I sat across from her at the bridge table.

"Julia, I've never been with another woman before. Physically, I mean. That time we kissed in Shangri-la was the first time I ever kissed a woman," she said. "That may explain why I ran out of the restaurant after we kissed."

"So, I'm your first girlfriend?" I asked. The word "girlfriend" flew out of my mouth before I could stop it. I watched in horror as it fluttered around the room and settled on Claire's shoulder. The fact that I used the word girlfriend to define the relationship so early on terrified me. Had I learned nothing from my many years of hysterical commitment? I broke out in a cold sweat and darted my eyes around the room, searching for an escape route.

"You're shaking. Are you cold?" she asked. "Do you want a sweater?" I nodded dumbly. She walked upstairs and returned with a sweatshirt, which she pulled over my head. When my head emerged, she kissed me. I didn't respond at first, but then my body took over. Before I knew it, I was laying on top of her, moving my hands up to her chest. Suddenly, I realized what I was doing and I jumped up.

"I've got to get going," I said, quickly making my way to the door. Flop trotted after me, misinterpreting my desire to get the hell out of there as an invitation to play.

"Julia!" Claire exclaimed. "What are you doing?"

What was I doing? The past year had been a blur of pain and malaise. My only real moments of pleasure had been spent with Claire. I leaned against the doorframe and rubbed my eyes wearily.

"I think I'm scared," I said.

"So am I," she said. She tentatively reached out and stroked my arm. "When you get home blink the boathouse light a few times and then I'll blink mine. That way we can say goodnight to each other."

As I backed out of her driveway, I could see the skyline of Chicago shining above the river. It never looked so far away.

* * * * * * * *

On the ride home, I called Carmen. It was almost midnight, but I knew she'd be awake. She rarely went to bed before dawn on a Saturday night.

"Julia!" she screamed over the din of bar noise.

"Where are you?" I screamed back.

"At Minsk," she yelled. "You'll never believe what just happened to me." I listened politely, knowing that the story would end with Carmen engaging in a mad makeout session with a strange woman in a bathroom stall.

"Julia, come meet me. Lots of cute girls here tonight," she said.

"Who are you there with?"

"Anne and Poppy, but they left a few minutes ago," she said. "Oooh, Julia! Did you hear that Anne left Tricia?"

"Yes. Do you know where Anne's living?"

"Yes!"

"Well, where is she?"

"With me. But she can't stay at my house because Grace thinks she is a bad influence. She thinks that Anne may give me ideas about leaving her. Oooh, Julia, if Grace only knew, huh? I don't need Anne to give me any bad ideas."

"Is Anne okay?"

"Yes, I think so. She's worried about the animals. She's going to call you and tell you to take care of them."

"Well, I can't." I told Carmen about the fight with Tricia.

"Oh, my God!" Carmen said, completely overwhelmed by the drama of it all. "Let's meet for a drink tomorrow and discuss this."

I said I couldn't because I had dinner plans with Claire. And then I told her about the evening with Claire and that I was the first woman Claire ever kissed.

"Julia, that's like dating an Amish person," she said. "You know they've had no experience in the world and it's up to you to show them. That's a lot of pressure, Julia."

"Do you know anyone who is still with their first girlfriend or has anything good to say about their first girlfriend?" I asked.

"No, first girlfriends always break your heart. Always! And now you are a first girlfriend. You must do this right. A lot is riding on you. You can be the first good first girlfriend in history! We are all counting on you, Julia."

* * * * * * * *

When I arrived at the boathouse, I discovered that Eric had dumped a pile of laundry on the floor for my mother to wash. I lugged the clothes into the laundry room in the house. As I tossed Eric's clothes into the washer, I remembered that I was wearing Claire's sweatshirt.

When I pulled the sweatshirt off, I caught a whiff of Claire's scent. I held the sweatshirt to my face and breathed in deeply.

As I was sniffing the fabric, my mother walked into the room. I jumped in alarm. It reminded me of my teen years when I would sneak out of the house after curfew. When I'd return, the house would be dark, and I'd assume that I had escaped undetected. But then I'd see the orange glow of a cigarette hovering above the couch and the tinkling of ice in a highball glass and I'd realize that I was busted.

"What are you doing?" my mother asked, staring at me suspiciously. I was still holding Claire's sweatshirt to my face.

"Smelling this sweatshirt," I said, dropping it into the washer.

"Why?"

"Mom, don't ask questions that you don't want answers to," I said. I gave her a peck on the cheek and dashed out of the house, skipping across the yard to the boathouse.

I looked across the river toward Claire's house. I flipped the boathouse light on and off. I smiled as Claire's light blinked twice in response.

CHAPTER 12

The next several weeks passed peacefully. I felt as if I'd been ripped out of my frantic life and transported to a dream-like existence that allowed me to crawl back into childhood after many difficult years in the trenches of adulthood. Like most happy dreams, I knew that it could quickly warp into a dark, distorted version of itself, one that would cause me to wake up screaming in terror and longing for my old, messy life. But, for the moment, I was content.

Claire and I settled into a cozy routine after my move to the suburbs. On nights that we didn't play bridge, I'd meet Claire at her house where she'd greet me armed with the entertainment section of the newspaper. She'd read off the events she circled earlier that day, glancing at me expectantly to gauge my enthusiasm for a particular event. Her curiosity about the world knew no bounds—she was equally excited about attending a chamber concert as she was about going to a bake sale.

The very fact that our dates were so mundane made them exotic. I was accustomed to courtships that played out over cocktails and confessions about sad childhoods. But each date with Claire was as wholesome and thrilling as a grammar school field trip. They held the allure of being taken out of your element for a brief adventure before returning to the safety of your parents' home at the end of the day. I soon began to view Chicago and its suburbs as a strange, foreign land filled with interesting people, fascinating attractions, and an extraordinary number of historical markers commemorating the life and travails of a Civil War-era character provocatively named Mother Bickerdyke.

Every Monday we attended free lectures at the University of Chicago on subjects that were so esoteric they left me doubting my command of the English language. We went to a museum that specialized in bizarre surgical implements and a tiny zoo that housed only barnyard creatures and, inexplicably, a penguin. We traveled to a rundown amusement park charmingly called Fairyland whose chief attraction was a roller coaster that bumped down an ancient track at a snail's pace. Each car offered only one narrow seat for two passengers, so you had to wrap your legs around the person sitting in front of you. The sensation of rumbling down the rickety wooden rails with my pelvis firmly pressed against Claire's shapely behind provided an unexpected but satisfying sexual experience. We rode the roller coaster at least a dozen times that day.

* * * * * * * *

When you enter a relationship, you often realize that the person you're dating is not necessarily the person you first became infatuated with. In most cases, this is not a positive turn of events. You learn, for example, that she participates in a revolting breakfast ritual that involves raw eggs and syrup or you realize that she has no friends and hates animals. Or you discover that she has an extra set of nipples, which happened to me the first time I slept with an accountant named Denise. The nipples weren't the problem. The problem was that she never warned me about them, so I gasped in surprise when I first spotted them plastered beneath her breasts like a couple of useless radio dials. I had no idea what to do with them and she didn't offer me any clues. Mainly I just avoided them or paid them polite but limited attention in the same way you'd acknowledge a crazy aunt at Thanksgiving before leaving her for your mother to deal with. The extra nipples came to define our relationship. If we couldn't talk about the nipples, how could we ever hope to communicate about anything else?

With Claire, though, there were no bad surprises. Her quirks and habits only endeared her to me more: the way she tugged her hair when she was nervous; her insistence on cleaning with a lethal blend of ammonia and bleach, dismissing warnings about the use of ammonium chloride as "propaganda from the Poison Control Board"; and her wacky yet touching devotion to her brothers and widowed father. They called her constantly, asking advice on everything from dating to how to start a lawnmower. At least once a week her father phoned with a question about laundry detergent.

The fact that we weren't having sex made our relationship more exciting. That feeling of anticipation that happens before you sleep with someone coursed through every encounter. My body would shake with violent longing each time Claire brushed against me. We'd have long, passionate kissing sessions that went nowhere, and yet left me feeling as if I'd just had the best sex of my life.

In the first weeks of our relationship, Claire was timid and allowed me to set the limits on our desire. But as we grew closer, she became the aggressor. She'd try to wrestle me out of my clothes and lead me into the bedroom. I'd resist, reminding her that I was her first girlfriend and she was not yet ready for sex.

"But I am ready," she'd say, smiling a half smile that revealed her slightly uneven front teeth. It's always the physical imperfections that transform an ordinary person into someone who is unbelievably sexy.

"No, you're not," I'd say, swatting her hands from my breasts. What I really meant, of course, was that I wasn't ready. My history of failed relationships had inexorably linked sex with disaster. So the thought of having sex with Claire caused a reverse Pavolvian response. Instead of salivating at the prospect, my mouth would grow dry as I'd imagine our first lovemaking session leading directly to a breakup.

Our most passionate episodes followed our bridge games. When we started dating, we played every Tuesday and Friday at the club. The effects of that type of mental intimacy made us crave each other all the more. It got to the point that just the thought of playing cards with Claire made me swoon with desire. We increased the frequency of our bridge dates—first to three nights a week, and then to four nights. Ostensibly, we did so to prepare for the Wisconsin tournament we planned to play in with my parents in late October. But the underlying reason was that bridge had become an intellectual form of foreplay, as seductive and intense as a caress.

* * * * * * *

I spent most of my days at my father's office, where I concentrated on closing down the law practice and completing the reams of paperwork necessary to begin the condo conversion of Eric's lakefront building. It was almost impossible to get any work done amid the constant roar of male voices debating who was the greatest heavyweight fighter of all time and arguing about the sexual charms of certain television vixens. The older men favored busty blondes who were destined for troubled marriages and repeat visits to the Betty Ford Center. The younger guys preferred anorexic waifs who always seemed to be in a foul mood, probably because they were starving to death. The conversations always—always!—ended with the old men accusing the young guys of being fags. It never failed to amaze me that men continue to rule the world considering how easily distracted they are by female flesh and sports statistics.

I rarely went into the law office. When I did, I'd arrive early so I was well entrenched when Tricia arrived. We avoided each other artfully. It was like a French farce, with one of us opening a door only to have the other slam her door.

Tricia and I didn't speak until the first week of October, almost two months after I moved out of the two-flat. It was a glorious autumn day, one of those crisp mornings that make you want to drink cider and wear flannel. I was staring out my office window, tingling from a particularly intense makeout session with Claire the night before, when there was a knock at my door. It was Tricia.

"Julia," she said formally.

"Hi," I responded warmly. I'd spent a lot of time thinking about how I'd react when Tricia and I finally spoke to each other. I planned to be cold and businesslike. But she happened to catch me when I was still in a dreamy mood with thoughts about Claire.

"The toe case is going to trial in two weeks," she said.

I nodded, adjusting my expression to match Tricia's look of barely repressed rage. "How are things going with it?"

"Okay. I have to finish completing the exhibits and preparing the witnesses."

"Do you need any help?" I asked. I didn't expect her to accept my offer. In fact, I doubted that she'd even want me sitting next to her in the courtroom. Over the years, Tricia had fantasized about how we'd handle a case that finally made it to trial, right down to our seating arrangements. In her scenarios, I was always seated to her right, keeping quiet and staring at her in adoration.

"You're better at details than I am," she said. She was standing at the edge of my doorway, being careful not to invade my sanctuary.

"So, is that a yes?" I asked.

She nodded. "We can start reviewing the depositions and making the exhibits this week. And I want to prepare witnesses this weekend. Does that work for you?"

I flipped open my calendar. The words "insect rally" were scrawled across the weekend dates. It was the endangered insect rally in Springfield that I promised Claire I'd attend the night we went to The Medieval Palace. I chuckled and began to tell Tricia about the rally, but when I looked up at her she was tapping the doorframe with impatience. "This weekend is bad. Can we start on Monday morning?"

"Fine," she said, retreating to her office.

Lonnie rolled her chair outside my office. Up until this point, she had refused to get involved in our spat. Now, though, she gave a frown of concern before wheeling back to her desk.

* * * * * * * *

The following Saturday, Claire and I planned to drive to Springfield for the insect rally with Kelvin and Max. But, first, Claire promised my mother that she'd give a lecture on the life of honeybees at the Scandinavian Club.

The Scandinavian Club was housed in a charming carriage house not far from my parents' home. Inside, the club was decorated in the traditional Scandinavian colors of white, blue, red and yellow. On the walls were photos of several generations of members. One picture featured my mother and me in matching frocks at the first mother-daughter fashion show. My mother, poised as ever, smiled coolly at the camera while I appeared out-of-focus, tugging at the hem of the dress she had stuffed me into.

When Claire and I arrived at the club, we were greeted by Gert Swensen, a beautiful, dark-haired Dane who grew up in Manhattan. Like most people from Chicago, I was awed and intimidated by New Yorkers. Gert represented both the best and the worst of that city—glamour, sophistication, wit, and a tendency to treat anyone who was not from New York like a rube. Gert was one of the few people who my mother considered to be her equal. They were behind every major decision at the Scandinavian Club and my mother often deferred to Gert's judgment. It was Gert who made the controversial decision to allow Icelanders into the club, even though they aren't officially Scandinavians. And it was Gert who dreamed up the theme for the next mother-daughter fashion show: Show Your True Colors. The mother-daughter teams would dress in clothes that represented the colors of their ancestral country's flag.

My mother appeared from the club's kitchen holding a butcher knife. When she spotted us, she pointed the knife at me threateningly and made her way across the room. "Oh, my God, what are you wearing?" my mother asked me.

"We're you planning on playing rugby this afternoon," Gert asked, taking a sip of wine and coolly appraising me. I was wearing jeans and a stripped cotton jersey.

"Claire and I are going on a road trip to Springfield this afternoon so I'm dressed for comfort," I said.

"There are more important things than your comfort, Julia," said my mother, glancing around the room in embarrassment. "What about my reputation?"

"Mom, if I didn't care about your reputation I would have worn those green Capri pants you gave me for my birthday."

"Julia's shirt is new. I was with her when she bought it," Claire said in my defense.

"Of course you were, dear," my mother said absently. She had lost interest in the conversation and was peering across the room at Marilyn Lingerman, a hopelessly dotty woman who was scared to death of my mother. Marilyn was chatting happily with a group of ladies until she saw my mother staring at her. She nervously waved in our direction, forgetting that she was holding a punch cup. Bright red liquid streamed down the front of her dress. My mother and Gert clucked in despair and marched across the room to take control of the situation.

After a lunch, Claire gave her presentation on honeybees. When she first took the podium, her hands shook and her voice squeaked with nerves. I grasped the sides of my chair, expecting the worst. But as she warmed to her subject, she proved to be a lively and engaging speaker. I felt a surge of pride as I watched her speak with a confidence I didn't know she possessed, entertaining her audience with fascinating anecdotes that made us feel a kinship with the bugs. Several women got teary eyed when Claire told of the sorry fate of worker bees, which spend their miserable little lives toiling for their queen. I glanced at my mother meaningfully to see if she picked up on the symbolism of the story. But she was too busy nodding importantly and surveying the room, making sure that everyone was paying attention to Claire.

* * * * * * * *

Following the luncheon, we met Max and Kelvin in the parking lot of the Scandinavian Club. Max drove an old conversion van that had captain chairs, shag carpeting, and a ratty daybed that served as a backseat. It reminded me of the type of vehicle pedophiles drove in the stranger-danger films we were shown in grammar school. The back of the van was filled with entomology gear—tubs of chloroform, specimen jars, and small, sharp instruments that resembled dental tools. Max told us that he had been stopped for speeding once and when the cop saw the contents of the van he immediately hauled Max in for questioning.

The boys, who were spending the night at a motel in downtown Springfield, dropped us off at a lesbian bed-and-breakfast that Claire discovered on the Internet. After the van pulled away from the curb, we stood staring at the structure, too terrified to enter. It was an old, wooden house with peeling paint and metal bars across the windows

"It didn't look like this on the website" Claire said with a frown.

"Were there photos on the website?" I asked.

"Well, no. But there was a sketch," she said. We sighed in unison and reluctantly ascended the stairs.

We were welcomed by a self-important woman with flaming red hair and a foghorn voice who introduced herself as Rusty and announced that she was an expert on Abraham Lincoln. There was Lincoln memorabilia everywhere—on the walls, on the shelves, on the draperies. For the next half hour Rusty talked non-stop about Lincoln, telling increasingly far-fetched stories about his homosexual exploits. Finally, in an uncharacteristic huff of impatience, Claire asked Rusty to show us to our room.

The house did not seem to be occupied by any other guests. It smelled, not surprisingly, like cats and mold. Rusty led us to our room, which was on the third floor. When she opened the door, she gestured to a tiny twin bed and remarked that Lincoln had shared a similarly narrow bed with a close male friend for years. Then she wandered away blathering something about the Missouri Compromise of 1850.

I stood just inside the room, mesmerized by a painting on the wall of a human foot. When Rusty wasn't giving tours of Lincoln landmarks she was working on her "art," dreadful paintings of human body parts. The painting above the bed was a greenish foot against an eerie background of purple. I was just about to suggest that we call a cab and join the boys at the motel when Claire pushed me onto the bed.

The first time you have sex with someone is usually a disappointment. The combination of nerves and high expectations inevitably leads to letdown. Typically, it takes a few weeks until you feel comfortable enough with each other to experience good sex. But with Claire, there was none of that awkwardness. It was all warmth, smooth movement, meaningful eye contact, and a blast of ecstasy that left me temporarily blinded. When we finished, we lay in the sliver of a bed, overwhelmed by the passion of the previous hour. I may have uttered "wow" at one point, but that's all we said until we fell asleep in happy exhaustion.

The next morning, I woke feeling defenseless against the emotional onslaught of the previous evening. When I felt Claire stir beside me, I closed my eyes tight and pretended to be asleep. She dressed and quietly left the room. I jumped up, dashed into the shower, and was pulling a sweater on when she returned.

"You're dressed," she said with disappointment. She was carrying a small tray that held a pot of tea, a cup of coffee and some muffins. Claire drank tea, not coffee, something I'd consider an affectation in anyone other than her.

"I don't want to be late for the rally," I said nervously.

"It's six in the morning," she said, setting down the tray. She slipped my sweater over my head. "We have plenty of time"

Afterward, we lay in bed drinking our now cold beverages. Claire was telling me a story about the time she did field research in Nebraska. The story had something to do with a vindictive caterpillar. I pulled Claire close to me and thought about the role free will plays in falling in love.

I refused to accept the common belief that the human heart is a thoughtless, bumbling oaf that has no capacity to resist poor choices. That it casually ignores cues from the brain when that far more sensible organ waves its little gray arms in alarm at advancing romantic danger. Rather, I believed that you can control your heart. You can talk sense into it when, say, it wants to chase after a woman who has left it bleeding on the roadside. You can gently prod it to fall in love with someone who is stable and sane. And, once it warms to the foreign thrill of emotional well-being, you can convince it that it's time to take a risk on something that you've never chanced before.

"Hey, Claire," I said, propping myself up on my elbow. "Let's move in together."

The smile melted from Claire's face. "Oh, Julia, I don't think so."

"You don't want to live with me?" I asked, feeling my emotional high quickly transform into a sickening panic. I was momentarily stunned by a stab of empathy for every former girlfriend who took the terrible risk of inviting me to live with them.

"Julia, we've been together for only two months. I was with my husband for four years before we got married," she said.

"Yeah, and look how well that turned out," I said with a snort.

"It didn't turn out badly," she said quietly. "I still love him."

"You still love him?" I asked shrilly. "I wish you would have told me that before last night." I reached to the floor and found my clothes. It was becoming clear that I was about to be humiliated. And I refused to be humiliated and naked at the same time.

"That's not what I meant and you know it." Claire reached out to touch my hand but I jumped away from her.

"Yeah. Okay. Fine. Forget I said anything about it," I said, pulling on my jeans and stalking into the bathroom.

Claire knocked on the door. "Julia, let's just give it some time. Six months."

When I opened the bathroom door, Claire was standing in the middle of the room naked. She looked as vulnerable as an infant, but I refused to be touched by her appearance. I felt my heart quit the business of emotional risk taking and return to the practical chore of pumping blood.

"Get dressed or we'll miss the rally," I said coldly. I knew I was being unreasonable, but I didn't care. Ever since I'd moved into my parents' house I felt myself regressing. At first, I slipped back into adolescence. Now I had reverted back to infancy.

We left the rooming house in silence. As we waited outside for Kelvin and Max, Claire turned to me, pleading with me with her eyes. But I refused to look at her, and she was left shuffling her feet and tugging at her hair.

* * * * * * * *

When we arrived at the rally, we were greeted by a gaggle of anemic looking middle-aged men with straggly beards who looked in desperate need of mothering.

"Where are all the women?" I asked.

"Women?" said one of the men, as if he had never heard the word before.

There was a flurry of activity at the podium just as the rally was supposed to begin. The leader of the rally reluctantly stepped to the podium and told us that he had just learned that the insect was not really endangered. It wasn't even threatened. "Rather," he said, coughing nervously, "it's troubled."

"That make two of us," I said just loud enough for Claire to hear.

A disgruntled entomologist wadded up a picture of the troubled insect and tossed it to the ground. I picked it up and stared at the sad-eyed bug.

"Oh, well," said Kelvin, "I always wanted to see Springfield."

Shortly after we left Springfield, Claire tentatively laid her hand on mine. I didn't respond. So she picked up my hand and folded my fingers around hers. First one finger, and then another, and then another. She held my limp hand for the entire ride home.

* * * * * * * *

After Kelvin and Max dropped us off at the Scandinavian Club, I drove Claire home. When we arrived at her house I kept the car running.

"You're going home?" she asked, wounded. "Stay with me tonight. I feel terrible about what happened this morning."

"I can't," I said, staring out the front window. "I have to meet Tricia at the office early tomorrow to prepare for the trial. I need a decent night's sleep."

"Can you wait here for a minute? I have something to give you," she said. She ran into the house and reappeared with a package.

"What is it?" I asked, regarding the package as if it were a bomb.

"Open it," she said, bouncing in her seat, unable to hide her enthusiasm.

I pulled out a heavy sweater. It was a red with a large black reindeer on the front.

"It's the sweater I started knitting at Bravehearts. The one I was knitting when we first played bridge together," she said.

I stared down at it on my lap and couldn't help but smile. For the past several weeks she had been rushing to complete the sweater. I'd already guessed that she was making it for me, and I would have been very disappointed if I was wrong.

"Do you like it?" she asked. I nodded, looking at the sweater instead of her.

"Julia," she said, taking my hand, "I can understand that you want to be alone tonight. But will you come over tomorrow night? We need to talk about what happened this morning. I feel terrible about it. I'll make dinner!"

Claire loved to cook and she tried new recipes on me several times a week. It was such a change from past relationships, where my girlfriends weren't content to starve me emotionally, they wanted to deny me physical sustenance, as well.

I nodded weakly. She wrapped her arms around my neck and kissed me. As soon as I felt my body warm to the kiss, I pushed her away. "I'll see you tomorrow," I said.

When I arrived at the boathouse I looked across the river. Claire's light was blinking furiously. I reached for the light switch to respond, but then I stopped myself. Instead, I walked inside and collapsed onto the couch, trying not to think about Claire's insistent light flicking on the other side of the river.

* * * * * * * *

Tricia and I met at the office at seven the next morning. We greeted each other coolly and got right to work. We discussed the exhibits we needed to create for the trial and she ran through the particulars of the case. Our witnesses were scheduled to come in throughout the afternoon. Jean, our final witness, was due to arrive at the end of the day.

I was too numb from the previous day's events with Claire to be nervous about seeing Jean. When she walked into the office that afternoon I barely looked up at her from the exhibit I was work-ing on—a scaled-down model of the scene of the accident. Tricia began preparing Jean as I continued to work on the model.

After about an hour, Tricia clapped her hands and said, "Okay,

we're as solid as we're going to be. I'll see you next week, Jean."
She walked out of the office without saying goodbye. I sighed
sadly. If we were still friends, Tricia never would have left me
alone with Jean.

I looked up at Jean from the accident scene. She appeared tired
and slightly bloated. Her hair, which tended to get stringy at the
end of the day, hung limply at her shoulders. But it didn't matter.
I was always most attracted to her when she was not looking her
best.

"So," said Jean.

"So," I said.

"Do you want to get something to eat?" she asked. "There's a
new place in Boy's Town that's supposed to be great."

"We're going to Anne's restaurant," I said. In all the time we
were together, Jean had never gone to The Depression.

Jean opened her mouth to object, but finally nodded in weary
resignation.

* * * * * * * *

Anne was at the front register when we walked in. We hadn't
seen each other since she left Tricia, and I felt a surge of emotion
as I watched her frowning at the computer screen.

"Anne Garland using computer? So, it's true. Hell has frozen
over."

Anne looked up and laughed loudly. Anne was not the touchy-
feely type, so we didn't hug. Instead, we just stood there, grinning
at each other like a couple of idiots. Then Anne spotted Jean.

"Oh, hi," she said to Jean, glancing at me askance. A table full of
gay men called out Jean's name, and she strolled to their table.

"What the hell are you doing?" Anne asked, nodding in Jean's
direction.

"It's not what you think. Tricia and I just finished prepping Jean
for the trial. It starts next week."

"I knew it was coming up. How is Tricia handling it?"

"Okay, I guess." I said. "I think she misses you." As soon as I said
it I realized that what I meant to say was that I missed her.

"I just can't deal with her craziness anymore," Anne said, shaking
her head. "And I've heard that you've had it with her, too."

I shrugged. "At least we're on speaking terms now."

"Well, thank God for that. She needs one of us around to keep
her from imploding."

"It would mean a lot to me if you came to the trial," I said. "I
could use the moral support. So could Tricia."

"I'll try," she said. "I just don't know if I'm up to seeing Tricia right now. And, listen," she said, nodding in Jean's direction, "be careful with that."

I sat alone at the table for ten minutes before Jean joined me.

"Well, this is just like old times, huh?" said Jean.

"Yeah, you running off and leaving me stranded for hours," I said.

"Oh, I wasn't that bad," she said, wrinkling her brow.

"No, you weren't that bad," I said, flirting as a way to punish Claire in absentia.

She tossed her head back and laughed. "Oh, Julia, I've missed you." She reached over the table and placed her hands on mine.

"Oh, yeah? How does Michelle feel about that?" I asked, slipping my hands out from under hers.

"That's over. She and Cindy are back together." Jean chuckled grimly. "It was a mistake. Michelle and I should have never gotten together." She was trying to act casual, but I knew better. Like most people who rely on the power of their personality to propel them through life, Jean's self-esteem was extremely fragile. The first whiff of rejection would send her into a tailspin of insecurity.

"Are you okay?" I asked, resisting the urge to gloat.

She shrugged uncomfortably and glanced around the room, searching for a distraction. Her eyes lit up when she spotted an acquaintance near the entrance. I gritted my teeth as she waved him over and invited him to join us for a drink. He was a pompous pretty boy who spent the next half-hour ignoring me and enjoying Jean's rapt attention as he languidly relayed tedious gay boy gossip.

Jean gravitated toward the selfish and the self-absorbed, who were easily won over by her insatiable curiosity about the minutia of their lives. When we first met, I was amazed at her ability to get people to talk about themselves, but I soon realized that it was a clever strategy that kept her safe from revealing too much about herself.

Yet, when you spend enough time with someone, they reveal themselves to you in a thousand different ways. If not as a measure of intimacy, then out of sheer exhaustion. And it's often the things that they are trying to hide—the parts of themselves that they are ashamed to share—that are the very things that make you fall in love with them.

I began to feel old emotions bubble up from deep within the recesses of my damaged heart. The swell of unexpected sentiment left me feeling nauseous. When the waiter asked if we wanted to see the dessert menu, I shook my head in a panic and demanded the check.

* * * * * * * *

When I returned to my parents' house, I called Claire. She was groggy with sleep when she picked up the phone.

"I tried to wait up for you, but it got so late," she said. "Are you coming over? Dinner is cold but I could warm it up."

"No, not tonight," I said. "Claire, it's going to be a tough couple of weeks and I don't think I'm going to be able to see you until this trial is over."

There was silence at the other end of the line.

"It's just that I'm going to be complete wrapped up in this trial, and I won't have time to talk. And we'd better cancel the bridge tournament trip. I don't know how long the trial is going to drag on."

More silence.

"Claire?"

"Did you see your ex-girlfriend today?" Claire asked.

"Jean? We had to prep her for the trial. And then we went out to dinner."

"Dinner? You went out to dinner? We made love for the first time this weekend and you went out to dinner with your ex-girlfriend tonight? When you knew that I was making dinner for you tonight? And then you call me and tell me that you can't see me or talk to me for two weeks?"

Now I was silent.

"I'm sorry," I said, finally.

"No, I don't believe you are," she said, and she hung up the phone.

I rolled over and moaned. I officially had become a bad first girlfriend.

I stared out the window and watched a bee that was trapped between the windowpanes ram itself against the glass. Claire once told me that bees get dopy in the fall. They do dumb things like wander off from the safety of the hive and attack their friends.

"Hey," I said to the bee, "if you're so highly evolved, why are you so stupid?" I opened the window and watched as the bee stumbled into the dark.

CHAPTER 13

For the next two weeks, Tricia and I worked late into the evening preparing for the trial. Initially, we barely spoke to each other. But Lonnie tired of serving as our intermediary and we were forced to settle into a working relationship of cool diffidence, treating each other as politely as a couple of strangers trapped in an elevator.

A few days before the trial, as Tricia worked on her questions for our medical experts, I stared out her office window in the direction of the suburbs. It was Tuesday, one of the nights Claire and I played bridge at the club. I had been so busy preparing for the trial that I hadn't had much time to think about Claire. As I looked out at the gloomy street, though, I wondered if Claire had found a new bridge partner to replace me.

"Julia, what's with you today? I just asked you the same question three times and you still haven't responded," Tricia said. She was wearing my old orange Elvis Costello tee-shirt that advertised his "Get Happy" album. She had coveted the shirt for years. On several occasions she kidnapped it, leaving ransom notes demanding things like Esperanto lessons, jars of Vaseline, or a small monkey. I finally gave her the shirt as a present on her thirty-fifth birthday. When she unwrapped the gift, she held it up dismissively. "Great gift, Julia. A ten-year old tee-shirt with holes in it," she said.

It suddenly seemed incomprehensible that Tricia knew nothing about my relationship with Claire. For the past decade, Tricia was always the first person I turned to when I had romantic problems. Even though her standard advice was to introduce sex toys into the relationship, I always felt better after confiding in her.

As I contemplated whether to tell Tricia about Claire, Lonnie called out from the reception area that our Chinese food delivery had arrived. Normally, Tricia would have jumped to her feet and pushed me out of the way in a rush to get at the food. But now she remained seated at her desk, looking at me with guarded concern.

"Are you okay, Julia?" she asked. "Is there something you want to talk about?"

Unexpectedly, I felt tears well up in my eyes and I bit my lip to keep from crying. I stood at the window immobile, unable to break through the wall of pride separating Tricia and me.

"I'm fine," I said, gulping down a sob. "I'm just tired and hungry."

Tricia held my gaze for a moment, willing me to make the first move. Finally, she closed her eyes and shook her head. "Okay, let's eat."

* * * * * * * *

On the day before the trial, my mother called me at the office to finalize plans for the bridge tournament in Wisconsin, which was taking place the weekend after the trial.

"I can't make it, Mom," I said. I was sitting on the floor of my office, leafing through a stack of depositions with the phone pinned under my chin.

"There is no reason why you can't play in the tournament on the weekend," my mother said. "You don't have to be in court on Saturday, do you? I mean this isn't Communist Russia."

"Mom, I'm in no mood to argue," I said, rising from the floor stiffly.

"Well, isn't Claire going to the tournament?"

The mention of Claire's name caused a sharp pain in my stomach.

"I doubt it," I said.

"Why not?" my mother asked.

"I don't know, Mom," I said hoping my irritation would make her drop the subject.

"Claire didn't attend this week's fashion show committee meeting. When I called her to ask where she's been she said that she's been working long hours. But, Julia, let's face it, no one spends that much time with bugs. What's going on between you two?"

"Nothing," I said, shifting the phone to the other ear.

My mother went silent for a moment. We both recognized that the conversation had entered dangerous territory. Although she'd always been vaguely supportive of my lifestyle, she showed it mainly by pretending that she had no idea I was a lesbian.

"For whatever it's worth, your father and I are very fond of Claire," she said.

"She's fond of you, too. God only knows why."

"I just wanted to enter that into the record," she said.

"So entered," I replied.

* * * * * * *

Later that evening, Tricia read her opening statement to me. The statement managed to turn Jean's brief encounter with the tow truck into an epic drama on the scale of *Gone with the Wind*. At the end of the reading, I broke out in applause.

"Do you think I should change the part about the driver's drinking history?" Tricia asked, flipping through the pages, making mad notes in the margins.

"I think it's perfect, Tricia. Truly elegant," I said, slipping into my jacket. It was almost midnight and we had to be in court early the next morning.

"Sit down and let me read it again," she said with irritation. She read through the statement a dozen times until I told her I couldn't take it anymore. I grabbed my briefcase and headed out the office door.

"Julia," Tricia said in almost a whisper.

I turned and looked at her. She was slumped against a wall, chewing on her lower lip. Tricia always appeared to be larger than life and in command. But now, with her wilted expression and ill-fitting blouse, she looked as small and timid as a little girl.

"I'm scared," she said.

I took a step toward her, but then I stopped myself. We hadn't had any physical contact in two months. I stood on the other side of the room wondering how to bridge the deep divide between us without appearing mawkish and anxious to go to sleep.

"Hey, Tricia," I said, finally, "do you want to polka?"

A smile slowly crossed her lips. "I get to lead," she said.

I put a polka CD on the stereo. Tricia and I met in the center of the room. As the Andrew Sisters began to sing "The Beer Barrel Polka," our eyes locked for an instant. In that moment, before Tricia slapped my shoulder and we began spinning around the room, the months of anger, resentment and hurt melted away.

In coming years, whenever Tricia and I would reminisce about the toe trial we'd never discuss the fight. Instead, we'd talk about the night before the trial, when we danced the polka. We always wondered what passersby on the street thought when they looked up at our office windows and saw us dancing around the furniture at midnight.

"They must have thought we were in love," Tricia would say.
"They must have thought we were lunatics," I'd respond.

* * * * * * * *

I arrived at court early the next morning. When I opened the
door to the courtroom, I paused for a moment before entering the
room. I hated trial work, yet I always felt a sense of awe whenever
I walked into a courtroom. It was, I suppose, the same sensation
that true believers feel when they enter a church. I'd witnessed
the justice system fail time and time again, yet it never completely
shook my faith that right would win out in the end.

I deposited the exhibits in the evidence room off the courtroom
and went to breakfast. When I returned to the courtroom, I found
Tricia sitting at the plaintiff's table, her hands folded primly on a
notepad, staring silently at the judge's bench. As I approached her,
I realized that there was something different about her. Her back
was hunched and her thighs were overflowing the chair.

"Tricia?" I asked, not recognizing this bulky figure.

"God, you startled me," she said. She was wearing a cheap suit
that looked like it was designed for a nun. She also had managed
to gain fifty pounds overnight.

"I've dieted my entire life and now it comes down to this," she
said, grabbing a handful of blubber in her fist. Tricia was wearing
a fat suit under her frumpy clothes. She had learned from Humble
Al that juries like chubby, dowdy attorneys.

We walked into the exhibit room where we fiddled with the
foot skeleton that our medical witnesses would use to show the
damage to Jean's toe. Tricia was nervous and distracted, yet she still
managed to be inappropriate. She removed the two tiny figures
that represented Jean and the tow truck driver from the accident
scene model and smashed them together in a perverted display
of toy sex.

Someone knocked on the door and we both jumped. It was Joe,
the baliff, who I knew from my days as a defense attorney. "Ladies,
the defense team has requested a meeting," Joe said with a wink.

"What do you think this is about?" Tricia asked. It usually irritated
Tricia that I had more courtroom experience than she did. But she
was too nervous today to pretend that she didn't need my help.

"I have no idea," I said.

We followed Joe to a conference room that was occupied by
Mahoney and a sharp team of attorneys from Trident Towing. They
were all well-groomed and dressed in expensive suits. Mahoney
looked exactly as I'd pictured him. He was slim and boyish with
carefully tussled blond hair. The type of golden boy every parent

wants their daughter to marry until they learn he has slipped a drug into her drink and given her to his fraternity brothers for a gangbang.

Mahoney gestured at two empty seats. The Trident attorneys had taken the regular conference chairs. The remaining seats were small, metal stools. When we sat down, our heads barely surfaced above the tabletop.

"Well, girls, today is your lucky day," Mahoney said snidely. "In spite of the fact that you have behaved completely unreasonably, the owners of Trident want to settle this case. I argued against this offer because I was looking forward to burying you, but," he said, pressing a delicate hand over his heart, "they don't want me to waste my time. So the offer is $450,000."

I gulped audibly. Tricia reached under the table and clutched my knee. Her expression, though, remained cool and unreadable.

"We'll have to discuss the offer with our client," Tricia said in a measured tone.

"Of course you will," Mahoney said, packing the remark with condescension. "And you'll also tell her what a generous offer this is, won't you, girls?" He rolled his eyes at the bank of attorneys, who chuckled on command.

Tricia gave a curt nod and we left the room. We managed to walk all the way to the evidence room before embracing each other.

"That's almost a half-million dollars!" I exclaimed. "For a half a toe! Tricia, I will never call you an idiot again!"

Tricia's face darkened and she dropped her hands from my waist. She glanced up at the ceiling and chewed on the pad of her thumb.

"No, Tricia! No!" I said, falling against the wall in despair. "Don't tell me that you're thinking about rejecting the offer."

Tricia placed a hand on my shoulder. "Julia, just hear me out. If they're willing to settle for that amount they are genuinely scared that the jury will award us much more."

"Better than a half million?" I said, trying not to scream.

"It's worth a shot," she said. "Look, I'll be honest. If it was any other client, I'd say let's take the money. It would kill me, but I'd do it. But we've got a strong case and, although I am loath to admit it, Jean is a very likeable witness. That surface charm she used to lure you into her web is going to play very well with the jury, and Trident knows it. If we are really going to dissolve the practice, let's have a proper swan song. We can have some fun with this, Julia."

"Tricia, if we don't tell Jean about the offer she can sue us for malpractice. Mahoney probably will offer to represent her in the malpractice case pro bono."

"Okay, how about this," said Tricia. "We'll tell her about the offer, but we won't advise her one way or the other. If she wants to take it, I won't try to talk her out of it."

Just then, Joe knocked on the door. "Ladies, court will be called to session in ten minutes and your client still hasn't arrived."

"I can't believe her," I said, suddenly remembering all the things that irritated me about Jean. "I told her to get here at least a half hour before start time. Now, we won't have time to accept the offer even if we wanted to."

Tricia tossed her hands up in mock helplessness. But, then, Jean appeared from behind Joe's wide back. I felt such a wave of relief that I embraced her. Joe raised his hand up to his mouth and giggled, pleased that we had fallen for his joke.

Tricia shut the door and cleared her throat. "Have a seat, Jean."

Jean looked at me quizzically and leaned against a table. Tricia explained Trident's offer in a dispassionate tone.

"Wow," said Jean, running her hand through her hair. "That's a lot of money."

"Yes it is," I said, unable to keep myself from encouraging her. Tricia reprimanded me with a stern frown.

"It's tempting," Jean said. "But I think we can do better. Don't you, Tricia?"

I began to object, but Tricia raised a silencing hand. "Jean, we have an excellent case, but you never know what a jury will do."

"What do you think I should do, Julia?" Jean asked.

I glanced at Tricia. She was clutching the side of the exhibit desk with such force that her knuckles had grown white. I knew that she was doing everything in her power to keep herself from shoving me aside and pulling Jean into the courtroom.

"I think Tricia is going to blow these Trident Towing jerks out of the water," I said. Tricia gaped at me in surprise. "I think Tricia is going to get you a million dollars for your worthless toe."

"That's good enough for me," Jean said, gazing at me soulfully. "I trust you." She leaned over and kissed me on the lips.

Joe knocked on the door and told us that it was time to take our seats. Jean walked out of the room and I began to follow her, but Tricia tugged my skirt and pulled me back into the room. She slammed the door and pretended to gag.

"Are you doing that because you are disgusted that she kissed me, or are you preparing to choke?" I asked.

"A little of both. Now if we don't get her a million dollars you'll have to get back together with her just so she won't sue us," Tricia said. She nervously tugged at the collar of her polyester pink blouse. A bit of the fat padding poked out at the neckline. "Julia, we don't have to do this. We can take the offer. I'm fine with it."

I glanced at the exhibits on the table. We had spent the past two weeks creating the exhibits and suddenly they looked like the sloppy work of a toddler.

"Tricia," I said, reaching over to adjust her fat suit, "if anyone can pull this off, you can. Now let's get out there before I change my mind." Tricia reached for the door, but I placed my hand on her shoulder before she could open it.

"Hey, isn't there something you want to ask me?" I said.

She stared at me in confusion for a moment, and then she let out a small chuckle. She extended her arms at her sides and slowly turned in place. "Julia," she asked, "how do I look?"

I took took it all in: the orthopedic shoes, the support hose, the polyblend suit, the hair arranged into a messy bun. "Tricia," I said, "you look like a real lawyer."

She turned to admire herself in the small mirror on back of the door. "You're right, Julia. I really do."

* * * * * * * *

We walked into the courtroom and took our places next to Jean at the plaintiff's table. There were only a few spectators in the audience. I recognized them immediately as courthouse groupies, old guys and housewives who were hoping to hear a juicy murder or rape trial. The door of the courtroom opened behind us. It was my parents. They ignored Joe's rough command to take a seat and walked directly to our table.

"Oh, just look at you two," my mother said, ignoring Jean, who was desperately trying to win her attention with a wide smile. "You look just like lawyers on television."

I jumped up and escorted my parents to the gallery. "Mom, you have to be quiet or you'll get us in trouble," I said. For once in my life, I was happy to see them. Tricia's parents had retired to Florida and she was currently at war with all her sisters, so there was no one from her family in the gallery. I made a silent prayer that Anne would arrive before we started.

"Not a word, I promise," my mother said in a stage whisper. She then proceeded to chat loudly with the other people in the gallery as I returned to our table.

"Julia," my mother called out. I turned and she motioned me over. "Is Tricia gaining weight?"

"No, she's wearing a fat suit," I said, smiling affectionately at Tricia's back. The pressure from the chair was making the foam bulge and it looked like her back had grown a set of breasts.

My mother sighed. "I hope you two know what you're doing."

The defense team entered the room in lockstep, as menacing and efficient as Nazi Storm Troopers. Mahoney paused at our table and looked down at us in contempt. "So what's your answer, girls?" he asked.

"Our client would like to proceed with the trial," Tricia said.

"Then you have a fool for a client," he said with a huff.

"Correction. Our client has fools for attorneys," Tricia whispered in my ear.

* * * * * * * *

Judge Wilma Daley entered and we all rose, each of us trying to impress her with a smile. Tricia and I had spent many hours speculating on whether Judge Daley was a lesbian. She was as tall and fit as a professional golfer, with short steel-gray hair and a sour expression. Early in the case, Tricia considered trying to seduce her but I talked her out of it. I didn't doubt that Tricia would be successful—she usually was—but I feared that sleeping with Tricia would backfire and prejudice the judge against us.

I was too nervous to enjoy jury selection, usually my favorite part of any trial. There is something about taking the witness stand that makes people want to confess their sins. When I worked in the public defender's office, the prosecutors and I would place bets on which juror candidate would be the first to blurt out that they were involved in an adulterous affair.

After the jury was selected, we broke for lunch. Tricia spent the break alone rehearsing her opening statement. When my parents and I arrived back in the courtroom following lunch, Tricia jerked around with such force that she toppled off the chair.

"Are you okay?" I asked, rushing to her aid.

"Just a little nervous," she said, dusting herself off. "But I'm ready." The door opened and Tricia spun around again.

"Are you expecting someone?" I asked.

"I thought Anne might show up. She called last night to wish us luck," she said, shuffling the pages of her notes. "I thought she might be here for the opening."

"Anne isn't here, but I am," I said, patting her back.

"Well, that's wonderful, Julia," she said, refusing to indulge my sentimentality. "But where the hell is our client?"

Seconds before the judge entered the room, Jean rushed into court, smiling an apology before falling into her chair. The judge walked to her bench and nodded brusquely before asking Tricia to begin her opening statement.

"Are you wearing underpants today?" I whispered.

"Of course not," she said.

"Good, you do your best work when you're not wearing underwear," I said.

"That's what I've been told," she said waggling her eyebrows lasciviously.

Tricia stood and turned to face the jury. She spoke in an unusually soft voice as she laid out our case in a gentle, logical way, almost as if she was apologizing for taking the jury's time.

As Tricia spoke, Mahoney shuffled his papers and whispered loudly to his colleagues in an attempt to distract the jury. I silently cursed myself for not instructing my mother to misbehave during Mahoney's statement. Immediately after Tricia finished speaking, Mahoney bounced up from his chair and launched into his opening statement. His voice sounded shockingly harsh compared with Tricia's subdued tone.

After opening statements, Tricia began calling our medical witnesses, who testified to the devastating effects of losing part of a toe. Tricia decided to put Jean on as our final witness. Clients are sometimes the weakest part of your case. You often hide them in the middle of your witness rotation, hoping that you can recover any damage they do with stronger witnesses. But Jean was a fantastic witness. She was articulate, polite, and appropriately alarmed about the loss of her toe. When Mahoney began his cross-examination, Jean deflected his hostility with an easy charm that left him flummoxed.

As I watched Jean on the stand, I remembered why I fell in love with her. I'd been focused on her faults for so long that I'd forgotten about the things that endeared her to me. I had worked hard to block her good qualities from my memory because anytime I remembered her lovable traits it made me want to cry. It was much easier to think of her as someone who didn't know how to pronounce "viscount;" who chewed her food loudly; who betrayed me.

When Jean left the witness stand, she winked confidently and returned to her seat next to me. I patted her knee and told her that she'd done a great job. I allowed my hand to linger on her knee as Tricia announced that we were resting our case.

The judge looked at her watch and asked if we wanted to continue the trial the next day—meaning was there any hope that we could agree to a settlement with Trident? Mahoney, trying to recover from his impotent attacks on Jean, jumped to his feet and strutted in front of the jury. "Your honor, I'm feeling pretty good about our case. Unless I suffer a debilitating stroke tonight I'm certain that we're going to win." Two members of the jury scoffed at his impudence. Another juror, who had the lopsided facial features of a stroke victim, sputtered to her neighboring jurors in outrage.

* * * * * * * *

I arrived at the courthouse early the next morning. Tricia was there already when I entered the room.

"Did you get any sleep?" I asked. Tricia had a hard time sleeping under the best of circumstances. She wandered from bed to bed, hoping that a change in scenery would lull her to sleep. When we lived together, I'd wake to find her sleeping next to me at least once a week.

"Barely. The worst thing was that I couldn't even drink. I was afraid that if I started to drink I wouldn't be able to stop," she said. "What did you do last night?"

"I had dinner at my future sister-in-law's home," I said. Gretchen invited the families to her co-op for dinner in an attempt to make peace before the wedding. At first my mother refused to attend, but she finally agreed after it became clear that my father and I had no qualms about going without her. The evening was disappointingly anti-climatic. Mr. Berger proved to be oddly charismatic. He kept my mother's cocktail glass filled to the brim and charmed her with self-effacing stories about German rigidity. My brother was uncharacteristically solicitous, pulling out my mother's chair at dinner and encouraging Gretchen to allow my mother to help with wedding planning. Mrs. Berger sat sullenly at a corner of the table, hurt that no one was paying attention to her.

"Are your parents coming to court today?" Tricia asked.

"They had to leave for a bridge tournament in Wisconsin," I said. My mother made one final plea for me to join them before they left that morning. I told her the only thing I planned to do that weekend was drink my way through her liquor cabinet.

"Well, don't drink all the vodka," my mother said. "I'll need it after a weekend playing bridge with your father."

* * * * * * * *

About five minutes before court was called into session, Jean bounded into the room. As she pranced past the defense table, Mahoney glowered at her. He looked like he had had a bad night. There was a hint of darkness under his eyes, and he had forgotten to rumple his hair.

"Julia, can I speak with you in private?" Jean asked.

"Can it wait? We're going to start any second," I said, glancing at the jury room.

"It will just take a minute," she said, grabbing my wrist. I shook my head at Tricia, but she was too busy studying her notes to notice.

Jean led me into the evidence room and shut the door. She reached into her purse and pulled out a small package. Jean had bought me many gifts when we were together. They were usually very expensive, totally impersonal, and terribly disappointing.

"What is it?" I asked suspiciously.

"Open it," she said, rocking back on her heels.

I carefully peeled off the wrapping paper and spotted a small blue box that read Tiffany's. I had never been interested in jewelry, but I couldn't help but let out a gasp of awe when I saw that famous name. In the box was a bejeweled broach in the shape of a bumblebee. I carefully removed the pin from the Tiffany's box and stared at it in amazement.

"Jean, this must have cost you a fortune," I said. "I can't accept it."

"I want you to have it," she said, pinning it to my suit jacket. The pin was hideously ugly in the way that only really expensive jewelry can be.

"You can't afford this," I said.

"I'll be able to afford it after the trial," she said.

"You can't count on that," I said. "There's an excellent chance we'll win the case, but even if we win, who knows how much money the jury will award you. There was contributory negligence—you were jaywalking after spending the evening in a gay bar. If there's one homophobe on the jury, that could slash your award to practically nothing. Things seem to be going well, but juries are unpredictable."

"I know something about being unpredictable," she said, blithely ignoring my predictions of doom. "Julia, I'd like to start over again."

"I don't know, Jean," I said unconvincingly.

"You don't have to answer now," she said. "Come over tonight and we'll talk."

I nodded numbly. Jean leaned in to kiss me. As the kiss evolved into a passionate clinch, Tricia slammed open the door and sent Jean flying against the wall.

"Hey, tubby, be careful. You don't know your own strength," I said, picking Jean up off the floor.

"Were you two planning on spending the rest of the day in here?" Tricia asked. "Mahoney is just about to begin his electrifying defense."

Mahoney was so cocky that he called only one witness, a doctor who testified that losing a toe under the weight of a truck wouldn't be painful.

When the judge asked if Tricia wanted to cross examine the witness, she jumped to her feet and said, "You bet I do."

"Dr. Howard," she said, using her normal tone of voice for the first time in the trial, "are you saying that if a tow truck came crashing into this courtroom right now and ran over the jurors toes, they wouldn't feel a thing?"

Every juror cringed. That's when I knew we won the case.

* * * * * * * *

Immediately after the defense rested, the courtroom door opened and Anne walked in. I tapped Tricia on the shoulder and motioned to the gallery. She spotted Anne and smiled. "She's here in time to hear my closing argument," she said. "It's even better than my opening."

In Tricia's closing argument, she reviewed the facts of the case and then she asked the jury to award Jean $1.5 million in damages. Tricia wrote the figure in black marker on a large sketchpad that was placed in front of the jury. She explained that she came to that figure after performing a complicated series of calculations based on medical expense, pain and suffering, and mental anguish. However, I knew that she had pulled the number out of her ass the day before the trial started. I told her that when the jury heard the figure they'd laugh her out of the courtroom. But when she scrawled the figure on the sketchpad, the jurors didn't even chuckle.

The judge gave the jurors instructions and released them to the jury room to deliberate. As Joe closed the door behind the final juror, Tricia turned to me and said, "Let's go get a drink."

"Are we allowed to?" I asked.

"We can take heroin if we want as long as we get back in time for the verdict."

Tricia, Jean and I went to a loud diner across the street from the courthouse. Just as Tricia polished off her second cocktail, her phone rang. The jury had reached a verdict and we had to get back to court.

"Is this good or bad?" Jean asked. I shrugged. I didn't want to tell her that if a jury makes a quick verdict in a civil case, it usually isn't in favor of the plaintiff because figuring out a monetary award can take hours or days.

The court was called to order and the jurors filed in. The judge asked the foreman to read the verdict. I glanced at the defense table. Mahoney was smiling smugly, but I noticed that his Adam's apple was trembling.

The foreman opened the paper and cleared his throat. "We, the jury, find in favor of the plaintiff. We award damages in the amount of $600,000, less 15 percent for contributory negligence." That equated to an award of $510,000—$60,000 above Trident's final settlement offer.

"Well, I think this calls for a drink," said Tricia.

"I'm buying," said Jean.

"Oh, you bet you are," said Tricia. Then she looked at me. "Shangri-la?"

"Where else?" I said.

Jean raised her hand in a halting gesture "You two probably want to celebrate alone. Here," she said, pulling a twenty dollar bill out of her wallet, "have a drink on me." She hugged Tricia and then she grabbed me and whispered, "Come over to my place when your done. I'll be there."

"Big spender," Tricia said, holding the twenty dollar bill as if it was used tissue.

* * * * * * * *

Tricia and I settled into our regular booth at Shangri-la and ordered Mai Tais.

"Nostrovia!" Tricia said.

"Skol! You were remarkable, Tricia," I said.

"It's true. I was," she said.

We drank deeply from our cocktails and glanced around the room. The first time we came to the bar was the day we opened the practice. The bar had been a popular watering hole in the sixties but it had long fallen out of fashion by the time we began frequenting it. At that time, the clientele was mainly middle-aged businessmen trying to drink back a piece of their youth. Now, thanks to a revival in tiki chic, the bar was once again a hot spot, filled with young Republicans and wealthy college kids.

"We're going to have to stop hanging out here," Tricia said. "It's becoming much too hip."

"We'll never abandon Shangri-la," I said.

"Oh, yeah? Do you really think we'll keep coming here after we close down the practice?" she asked.

In the excitement of the trial I'd almost forgotten about closing the practice. Although I had completed the paperwork for the final dissolution, we had never sign it.

"Julia, do you really want to leave the practice?" Tricia asked, staring into her drink. "It would kill Lonnie. She's rather attached to you."

"Tricia, there's one thing I realized over the last few days. You shouldn't be wasting your time doing real estate work. And I don't have the stomach for litigation. This is how we should end it for us...with a big win."

We turned silent and glanced around the room. In spite of our polka détente, there was still a lingering emotional stiffness between us. It would take weeks before we d shake the remnants of awkwardness and return to our old, careless friendship.

"So are you planning on sleeping with Jean tonight?" Tricia asked.

I sighed and took a sip of my drink. And then, finally, I told her about Claire.

"The one with the bugs? I really liked her, Julia. She seemed sane and nice. So unlike any other woman you've ever dated."

I started to explain what happened between Claire and me but I was overcome by an unexpected wave of sadness and I couldn't finish the story. "Bottom line, I screwed things up with Claire," I said. "Anyway, I'm meeting Jean later tonight and you know how much self-control I have."

"Have dinner with Anne and me instead," Tricia said. "Just the three of us."

"No, I promised Jean I'd meet her. I've got to play this one out to the finish."

Tricia nodded her head slowly. "I've spent a lot of time with Jean over the past several months. She's really not so bad. But, Julia, I don't think she's right for you."

"I don't know, Tricia. I think that Jean and I truly deserve each other."

* * * * * * *

After leaving Shangri-la, Tricia took a cab to The Depression and I drove to Jean's apartment. Miraculously, I found a parking space directly in front of Jean's apartment. Her neighborhood was so congested that I usually couldn't find a space within a mile of her apartment. I decided to interpret the convenient parking space as a sign that I was doing the right thing. When I reached down for my keys, the bumblebee pin jabbed me in the chin. I yelped in pain and rubbed a streak of blood across my face.

As I looked in the mirror and cleaned off the blood, I slowly realized what a mistake it would be to sleep with Jean. We'd wake the next morning regretting what we'd done, and then we'd waste the next few weeks going through the motions of rekindling our relationship. It would be a sad exercise that would kill any remaining feelings of warmth between us.

I started the car and drove to The Depression. I spotted Anne and Tricia at the counter. Anne was laughing at Tricia, who was talking rapidly and flailing her arms wildly above her head. I took a moment to savor the scene. Then I walked over and joined them. By the end of the evening, I realized that even though it seemed that everything had changed between us, nothing really had changed at all.

CHAPTER 14

Early on a Sunday morning the following spring, I woke up confused. I blinked my bleary eyes and glanced around my bedroom, trying to remember where I was. This had been happening a lot lately. It was the result of too many moves in too short a time. I pulled myself up in bed and dragged my hand through my hair. Norm jumped onto the bed and rubbed his back against my chin. I petted him absently and looked out the window. The sun was rising and it was shaping up to be a bonny morning. I yawned and stretched happily. Then, suddenly, I remembered what I had to do that day. I fell back into bed and groaned.

Claire, who was burrowed under the blankets, began to stir. In the morning, I'd often crawl into her cocoon and sing "Let's Do It" to wake her, which never failed to make her wiggle with delight. But I was too busy fighting off an anxiety attack to entertain her this morning.

"It's going to be a big day," Claire said, wiping the sleep from her eyes.

"Don't remind me," I said, trying to be crabby but finding it impossible in the face of Claire's relentless good cheer.

Flop was sprawled at the foot of the bed. When he heard my voice he crawled up the bed, creating a wall of dog between Claire and me. Flop could stretch his small body in such a way that it took up the bulk of the bed, leaving me with just a sliver of space to work with. Claire encouraged me to shove Flop out of my space, but I didn't have the heart to do it. In spite of my best efforts to resist his charms, I had developed the type of neurotic attachment to Flop that left people quietly questioning my sanity.

Flop spotted Norm and merrily chased him off the bed. They ran out of the room in a fit of barking and hissing. The day had officially begun. I followed the animals into the kitchen, sighing wearily as I passed the cardboard boxes that lined the halls. Today would mark the fifth time I'd moved in a year.

I made a pot of egg coffee, the only type of coffee Claire drank. It involved blending a mixture of eggshells, coffee grounds, egg yolk, and cinnamon, and then brewing the concoction over an open flame.

"Danish coffee," my mother said approvingly when Claire made a large pot of the brew for Gretchen's bridal shower.

"Actually, Astrid, it's Swedish," Claire said.

"Well, they must have gotten the recipe from the Danes," my mother said. "The Swedes have no sense of adventure. They would have never dreamed of using eggshells in coffee. Remember, dear, when the Danish Vikings were out conquering the world, the Swedes stayed home, tending to their cows and waiting for handouts."

My mother had tempered her views on Swedes considerably over the past several months out of respect for Claire. However, she couldn't resist educating Claire on her own delusional version of Scandinavian history.

As the coffee brewed, I wondered whether I should wake Tricia. She was moving that day too, and she hadn't even begun to pack. "I'm only moving downstairs, Julia," she said earlier in the week when I badgered her to start packing. "It's not like I'm traipsing all the way to the suburbs, like some other idiot I know."

The idiot she was referring to was me.

I moved back into the two-flat in December after life at my parents' house had become unbearable. The planning for my brother's wedding was escalating to a bloody climax. Gretchen and her mother had joined forces and were proving to be worthy adversaries. I knew that my mother would triumph in the end, but I feared I might be one of the casualties lost in battle. So, I returned to the safety of the two-flat in my old, bullet-scarred neighborhood.

Now, six months later, I was returning to the suburbs and Anne was moving back to the two-flat. She was going to live on the second floor, and Tricia was moving to the first floor.

I poured two cups of coffee and walked up the back steps. I strolled into Tricia's bedroom and sat on the edge of her bed. Tricia was laying next to Pat, a woman Tricia had been dating for the past several weeks. Pat was the latest in a string of women Tricia had dated since the toe trial. They met when Pat gave an estimate on remodeling the kitchen on the second floor. The kitchen was one of the incentives Tricia used to lure Anne back to the two-flat. Tricia also vowed not to interfere in Anne's relationship with Poppy, a promise she had no intention of keeping.

Tricia pretended to be smitten with Pat, but we both knew the relationship wouldn t last. I felt bad about it because in spite of Pat s surly attitude and her habit of spitting in public, I liked her. Pat was a recovering alcoholic who owned a contracting business with an all-girl crew. I introduced her to my brother, who was always on the lookout for people who could make his life easier. Pat quickly took control of his construction sites, leaving Eric free to enjoy the war between his fiancée and his mother to baby him.

I sat down hard on the bed and bounced on it until Tricia woke up.

"Jesus, Julia, what time is it?" she asked.

"It's moving day! Time to pack," I said. Pat cursed me and turned over on her belly. I handed Tricia a cup of coffee, which she accepted grudgingly.

"You are planning on moving downstairs today, aren't you?" I asked. I took every opportunity to remind her that living in the same apartment with Anne was not an option. "Anne is going to have her stuff here this afternoon. You need to be out by then."

"Well, Anne and I might have to live together up here for a couple of days," Tricia said coyly. "I'm too busy to pack today."

"Too busy doing what?" I said.

"I'm driving out to the suburbs this morning to attend a mother-daughter fashion show," she said with a smirk of triumph.

I gulped in horror. "How did you find out about it?"

"Claire offered to sell me tickets to the show and so I purchased an entire table," Tricia said, reveling in my misery. "It's such a good cause, I simply couldn't resist. We'll all be there. Me, Annie, Carmen. Personally, I can't wait to see what the Scandinavian smart set will be wearing this season."

I clutched my aching stomach and moaned. "Sometimes I hate you," I said.

"Sometimes I hate you, too," she said.

I grabbed a pillow and held it over her face until she thrashed out from under it. We fell to the floor and wrestled until Pat threatened to kill us if we didn't shut up.

I stomped down to my apartment, intent on yelling at Claire for telling Tricia about the fashion show. But then I found her standing at the stove, humming happily while cooking an elaborate omelet, and I felt the anger melt away. I returned to bed and curled up in the fetal position while I waited for Claire to call me to breakfast.

* * * * * * * *

On the evening we won the toe trial, I worked up the courage to phone Claire. I punched in her number and closed my eyes tight, expecting her to slam down the phone when she heard my voice. I couldn't have been more surprised when Mardelle, one of my mother's cleaning ladies, answered the phone.

My mother kept a stable of several cleaning ladies on her payroll. The women rotated their visits because no one person could put up with my mother's outrageous demands on a weekly basis. The house would be immaculate when they arrived and the women would be close to nervous collapse after spending hours trying to find a speck of dust before my mother did.

"What are you doing at Claire's house, Mardelle?" I asked.

"I'm taking care of her puppy while she's out of town," she said.

"Where did she go?" I asked.

"She went somewhere with your mom. Imagine spending an entire weekend alone with your mom, the poor thing," said Mardelle. In spite of her tough talk, I suspected there was nothing Mardelle would rather do than spend a weekend being intimidated and persecuted by my mother, her one true love.

I hung up the phone and merged onto the highway, heading north to Wisconsin and the bridge tournament. About an hour later, my phone rang. It was my mother.

"Julia, your father has come down with a terrible flu and I need you to drive to Madison to play with me in the bridge tournament," she said. It was such a lousy lie that I almost laughed. My father had the stomach of a goat. He could consume motor oil and not get sick.

"Mom, I'm so exhausted from the trial that I don't think I can manage a weekend of bridge," I said, smiling to myself as I crossed the Wisconsin state line.

"Julia, you're a young woman. You have no business being tired at your age. Now get in your car and drive up her tonight," she demanded.

"Sorry, Mom, no can do," I said. Although I was touched by her obvious ploy to get Claire and me together again, I wasn't going to make it easy on her.

My mother sighed and rethought her strategy. "Julia, I'll make you a deal. If you come to Wisconsin tonight I'll stop pestering you to perform in the fashion show."

"Can I get that in writing?" I asked, knowing full well that she'd conveniently forget her promise as soon as I caved to her wishes.

I arrived at the tournament just as the final game of the evening was ending. The tournament was held in an enormous sports arena, which was packed with hundreds of people playing cards.

In spite of the crowd, the room was eerily quiet as players silently concentrated on their cards. I scanned the room, hoping to spot Claire. Suddenly, I heard my mother's voice break though the crushing silence.

My mother was sitting at the far end of the arena. When she spotted me, she called out my name. Dozens of people turned in their chairs and glared at me in irritation. Players at neighboring tables loudly shushed my mother but she ignored them. I made my way through the maze of tables until I was standing directly behind Claire's chair. Claire continued to study her cards, refusing to look up at me.

"I thought you didn't have anyone to play with," I said to my mother.

"I never said that, Julia," my mother said. "Think back to our conversation. Think! All I said was that your father isn't feeling well."

"Do you mind?" one of their opponents barked. "We're trying to play."

"We have just one more hand, Julia. Your father is in the hotel room, probably ordering everything on the room service menu. I'll sneak over and catch him in the act and then you and Claire can play in the next game."

They finished the game, and my mother raced off to the hotel, leaving Claire and me alone. I stood next to my mother's vacant chair, waiting for an invitation to sit down.

"Your mother told me that you won your case," Claire said, fiddling with a pencil on the table. "Congratulations."

"Tricia did all the work. I was just there to make sure she didn't get tossed into jail in the process," I said. I ran my hand along the back of the chair. "Can I sit down?"

Claire shrugged noncommittally. I sat down and glanced around the room. It was almost midnight. Players were finishing their games and stretching off a long day of bridge. In the reception area, crews were dragging out kegs of beer. The tournament was officially over for the day, yet some people were grabbing beers and bringing them back to the playing tables.

"There's a special game that starts at midnight," Claire explained. "It's called Play 'Till You Drop. You keep playing until you lose to another partnership and then you get to go to bed."

"Would you like to play together in that game?" I asked.

"Okay," she said with a shrug, "if you're not too tired."

"I'm wide awake," I said.

"So, your mother tricked you into coming here?" Claire asked.

"She thinks she did," I said with a laugh. "I was on my way here when she called. I knew you were here and I wanted to see you."

"If you wanted to see me why didn't you just call me?" she asked, looking directly at me for the first time.

"I was afraid to call. You were mad at me."

"I still am."

"Then why did you come here with my parents?"

"Your mother is impossible to say no to. She called me yesterday and insisted that I drive up with them." Claire looked down at her hands again. "You really hurt me, Julia. I'm very upset with you."

A tournament director yelled that it was time to start the game. Two burly guys who looked like they had slammed ten beers in the past fifteen minutes lurched toward our table.

"You have every reason to be upset. But you'll get over it," I said. "It would be easy for you to find a better girlfriend than me. But you are never going to find a better bridge partner."

Claire tried to suppress a smile as our opponents joined the table. As we reached for our cards, her fingers brushed against mine. I was overwhelmed with a familiar wave of desire. I glanced across the table and grinned at Claire. In that instant, we silently agreed to throw the match. The sooner we lost to our opponents, the sooner we'd get to retreat to her hotel room. We had better things to do that evening than play bridge.

The next morning, we met my parents for breakfast. Shortly after our meal was served, a tournament director who had a crush on my mother approached us. He was a slight, preppy fellow who looked like he spent most of his days on a yacht. The previous day, he hovered over my mother, whispering playing tips in her ear and offering to give her free bridge lessons in his hotel room.

"Good morning, Larry," my mother said brightly. "Tony, this is the nice man who offered to give me private bridge lessons."

My father glared up at him menacingly from his mountain of pancakes. Larry cleared his throat nervously and changed the subject.

"And who are these lovely ladies?" he asked.

"This is my daughter, Julia," my mother said, nodding her head at me. Then she reached across the table and patted Claire's hand. "And this is my other daughter."

Claire choked back a sob of surprise and her eyes welled up with tears. I frowned and shook my head at my mother. Claire may have been taken in by my mother's manipulative charm, but I knew exactly what she was up to.

* * * * * * * *

On the morning of the fashion show, I ate breakfast as slowly as possible. I knew that when I finished we'd have to drive to the suburbs.

"Can't you call my mother and tell her I'm too sick to perform?" I asked as Claire tried to pull me away from the kitchen table. "She likes you more than she likes me. Maybe she'll believe it if it comes from you."

"I promised her that you'd be there," she said. Lately, whenever my mother wanted me to do something, she'd go through Claire. I had read stories about parents who refused to have anything to do with their daughter's lesbian lovers. I wondered why I couldn't be so lucky.

When Claire and I arrived at the Scandinavian Club, we were greeted by my mother and Gretchen, who was wearing the ugliest dress I'd ever seen. It was a puffy pinafore in gold, black, and red—the colors of the German flag.

"Is it really necessary that I wear this, Astrid?" Gretchen asked.

"Gretchen, the theme of the show is 'Wear Your True Colors.' Now, it's not my fault that the Germans chose those dreadful colors for their flag," my mother said gaily.

A few weeks earlier, Gretchen surprised my mother by agreeing to participate in the fashion show. My mother interpreted it as an elaborate scheme to weaken her power in the final stages of wedding planning. In retaliation, she found the most hideous outfit imaginable for Gretchen.

My mother was dressed in an elegant red knit dress with a red and white silk scarf tied fetchingly around her neck. When we entered the dressing room, she handed me my outfit, a tasteful red-and-white sweater set and skirt. My mother and I were representing the colors of the Danish flag. However, in a last-minute act of defiance, I tied my hair back with a green bow. The green bow, combined with the red and white outfit, symbolized the Italian flag. Claire wore the colors of Sweden, a blue-and-white checked dress that made her look like a sexy 1950's housewife.

After I dressed, I peeked out from behind the curtain. Tricia, Pat, Anne, Carmen and Poppy were in the front row. The strains of ABBA's "Mama Mia" came pounding out of the speakers, signaling the start of the show. My mother yanked me backstage and gathered Claire, Gretchen and me around her. Too soon, I heard the opening notes of a Danish rock band's version of "Wonderful Copenhagen" and the four of us took the stage. As we made our way down the catwalk, the emcee described our outfits, struggling to put a positive spin on Gretchen's awful frock. I briefly considered abandoning the catwalk and stalking out of the club, but then I felt Claire squeeze my arm. Her face was flush with embarrassment and I realized she was as mortified as I was. She had so enjoyed the hours she spent planning the event with my mother that I assumed she was actually looking forward to participating in the show. But now I knew that she simply liked to spend time with my mother, which was a whole separate problem that didn't have to be dealt with at the moment.

As I glanced at my mother, who was clutching Claire's arm possessively, and then looked toward the audience, where my friends were gaily heckling me, I was reminded of something Claire once told me about bees. She explained that for some social insects, sex is a cooperative affair with complicated divisions of labor. Thousands of members of a family of bugs work selflessly to promote the romantic coupling of a choice few, maiming or killing any undesirable players who try to woo their comrades. I smiled fondly as I wondered whether Claire and I would be together without the benevolent interference of my mother and my friends.

At the end of the catwalk, my mother wrapped her arms around Gretchen, Claire and me. "No one can accuse me of being a racist!" my mother exclaimed. "Look at my family. An Italian, a Swede, and a German!"

"You're a regular United Nations, Astrid," Tricia shouted.

* * * * * * * *

Claire and I joined our friends for the post-show luncheon. As I gulped down a glass of wine, Tricia huddled with one of the waitresses, who had set down her drink tray and was gesturing to her head in alarm.

"Julia, we have a new client," Tricia said when she returned to the table. "That waitress' husband lost part of his ear in a bar fight. An ear! That's practically a brain injury. I bet I can get two million dollars for it."

I dropped my head into my hands and groaned.

"I thought you two had dissolved your partnership," Poppy said.

"They tried. It didn't work," Anne said, wearily acknowledging her own failing attempt to end her relationship with Tricia.

Over the past six months, I had tried on several occasions to get Tricia to sign a dissolution agreement. But she always found an excuse not to sign. She'd suddenly have an emergency dental appointment or she'd spill coffee on the papers. Finally, I conceded defeat and agreed to remain in the practice if she agreed to invest the money we made in the toe trial in real estate. We used half of the money to partner with my brother in his newest condo project, a development that catered to Yuppies with more money than taste. With the other half, we bought an apartment building on the lake, which we planned to convert into affordable condos for low-income families. We convinced my brother to invest in the building after explaining the extraordinary tax benefits that result from helping the poor.

"We're going to be millionaires, Julia," Tricia said after we signed the agreement with my brother.

"Yes, and no one had to lose a limb for that to happen," I said.

Carmen spent most of the luncheon flirting with a pretty blonde, who was the wife of one of the member's sons. At one point, they disappeared into the bathroom together. Minutes later, Carmen trotted out with lipstick smeared over her face. "Bad news, Julia," she said. "Your mother caught me kissing that lady in the bathroom. I don't think she's happy."

My mother walked into the room and glared at our table. Tricia raised a glass to her. "Lovely party, Astrid."

My mother sighed so loudly I could hear it all the way across the room.

* * * * * * * *

After lunch, Claire and I drove to her house. When we arrived, the movers had already finished their work and were gone. The living room was so cluttered with boxes we could barely squeeze past them. We stared at the mess silently, overwhelmed by the unpacking job that awaited us.

"We might have to look for a bigger house sooner than we'd hoped," Claire said.

"I'm not moving again for at least a year," I said. "Besides, you get used to living with boxes. They become like friends after a while."

Claire and I made the decision to move in together several months before. We agreed to wait until after the fashion show, reasoning that if we could make it through the hell of countless dress fittings without breaking up, then we belonged together.

As we navigated through the living room, I discovered Flop trapped in the forest of cardboard. I scooped him up and we went upstairs to the bedroom, where we collapsed on the bed. Claire reached to the nightstand and picked up a magazine. The room was hot and stuffy from the afternoon sun that was pouring through the window. Claire fanned herself with the magazine as Flop gnawed on a chew toy at our feet. I stilled Claire's hand so I could read the cover of the magazine. It was our monthly bridge magazine, a glossy publication that offered tips on bidding and reported the scores from recent tournaments.

"When did you get this?" I asked, taking the magazine from

her.

"This week," she said.

"I wonder if the results from the Indianapolis tournament are in it," I said, leafing to the results page. I found our names under the tournament listing. We had placed first in six of the eight games we played in at the tournament.

"I guess this means we're good partners," she said when I showed her the results.

"I guess it does," I said.

Printed in the United States
95543LV00004B/8/A